M000114067

WOOD'S TEMPEST

A MAC TRAVIS ADVENTURE

STEVEN BECKER

THE WHITE MARLIN PRESS

Copyright © 2018 by Steven Becker

All rights reserved.

No part of this book may be reproduced in any form or by any electronic or mechanical means, including information storage and retrieval systems, without written permission from the author, except for the use of brief quotations in a book review.

This is a work of fiction. Names, characters, places, and incidents either are the products of the author's imagination or are used fictitiously. Any resemblance to actual persons, living or dead, businesses, companies, events, or locales is entirely coincidental.

WOOD'S TEMPEST

ONE

MAC WATCHED THE WEATHER-BRICK SWING, THEN STOP, and spin slightly. The primitive forecasting tool was more of a novelty than a predictor, and it proved inconclusive at best. October in the Keys could bring anything from a hurricane to a cold front, and the brick suspended from a piece of string reflected that mood. It was also an indicator of his own mood. His life had been in a nice groove, then came the call last week from Kurt Hunter, a special agent for the National Park Service stationed in Biscayne National Park. Since then, Mac's past, or at least the part of it that he'd rather forget, had come back to haunt him. With his mind spinning like the weather-brick, he finished the Yuengling and looked down the bar at Rusty, signaling for another by tapping the empty bottle on the bar.

Two beers was his self-imposed limit, enough to unwind after the day's events and the ride back from Miami, but facing a nighttime run to reach his island retreat, he needed to be careful. Rusty came by with a fresh beer and set it on the bar. Mac looked through the clear lid of the dry box containing a hard drive, with years worth of Gill Gross's research, sitting in front of him and wondered if it wouldn't be better to toss it. He knew what it contained and the trouble it could bring, but like a fresh ballyhoo to a mahi, he also knew he couldn't resist.

"You look like you've seen a ghost," Rusty said, taking the empty and tossing it into a recycling bin, something his daughter Julie had pressed on him.

Mac looked around the Rusty Anchor and, after a glance at the door to make sure that his past hadn't followed him here from Miami, said, "You know about Gill Gross getting killed?"

"Sure. Did some diving with him back in the day. You're not mixed up in that, are you? Been keeping an eye on the news."

"More than I want to be." Subconsciously, Mac pulled the dry box toward him, catching Rusty's eye. There were no questions. The two men had known each other for years and didn't have to speak to communicate. Mac tipped the bottle back and finished the beer. He pulled out a soggy twenty and laid it on the bar with a set of keys. "Thank Jesse for the loaner when you see him."

"Will do," Rusty said, picking up the empty bottle and bill. He went to the register, rang up the beers, and brought back change.

Mac pushed the bills toward him. "Better get home before Mel has my head."

"Probably thinks you're out with Trufante. Ain't seen him around in a while."

Mac's personal shit magnet rarely frequented the Rusty Anchor, preferring to hang out where there was less supervision —or at least without Rusty watching him. "His girlfriend split for Key West. He's been down and out lately."

"That's not a good place for him. She was different, but seemed to ground him. Boy needs someone like that."

Mac nodded. Trufante had a way of finding trouble, or trouble finding him. Either way, Pamela had been a good influence on the deckhand. "I'll be sure to say hello when I see him.

Probably go check the traps tomorrow." Mac glanced back at the weather-brick still spinning on the rope.

Rusty must have seen it too. The brick foretold the obvious: not moving equaled no wind, moving was a breeze, hard to see was foggy, wet was raining. There were all kinds of variations, but the locals were superstitious, and Mac and Rusty looked up at the twin TVs at the same time. One showed a ball game and the other was an internet feed of the local radar and weather conditions. Living on the island chain, the weather was the number one topic of conversation and dictated what most people did with their days. The local image was clear, but that wasn't what they were concerned about. The next image showed the Atlantic Ocean. What had started as an area of disturbed air off the coast of Africa last week now had a name and was spinning off the coast of the Dominican Republic. Mac had been looking at weather patterns for years and had been keeping an eye on this one since it had formed.

"No other weather comes to play, that thing'll be here inside a few days," Rusty said. "Gonna start buttoning up things around here in the morning."

Mac didn't respond. The worst fear of a man living on an island was less than a thousand miles away. "See ya around," he said, picking up the dry box from the bar and sliding the keys to The Beast toward Rusty. He had borrowed the rebuilt 1973 International Travelall belonging to Jesse McDermitt, who lived on a nearby island in the Content Keys. He was the closest neighbor Mac had, and along with Rusty, was one of the only men Mac trusted.

On his way out the door, Mac looked at the box again and wondered if Kurt Hunter fell into that category. His new wife, Justine, who worked as a forensics tech for Miami-Dade, had handed the box to him without explanation earlier today. Tucking it under his arm, Mac walked past the shack housing the Caribbean's finest full-time cook and part-time philosopher, Rufus. Mac almost stopped for one of his famous hogfish sandwiches, but with darkness unfolding, he decided he should get moving.

Hoping that Mel had cooked dinner was a crapshoot. Although she was a good cook, since Mac had installed satellite internet on the island last year for her, she often shifted into lawyer mode and forgot time. The past summer's red tide just north of their island had been one of the worst in decades, and her involvement as an advocate in the fight against Big Sugar polluting the coastal waters consumed her. He couldn't argue, after seeing the results firsthand when a king tide had brought the fish kills to his doorstep.

Thankfully, once he passed Rufus's shack, the wind took the smell in the other direction, and he continued down the path to the dock. The Rusty Anchor had a small turning basin with a deepwater channel leading to the Atlantic. It wasn't a marina, but did house several live-aboards. Mac waved to a couple on a trawler as he untied his center console and dropped to the deck.

After placing the box in the compartment below the wheel, he started the center console's single 250-horsepower engine and pushed off the dock. After spinning around, he idled out of the canal, smiling for the first time all day. Leaving land behind often did that. No matter how the world chose to conspire against him, the freedom of a boat rarely failed to put a smile on his face. Just before he pressed the throttle down, he heard his phone ring.

He could remember a time, not long ago, when he rarely turned his out-of-date phone on. Now he regretted he was attached to his like everyone else. Originally, he had justified it for the weather and navigation apps, not wanting to admit he would be lost without it. The ring startled him. Still jumpy from the confrontation with two of his old nemeses—Slipstream, an old-timer from Wood's day, and the state archeologist Jim DeWitt, who were both now in custody for the murders of Gill Gross and one of his backers—he pulled the phone from his pocket and, acting out of character, answered it without looking at the caller ID.

"We goin' tomorrow?" Trufante asked.

Mac thought for a second. "Weather's getting close. I'd like to get another day or two's soak out of them, but I'm thinking now we should just pull them."

"You the man," Trufante said. "What time you want me?"

"Be out at my place at seven." There was a moment's pause on the line. Mac could hear the background sounds of a bar while he waited for Trufante to answer. The longer the pause meant the longer he'd been there.

"Got a small transportation problem."

Mac thought about the swirling circle out in the Atlantic. Sometimes storms lingered; others blasted through the open water, growing in size and intensity as they sucked the warm moisture from the ocean. In the case of the latter, the far-reaching effects could start to impact them as early as tomorrow night. At this point he was certain it was going to affect the islands in some way. Odds were it wasn't going to be a direct hit, but it didn't have to be to cause damage. Leaving his stone crab and lobster pots out would mean losing them.

"I'll come get you. Keep quiet and out of sight and you can stay on the big boat overnight," Mac said, referring to his trawler that was out at the island. Having Trufante that close to Mel could mean trouble, and Mac hoped the mangroves between the lone pile where it was tied and the house would be enough of a barrier between them. "Where you at?"

"Pickled Pelican."

It took Mac a long second to place the bar. The Keys might

be paradise for tourists, but it was a harsh climate for businesses. They changed hands regularly, and keeping track of them was not on his radar. "I'm running out of the Anchor now. I'll pick you up in twenty minutes." He paused. "And don't make me come upstairs after you." He disconnected and pushed the throttle down. The boat leveled out, and without the weight of a T-top, which had been damaged during another Trufante episode, the hull was soon skipping over the small wind waves.

With the breeze blowing through what was left of his hair and the occasional mist of salty spray landing on his face, Mac found himself smiling despite his concerns. On the Atlantic side, he passed the mouth of Sister Creek, skirted West Sister Rock, and, staying to the ten-foot contour, rounded Knights Key. With the Seven Mile Bridge ahead, he set course for the fourth opening from the eastern end and cruised past the entrance to Boot Key Harbor before crossing under the new span of the bridge and entering the gulf. Once past the old bridge, he turned gradually to the east and followed Vaca Key toward the small breakwater that led to Keys Fisheries, where his smile faded.

Passing the turn to the right that led to a charter-boat marina, Mac headed straight until he found an opening between two lobster boats tied up against the concrete seawall. With little current inside the protected water, he idled in place, waiting for Trufante. The short tropical twilight was about to fade to night, and the security lights hadn't come on yet, but even in the low light, there was no sign of Trufante's six-five frame or his smile that resembled the grille of a Cadillac. Cursing under his breath, Mac pulled up to the dock and reached for one of the old, frayed lines he used to secure the boat.

With his head down, he crossed in front of Key's Fisheries and looked up at the large, palm-frond-covered bar set up on pilings. Glancing out at the boats in the marina, he was surprised to see the bar wasn't the only business that had changed hands here. It had only been a few weeks—maybe a month—since this had been Celia's domain. The flamboyant woman had helped Mac in the past, though the last time he had seen her it was to tell her the quad-powered boat he had borrowed was a total loss. The marina was dark and quiet, a stark contrast to when she used to run it. Then, it had been home to a fleet of blinged-out, quad-powered sportfishers that lit the night with their multi-colored LED lights. The story would come out eventually, but for now, he needed to haul the Cajun out of the bar.

After climbing the last step, Mac looked cautiously at the crowded bar overlooking the water. There were a few deck-hands he recognized, but none of the captains who would want to bend his ear about the bite. Mac was one of them, but at the same time kept his distance. His traps were always the farthest out, and the other captains, when they could pry any intel out of him, used his success or failure as a bellwether for where to set their traps. Mac was tight-lipped. His mate was not.

Trufante sat at the bar surrounded by a half-dozen people. They were staring at the TV, which showed the same image that Mac had seen at the Rusty Anchor. Trufante, as the local expert on everything, was regaling the crowd with old hurricane stories in exchange for drinks.

The crowd parted as Mac walked directly toward Trufante, whose Cadillac grin faded briefly when he saw him. After a quick calculation of how to maximize his benefactor's appearance, he turned to Mac. Knowing what he was dealing with, Mac grabbed Trufante by the arm and, without a word, pulled him away from the bar. With Mac gripping his right arm, Trufante reached back with his left and, at the maximum reach of his wide wingspan, was able to snag his drink off the bar.

With a few goodbyes, said backward as Mac pulled Trufante out of the exit, the duo headed downstairs to the parking lot.

"Them boys would have bought you drinks all night if you'd just be nicer," Trufante said as they passed several stacks of lobster traps.

"Being nice never got me anywhere," Mac muttered as he led the Cajun to his boat.

TWO

FROM ALMOST A QUARTER MILE OUT, MAC COULD SEE MEL, with her hands on her hips, standing on the beach. Between the low light and the distance, he couldn't read the expression on her face, but he knew what it was. There was no hiding Trufante on the twenty-four-foot boat.

With his mind trying to fabricate a story, even though he knew she wouldn't buy it, Mac slowed the boat and turned around a small whirlpool that disguised a coral head. The backcountry of the Keys was better marked than it used to be, but many small channels and hazards were navigated at the mariner's own risk. Without the standard green-square and red-triangular placards, the homemade markers were as dangerous as what they hid, offering no clues as to what they represented. Local markers, often only hand-driven stakes or pipes, some with jugs or buoys attached, others unmarked, were placed by residents. There was one that had a toilet seat hanging from it. The lone pile that Wood had sunk years ago inside a small deep-water channel that he had dredged leading to the island was a good example. Heading directly toward it would be a mistake. What it didn't tell you was that there was a large rock, submerged except at the lowest of low tides, that had to be skirted to reach the safety of the channel.

Privacy had been Wood's goal when he built the original structures on the island in the early nineties. The solitary pile was his concession to tie off a larger boat. Up the narrow beach, and behind a gate camouflaged by mangroves, lay a small clearing with a winch and an old truck axle that he had used to haul out his old skiff. The original house had been carefully sited so it would be invisible to the casual passerby. Unless you knew the island was inhabited, it looked like every other mangrove-covered key. Mac had left the old gate system in place, but since moving here full -time with Mel, his forty-two-foot trawler signaled his presence.

Once past the rock, he coasted up against his trawler. With its bow secured to the pile and a stern anchor deployed, Mac used the trawler to secure the center console. With the boat secure, he climbed over the gunwale and stepped into the thigh-deep water.

"Why?" Mel asked.

Mac could see her face and knew he was in trouble. "Got a storm out there. Figured it'd be best to pull the traps in the morning."

Mel had grown up here and knew the weather and water as well as Mac. She relaxed slightly. "He's staying on the trawler," she said, and walked away.

Mac waited until she was far enough along the winding trail before turning to Trufante. "Think you can stay out of trouble for one night?"

"Dude, I'm already down and out." Lifting one long leg, Trufante stepped onto the gunwale and across to the trawler.

"All right, then. We'll get an early start." Mac left him and waded toward the beach. Before he reached dry land, he remembered the dry box and went back for it.

"What'cha got there?" Trufante asked, popping a beer he had taken from the galley refrigerator.

Along with his nine lives, most of which he had already spent, Trufante had the instincts and eyesight of a cat. "Nothing." Mac subconsciously moved the box to his other hand and out of sight from the Cajun. He tucked the box into the crook of his arm like a football and started down the path. Mac noted the recent growth. It was a war to keep the brush at bay, and the three-foot-wide walkway had well-defined walls where the machete had done its work. Mac looked down as he walked, struggling to see the roots in the dim light. After a few hundred feet, he reached a large clearing that contained the house and a small storage shed.

The remodel, or rebuild, which it essentially was after the house had been firebombed by a rogue CIA agent several years ago, still looked new. The concrete piers that supported the single-story structure had replaced the old wood pilings that Wood had originally used. The additional ten feet of elevation would keep the house above all but the worst storm surges and allowed airflow through the upstairs living quarters. Off the grid, the house had solar panels along with a backup generator, which ran on propane. Water was heated by two 500-gallon black plastic tanks sitting on the roof. A small on-demand water heater, also fueled by propane, boosted the preheated water to a comfortable temperature.

Mac passed the shed and climbed the stairs to the house. Crossing the covered porch that wrapped around the structure to keep the sun and rain out, he opened the screen door and entered. The shell of the building had been upgraded, but Mac and Mel had chosen to keep Wood's original floor plan, with one bedroom in the back and a large great room with the kitchen off to the right. Though it seemed a little more crowded by bringing in the world through the addition of the satellite internet connection, it was plenty big enough for the two of them. Mac set the dry box on the table and went to Mel, who was sitting at an old table made from foraged driftwood, working on her computer.

"Heard the red tide's moving out," Mac said, then kissed her on the top of her head. He knew better than to expect her to fall into his arms.

"I hate to say it, but I'm hoping it was bad enough this time," she said, looking up and removing the reading glasses that she had recently succumbed to.

If there were a microphone present, the comment would have made the news, but Mac knew what she meant. In order for something finally to be done to stop Big Sugar from dumping millions of gallons of fertilizer into the water, the damage had to be newsworthy. This year's edition had been.

"Your boyfriend all settled in?"

He let it go. "Won't give us any trouble."

"If only," she said. "You hungry?"

"Famished. We have anything?"

"Got a couple lobsters I can throw on the grill with some corn," Mel said. Getting up from the chair, she went to the small kitchen and pulled two whole lobster, bigger than the ones the tourists overpaid for, and two ears of corn from the propane-powered refrigerator.

Mac took them and headed out onto the deck. He lit the grill, placed the food on, and sat back in his favorite chair. Mel came out a few minutes later with an open bottle of wine and two glasses. She took the chair next to him, and they sat in silence, listening to the crackling as the juices flowed onto the burners. Florida spiny lobster, known locally as bugs, were actually more like crayfish than the bright-red Maine lobster. The tails were the only edible part, but many locals preferred to cook them whole to keep them juicier. It was the same principle as grilling corn in the husk.

"How was your trip?" Mel asked.

"Complicated. I was hoping that finding the wreck of the *Sumnter* would stay off the radar, but it's likely to be all over the news. The only good thing is that it's in federal waters." Mac finished his glass and got up to turn the lobster. Mel held her empty glass out with one hand while she navigated her phone with the other. Mac filled both glasses and sat back down.

"Top billing from every major outlet," she said, skimming the newsfeed on her phone.

"That's what I was afraid of. Finally get something outside of the state's grasp, but this publicity's going to put it up for the highest bidder," Mac said, sitting back and thinking how many times, in the name of archeology, the state had screwed both him and Wood out of their finds. Federal waters, lying three miles offshore, were less restricted, but often too deep for the average salvor. Mac got up.

"What's up?" Mel asked.

"Be right back," he said, and went inside. After grabbing the dry box from the table, he brought it outside and set it between them. One at a time, Mac released the three clasps that made the watertight seal and opened the lid. Their heads almost collided as they peered inside.

Mac pulled back first.

"It's a hard drive," Mel said.

"Probably Gross's. Kurt's wife gave it to me as I was leaving." Mac got up and took the lobsters off the grill.

"Let's eat and I'll have a look," Mel said, picking it up and turning it in her hands. She was clearly more intrigued than Mac.

"Gross was like a pack rat. There's probably two decades'

worth of research to comb through on that thing. And half in archaic Spanish."

"Not much more I can do about Big Sugar tonight. Maybe I'll find something."

Mac gave her a look that clearly showed he thought not, and took the tray with the lobsters and ears of corn inside. Mel followed with the remnants of the wine, which he dumped into her glass before tossing the bottle in a bin.

Though Mac and Mel both tried to avoid it, their eyes kept returning to the hard drive as the flickering light from the oil lamp danced on the metal case. They ate in silence, lost in their own thoughts. Mac was worried about what the drive might reveal; Mel, clearly anxious to see what mysteries it held, in a rare case, finished her dinner before Mac. She picked up both their plates and took them to the sink, where she left them and returned to the table.

While she tried to figure how to connect the drive to her laptop, Mac went back to the kitchen, did the dishes, and brought back a bottle of Pilar rum and two glasses. After pouring two fingers into each, he slid one across to Mel and leaned back to watch her. Her eyeglasses were a new look, and he tried to decide whether he liked them or not, finally deciding that he did. In an unspoken competition, she had succumbed first to wearing them, claiming it was hard to read the computer screen, but he knew he would be right behind her.

Mac and Mel had known each other since she was a senior in high school and Mac was a twenty-three-year-old commercial diver looking for a change of scenery. After ditching his crazy girlfriend in Galveston, he had hitchhiked his way to the end of the world. His plan was to go all the way to Key West and seek out work with the famous treasure hunter Mel Fisher and his team, but in a pouring rainstorm, Wood had picked Mac up and his future had been sealed. The six-year age difference had been insurmountable then, but when they became reacquainted five years ago, it seemed like nothing. There were no regrets.

He sipped and watched Mel as she furrowed her brow, patiently trying each end of a pile of cables lying on the table. He was just thinking about how much she looked like Wood, when, with the same expression that her father had used, she crossed the thin line between patience and stubbornness.

"You have those tiny screwdrivers?" she asked, pushing away the pile of cables.

As much as Mac didn't want to know what was on the drive, neither did he want it ruined. "Why don't we take a run up to Key Largo after Tru and I get back tomorrow?" Tech gurus Alicia and her boyfriend, TJ, ran a dive shop. It was their passion and a good cover for their contract work with the CIA. Alicia had been a top analyst and TJ was a computer whiz.

Mel pushed the drive away and drank half the rum. "That is, if you two don't get into any trouble tomorrow."

Mac wasn't sure how they could, but knew if Trufante was involved, anything could happen. He finished his drink and went around the table behind Mel. Wrapping his arms around her, he lifted her from the chair and brought her back to the bedroom. Having the Cajun on either of their minds was not conducive to a good night's sleep, and he had a plan to fix that.

THREE

A STRANGE ANXIETY CREPT OVER MAC AS HE AND Trufante pulled in the traps and stacked them. It wasn't the fishing; the catch was good. A few shorts, but most of the stone crab traps were bringing in double digits of the tasty and expensive claws. Even though the sky was clear, between Ruth and the drive there seemed to be a cloud hanging over him. He had to admit that adding internet to the island had its advantages. A glance at the weather this morning had shown no change in the storm's trajectory, and as he had expected, it had picked up speed overnight.

"Not a bad haul for a two-day soak," Trufante said as he snapped the larger claw off a stone crab and tossed it back into the water. In an odd irony, his stump of a right middle finger, which had been lost to a sadistic drug dealer in a chum grinder, was the digit that the crabs tried to snap first when he pulled off their claw. Though it was legal to take both claws, leaving the crab with one pincer gave it a good chance to remain alive while it regenerated the other. Watching the crab get another chance, Mac wished that he could do the same in his life; once something crossed his path, it was forever a part of him.

"Just a few more of the stone traps, then we probably ought to pull the lobster traps and bring them in." He looked at the bin full of crab claws glistening in the sun. Trufante was eyeing the bin as well, calculating his cut. Lobster and crab fishing was all about risk and reward. The early-season lobster take had been good, but had tapered off after two months. Pulling those traps would get them to safety in case the storm came through, but with what Mac saw in the bin in front of him, if the storm didn't come, it was going to cost him. Losing even a couple of days when the crabs were around could cost him thousands of dollars. He could tell from the look on Trufante's face that he had calculated that as well, but Mac wasn't about to ask Trufante's opinion—risk was his middle name.

"Maybe ought to get these onto the island and stack 'em," Trufante said.

Mac knew what he was after. "Okay. Mel wants to go up to Key Largo. We'll get the lobster traps tomorrow morning." It was a rare circumstance where Trufante and Mel's agendas aligned. Mac looked forward, lining the bow up with the last string of traps, and started toward the next buoy. As they worked through the remaining traps, he started thinking about the hard drive and what might be on it.

THE CAREFULLY LIT pedestals displaying ancient clay pottery and the glass-covered cases of Spanish coins and artifacts made the conference room look more like a museum than its intended purpose, but as with everything else he did, Vince Bugarra was all about effect. To that end, he stared at the printout in front of him. A larger-than-life character in both physical size as well as personality, he crossed his tanned legs and waited.

The man sitting next to Bugarra had a laptop in front of him. Despite wearing thick glasses, the accountant squinted and moved closer to the screen. The man wasn't someone who would be his friend, but Bugarra knew the value of the man—while creative accountants were easy to find; good creative accountants were not.

"Preliminary numbers from the fundraiser are good." The accountant slid several printed pages toward Bugarra. "That incident with Maria Gross slowed things down for an hour, but we rebounded and should finish a couple of thousand dollars higher than last year." The man shrank back when he saw the pensive look on Bugarra's face.

"Can you move some of the charity money around? We need to show more growth."

"Yes, sir. Ten percent over last year should make the backers happy."

Bugarra nodded. The charities that had participated would make enough, but without showing year-on-year growth, his backers might not put up the money to run the event next year. It was easy to justify the three-card Monte game in his head: If the backers weren't happy, there would be no event; if there were no event, there would be no money for the charities. It was unfortunate about the incident. Maria hadn't been the same since, something that he would have to rectify. He wondered if the accountant could balance her moods as well as he did the books. With her father, Gill Gross gone, Maria was the only link left to his years of research. Getting his hands on that research had become a priority. His backers would up their antes the minute they found out he had it. More important to Bugarra personally was what Gross had been working on. "Do what you need to," Bugarra said, rising from the captain's chair. Like everything else in the room, the chairs were staged for effect.

"Right. What about the *Sumnter*?" the accountant asked.

"Whatever it takes to get the bid. If Gross was hiding it, there's something there. Just wish it wasn't in that damned park." Unlike most salvors, Bugarra was entirely comfortable paying off the state archeologists and keeping the lion's share of the profits, as well as the coordinates, for himself. With DeWitt locked up for accessory to murder, there would be a new representative for the State of Florida, adding another worry to his growing list.

Bugarra left the accountant fretting over his spreadsheets and walked down the hallway toward the door at the end. Made to look like a ship's hatch, the polished mahogany was fitted with gleaming brass fittings. After he entered a code into the pad concealed to the right, the electronic lock released and the door swung open, revealing a rendition of a captain's cabin. Bugarra walked around the plush chairs and passed the cut-crystal decanter of Appleton thirty-year-old rum, which, despite the early hour, he was tempted to taste. He almost surrendered, but things were moving too quickly to allow the alcohol to slow down his brain. One badly timed decision could cost him his fortune.

Moving around the large hatch-cover that had been made into his desk, he sat and pulled out his cell phone. There was a text from Maria, which he decided to ignore for a minute. Going to his contacts, he found the number labeled *Rat,* and pressed the connect button. He wasn't even sure if it rang before the Rat's nasal whine came over the line.

"Mr. Bugarra?"

"Did you find it?"

"I was able to access the Wi-Fi network in Gross's house, but I can't find the drive."

"What do you mean?" The Rat had earned his nickname by burrowing into every computer Bugarra had asked him to, including the state's secret database of permits—and their GPS coordinates.

"It's not physically there," he said apologetically. "If it was in the house, I'd find it."

"What about Maria's place? Maybe she took it."

"Checked that as well." He paused for a second. "Something you should know. Her browser history shows some recent searches for a guy named Mac Travis."

Bugarra slammed the phone down on the desktop, adding a real dent to the distressed top. He picked up the phone. "Did she find him?"

"She's craftier than I gave her credit for. Found some woman named Melanie Woodson, whom she emailed."

Bugarra's eyes bulged at the mention of Wood's daughter. This had moved above the Rat's pay grade. "Keep an eye on that and let me know if she gets a response." He cursed under his breath and started to rise. It took all his restraint to stay seated and avoid the decanter with its amber liquid that was calling his name. Instead, he picked up the printouts the accountant had given him and started scanning the lines. Running a salvage enterprise required him to wear several hats. It had been decades since he had been able to spend his days underwater looking for treasure. Now, he was a CEO, and that required the ability to present the numbers in front of him to anxious backers.

He threw the pages down in disgust, both from the information they contained and the way the name *Woodson* still floated in the air. The Shipwreck Ball, which he sponsored every year, had generally been a success. The fake galleon, usually staged near the beach of the Savoy Hotel for the event, was now tainted after Slipstream's failed attempt on Maria's life. It had cost well into the tens of thousands of dollars and lasted five years, only half its depreciated lifespan, but the run was over.

Next year he would have to find a way equally as creative and dramatic to part people from their money.

And Woodson. He hadn't heard that name in years, but it still left a bad taste in his mouth. Pushing the papers to the side, Bugarra opened a browser window on his computer and entered *Melanie Woodson* into the search field. The first results were her social media profiles. Scanning them, the first thing he noticed was how attractive she was, something that might be used in his favor. Further down the page of results were several business related links, which he opened and skimmed through. Satisfied, he leaned back and started to calculate a strategy to win the woman over. That, he was confident he could do, but Travis would have to be dealt with first.

The salvage business was a small community. The barriers to entry, between the equipment and the ability to finagle a permit from the state, required resources out of reach of most divers. With billions at stake, it was a ruthless occupation. Wood had been a guy lurking on the fringes, making most of his money from his ability to engineer and build or rebuild the bridges linking the Keys together. Along the way he had made some notable finds, but he was risk-averse and happy enough to build, fish, and dive. Travis was the same, but Wood's daughter was a different animal.

Two websites had given Bugarra a snapshot of her life. The Florida Bar Association and the ACLU both had extensive biographies on her. He only had to skim a few paragraphs from each site to know she had legal teeth and wasn't afraid to use them. He all kinds of people to do the "behind the scenes" work, but one of the keys to his success was the ability to do the heavy lifting himself. In this case, that meant a trip to the Keys.

WHEN HIS WORLDS ALIGNED, Mac got nervous. There was a large payday coming from the bin of stone crabs he and Trufante had pulled from the traps, just another harbinger that this storm was coming for them. Tru was actually a help. Together they stacked and tied down the crab traps in the old clearing, the second highest point on the island where Wood had kept his skiff. When that was complete, Mac sent Trufante to load the catch on the center console, while he went to the house to get Mel.

She was also in a good mood, and despite Trufante lingering less than a hundred feet away, she leaned in and kissed him. "Better get a shower," she said, wrinkling her nose.

Mac went through the house and stepped onto the porch from the back door in the bedroom, where he used the screened outdoor shower to clean the morning off him. Mel was dressed for town, and he knew better than to wear his usual cargo shorts and t-shirt. He found a pair of flat-front shorts and a button-down shirt that would be suitable for the dinner out he guessed was in his future, and left the house.

Trufante whistled his approval as they approached the boat, and he offered—and, surprisingly, Mel accepted—his help aboard the boat. Mac waded out and boarded, keeping a careful eye on the two of them. Both were happy now, but he knew from experience that that mood could turn on a dime and things would return to normal. With a "take it while I can get it" attitude, he started the engine and sent Trufante to the bow to release the line from the trawler.

With the sun just behind them, the water was brilliantly lit, displaying the palette of color that taunted thousands of amateur artists, and at the same time revealing the hazards below them. Without the help of the chartplotter, Mac navigated the winding route to Marathon by memory, and they soon pulled up to the dock behind Keys Fisheries. Mel went to the office while Mac and Trufante unloaded the catch. A half-hour later, with a large check in his pocket, Mac fished a dozen hundreds from his wallet and paid off an eager Trufante, who disappeared like a yellowtail with a barracuda in pursuit.

Mac shrugged, checked the lines, and, with Mel beside him clutching a bag with the hard drive in the dry box, walked to the parking lot. Mac thought he glimpsed Trufante walking upstairs to the bar as he opened the car door for Mel. Both were still smiling—a very unsettling occurrence.

FOUR

"WOULD YOU WATCH THE ROAD?"

Mac pulled his attention back to the two-lane road in front of him. As spectacular as the water looked from a boat, the view from the Long Key Bridge put it in a different light. It felt as if a magnet was pulling his eyes to the water as they passed the aqua flats. Shades of brown speckled with white-sand patches drew his eyes. He knew there were likely lobster or stone crabs there. Then, as they approached the center of the span, the blues became deeper, finally settling on an indigo that could only be described in paint color nomenclature. He knew the pass well. He and Wood had rebuilt the bridge together, and Mac remembered every pothole and cut that held lobster and fish.

His attention was brought back to the dry box sitting on Mel's lap. Hopefully, TJ would be able to download its contents. Mac was torn between hoping it would reveal the location of some long-forgotten treasure, or having nothing useful. There was something to be said for his disparate life. Some might call it boring, but he was satisfied. Mel had struggled with island life at first after leaving the ACLU and moving back from Virginia. The last year or so, her fight against Big

Sugar had given her the *why* she needed. Together they were happy. But Mac knew if there was something on the treasure hunter's hard drive, he would be like a sailfish stalking a bait ball. No way he could ignore it.

The late-afternoon traffic was light as they moved through Islamorada and entered Tavernier. With the majority of the bridges behind him, Mac focused on the road as they drove through his least favorite part of the island chain and entered Key Largo.

Mac turned right off US 1 and onto the side street that led to TJ and Alicia's dive shop. Mac checked the time; he hoped TJ would be back from his afternoon charter. Seeing the large red and white dive flag flying over the shop, he turned into the crushed coral driveway. The lot held a half-dozen cars, many with dive stickers. Running a business here was hard, especially in the off-season, and Mac was glad to see that the couple appeared to be doing well.

He parked off to the side, and they went to the shop. A buzzer attached to the door alerted Alicia, who sat behind the counter with her nose buried in a computer. She looked up and smiled, quickly coming around the counter and hugging Mel and then Mac. There was a special bond between Mac and the diminutive woman, who had been a desk-bound analyst when he had met her. He and Trufante had guided Alicia through her first field action. It was good to watch her grow from the shy and clumsy geek to a happy and fulfilled woman.

"How are you guys?" she asked.

"You look great," Mel said.

"Getting out as often as I can. With summer over, the dive business has slowed down. TJ's got the group today." She looked at a large digital clock on the wall. "Should be back anytime. Let me get him on the radio."

"No need. We can catch up while we wait."

A few minutes later, Mac heard TJ on the radio. He was already halfway down the dock, with Alicia and Mel right behind him, when he saw the converted sportfisher enter the canal. Mac waited with the bow line while TJ spun the boat 180 degrees and, using the wind, allowed it to settle against the dock. Mac climbed aboard with a line, while Alicia waited by the stern ready to toss the line to TJ.

With the boat secure, Mac and Mel stepped aside to let TJ and Alicia finish their business. The talk amongst the divers was all positive, and Mel helped several take pictures with TJ. With his short, sun-bleached dreadlocks, he looked the part of a Keys divemaster. Several customers tried to tip him as they disembarked, but he refused, urging them to come back for more.

A helping-hand chain was quickly formed to unload the dive gear, and soon it was just the four of them on the dock. "Business looks good," Mac said. With all the competition in the Keys, and most of the commercial dive boats packed like cattle cars running out to Pennekamp Park every day, Alicia and TJ had tried a different business plan. They offered custom-blended mixed-gas charters designed to maximize the divers' bottom time. The enriched oxygen blend known as NITROX generally came in thirty-two or thirty-six percent mixes. The added oxygen allowed longer bottom times by mitigating the effects of the nitrogen buildup in the divers' bloodstream that caused the bends, but it had a drawback. The richer mixes became fatal, causing oxygen toxicity at depth, making the tradeoff not always worth it. TJ had designed a program that gave the divers the optimum mix for each particular dive. This decreased the surface intervals between dives and allowed the dives themselves to be longer. The reviews were positive—most dive shops wouldn't be filling their charter boats on a weekday in October—but it was a lot of work, especially without a crew.

"Looking good there, big man," Mac said. Though muscular,

TJ's genetics configured him in the shape of a bowling ball, a stark contrast to Alicia's rail-thin figure.

"Keeping you busy down there?" TJ asked.

"Got something for you to look at if you have time." Without needing to be asked, Mac stepped aboard and started pulling the empty tanks from their racks and setting them on the docks. Each one had a piece of blue tape that indicated the percent of oxygen of each mix. He noticed quite a few in the mid-twenties. With standard air being twenty-one percent oxygen, he wondered what effect the slight increase had. "What's the twenty-six percent blend do?"

"Brewed that up for a 130-foot dive. With that mix, you can get almost forty minutes of bottom time."

Mac knew the standard dive tables by heart. With regular air, the bottom time for that depth was less than twenty minutes. "Nice—as long as they don't suck air, it's a big advantage."

After unloading and hosing down the boat, they moved upstairs to the apartment the couple lived in. Alicia offered beers to everyone, and they entered the War Room, set up behind a pair of doors that looked like a closet. The environment was stark and cold. At least a dozen large monitors lit up on the far wall after TJ pressed the spacebar on the keyboard at his command center that looked like Kirk's captain's chair from the *Starship Enterprise*. The screens were all showing the same image, but Mac knew TJ had the ability to mix them up as he needed.

Mel moved toward the captain's chair and handed him the dry box. TJ looked at it like it was a bomb.

"It's okay. Remember Kurt Hunter? His wife's a forensic tech for Miami-Dade. She gave it to me," Mac said.

TJ opened the lid and removed the drive. "No worries here. Give me a minute."

He got up and went to a wire shelving unit full of bins, the only piece of furniture placed against the side of the room. The monitors on the front wall and TJ's captain's chair made the room look full, but with the exception of Alicia's desk, there was no other furniture. He pulled out a bin and brought it to the chair. Pre-Alicia, TJ had been a big-time gamer, designing programs and winning competitions. His attention had turned to the real world after meeting Alicia. It was interesting how transferable his skills had been.

He found the connector he was looking for and plugged one end into the drive. The other end had a standard USB plug, which he inserted into a port in the chair. His hands flew over the keyboard, and several seconds later, the screen showed a list of the files on the drive.

"Who'd this belong to?" TJ said, scrolling through the directory.

"Gill Gross," Mac said.

"Ah, that would explain the structure."

The names of the folders were four-digit numbers, which looked like years. From the early 1600s to the mid-nineteenth century, just about every year had a folder.

"Can you open 1733?" Mac asked.

"Sure."

The 1733 Plate Fleet had been lost in a hurricane off the Keys. The wrecks had been found and salvaged in the seventies and eighties. They were now off-limits to salvors. Mac didn't expect to see anything new, perhaps just an insight into Gross's mind.

TJ opened the file, and Mac immediately recognized the name of the ships. None of this was new information, but Gross had done his homework. A similar file existed for the 1715 fleet that had met its demise along the east coast of Florida.

"Lot of information here," TJ said.

Another screen changed, and Mac turned to Alicia, who was pounding on her keyboard. Mel leaned over her. "Here's a list of every Spanish wreck by value," Alicia said. "We can cross-reference these to the years they were lost and see what Gross was up to."

"Or—" TJ stopped and hit several keys. The directory re-sorted itself, showing the most recent files on top. The two that TJ had opened were on top. He clicked the third.

"Showoff," Alicia said.

For the next several minutes, the room was filled with the sound of keyboards clicking and screens flashing. The data war between TJ and Alicia was well underway when Mac moved toward the door where Mel was standing, her face illuminated by the light from her phone. When he reached her, she handed it to him. Mac took the phone and squinted at the display. With a flourish, she took her glasses off and handed them to him.

Mac might have suffered, squinting to read the email if they were in public, but, rationalizing the use of the glasses to himself due to the low light in the room, he carefully put them on. The display was clear now, and he started reading.

Ms. Woodson,

Although we've never met, I feel that we should know each other. My name is Vince Bugarra of Treasure Hunters, Inc. Your father and I were acquainted and worked together back in the nineties. By the way, my deepest condolences on your loss.

It has come to my attention that you may be in possession of some data retrieved from Gill Gross's computer. I would like to speak with you about this at your earliest opportunity, and in that regard, I plan on being in the Marathon area for the next few days.

Sincerely, Vince Bugarra

FIVE

BUGARRA HAD TRUFANTE CORNERED IN THE BAR. SEVERAL inquiries had led him to the lanky Cajun. It had taken more drinks than he planned, and his patience with the deck hand's tales was waning. If drinks weren't going to be enough, he decided to throw money into the mix.

"They're old friends and there's a rather large reward for information ..." Bugarra let the sentence hang and got the reaction he wanted.

"So, you're interested in Mac and Mel?" Trufante asked.

It was as if Bugarra had wasted the last hour, but he had finally broken through. "You have a boat, we could go see them now." He pulled a stack of hundreds out of his pocket long enough for Trufante to see them, then slid the bills back out of sight.

Bugarra followed Trufante's gaze as he looked around the bar, then down to the marina below. He had overheard Mel saying something about heading to Key Largo. She had been secretive as usual around him, but he knew that Mac's center console was still tied up to the seawall near the lobster boats. Trufante tossed down his drink and seemed to do a calculation in his head. Bugarra waited, already knowing what the answer would be.

"Gotta be just a run out there and back. I can't have you in the house either. Just a quick look."

Bugarra could tell Trufante was wavering and decided to seal the deal. "One more for the road?" Bugarra looked down the bar, caught the bartender's attention, and ordered two shots of Pilar white rum. He had been dealing with people like Trufante for a long time and knew that the extra few dollars spent on top-shelf liquor, brands that they would never drink themselves, often paid dividends. Bugarra downed his in one gulp and watched Trufante roll the rum around in his mouth as if trying to get his taste buds to remember it. Finally, his large Adam's apple bobbed and he turned and led the way out of the bar, down the stairs, and across the parking lot. Bugarra sweetened the pot a little more once they were on the boat, sliding two hundreds into Trufante's hand as he pulled the keys out of a small compartment concealed in the console.

They didn't need the glow from the setting sun; Trufante's thousand-dollar grin could have lit the way to Mac's island. Bugarra was vaguely familiar with the area from studying charts, but as Trufante drove the serpentine route necessary to dodge the shoals and sandbars, he was quickly lost. At about the same time that the center span of the Seven Mile Bridge dropped below the horizon, they entered the cluster of mangrove-covered islands. By the time they had passed between a pair and cut behind another, he had no idea where they were. To make matters worse, the Cajun was driving by memory and the chartplotter remained off.

When Trufante cut the wheel hard to port and slid into an unmarked channel, he saw Travis's trawler tied to the solitary piling. It was the only sign of life Bugarra had seen—beside some birds—in the past forty minutes. Trufante stopped next to the large trawler, reached over the gunwale, and retrieved two dock lines, which he used to tie off the center console. Without a thought, he vaulted over the side and landed in what was for him calf-deep water. Bugarra looked down at his shoes and slowly took them off before joining Trufante in the water.

Together they waded to the beach. Bugarra wasn't sure where they were going until Trufante opened a gate, woven with mangrove branches to conceal it, leading to a well-worn path. As he followed, a touch of paranoia crept into his thoughts. If Travis had gone to so much trouble to disguise the place, there could be security cameras or even booby traps. He tried to match the Cajun's footfalls, but his shorter legs couldn't quite equal the taller man's stride. As they approached the clearing and he saw the house, Bugarra relaxed slightly. There were no turrets or concealed gun placements, just a new-looking stilt house. He doubted the door even had a lock. It was a strange phenomenon out in the boonies that if you were going to lock your house, it had better be a fortress. Often it was easier to leave the doors open and let anyone take what they needed without doing damage.

Trufante confirmed that by walking upstairs and letting himself into the house. He entered, only to return a minute later with a beer in hand. "You seen what you want? We gotta go."

Bugarra took one more look around the clearing and climbed the stairs to the house.

"The deal was to see the place, not search the house."

He walked past Trufante and went inside. In another life, he would have called it tasteful; in his current one, it seemed small and cramped. On the dining room table was an open laptop. After a quick scan of the bedroom, he came back and sat in front of it. Hoping there was no password, he pressed the spacebar and waited for the computer to come to life.

The email program had been left open, and he skimmed the

inbox, noticing his own. Wondering if he should delete it, he opened it and looked up when he heard Trufante enter.

"I'm gonna drink one more beer and we really gotta go." He went to the small refrigerator and took out two beers.

One he opened, and Bugarra thought he was going to offer the other to him, but Trufante walked out, saying something about a "boat beer." Knowing he was running out of time, Bugarra focused on the emails. It appeared Ms. Woodson was involved in the good fight against Big Sugar, something he could side with her on. The salvage business was more efficient in clear water, and the sugar magnates around Lake Okeechobee were clearly responsible for the decrease in visibility over the last few years.

He had a measure of her, at least, and opened the Finder app, skimming her files. Computers weren't in his wheelhouse, but he had people for that, and took several pictures of her recently opened files. Overall, he decided the trip had been worth it. There was no sign of the hard drive or its files, but he knew his Sun Tzu and how important it was to know your enemies.

"Beer's about empty. I'm heading to the boat with or without you," Trufante called up from below.

BUGARRA LEFT QUICKLY and walked down the stairs, thinking the Cajun might be crazy enough to leave him. There was no sign of Trufante in the clearing, so he continued onto the path. After closing the gate, Bugarra saw him sitting on the rocket launcher drinking his beer and grinning.

MAC AND MEL entered the War Room. The keyboard battle

was over, though there was no obvious winner, and their attention was quickly drawn to the screens. Two images were displayed side by side. Mac knew one. "That's the *Sumnter*. We just dove her."

"Gross had completed a good deal of research on several immediate pre-Civil War era vessels," TJ said. "It looked like that had become his focus, but the 1628 file was recently opened as well. From what we figure, that's where the money is, unless you're Vince Bugarra, who needs to salvage just enough Spanish gold to keep his backers lined up. He makes his money fundraising."

The other screen showed the face of a man. It was a stark drawing, with heavy brows and a large nose. "Who's that?" Mel asked.

TJ looked down at a file. "Moses Henriques. Seems he was a pirate who captured the 1628 fleet. That treasure was supposedly taken to an island in Brazil."

"Was it ever found?" Mac asked.

"Doesn't look like it, but that's way out of Gross's wheelhouse."

Mac agreed. "This is all research. Are there any logs or anything that shows if he dove it?"

"There's enough on here to keep me busy for several months. I'll keep going on it," TJ said.

"Can I get a copy?" Mel asked.

"Sure thing. I'll copy the files onto my server and give you the originals back," TJ said.

"Might ought to burn it to a flash drive or something we can easily access," Mac said. "I'd also like to get the original back to Kurt before someone finds out it's missing."

"Roger that," TJ said. He got up and walked back to the shelves, where he pulled a flash drive from one of his bins. After inserting it into a port in the chair, he hit some keys and, a few minutes later, pulled it out. "You need to check anything out, let me know. Business is good, but getting spotty during the week."

"Cool," Mac said, and took the offered flash drive and the original hard drive back. "Appreciate you doing this."

"We just wrapped up a contract. It'd be fun to get into something for someone without an alphabet soup name."

Mac knew he was referring to the CIA. He looked over at Mel. "We ought to get going. Long ride back."

"And we've done it in the dark before," Mel replied. "Be a little social, Mac. Bad enough you're like a hermit out there. Scary how similar you are to my dad." She turned to Alicia. "Where can we take you to dinner?"

TO SAY he suffered through the meal was not exactly accurate, as Mac enjoyed another bite of his ribeye. Most tourists sought out fresh Keys seafood, but with residents' freezers generally loaded with it, they were often the opposite, getting their meat fixes from the restaurants. He liked the couple and could tell that Mel needed this. Still, he was worried, and his mind wandered from Bugarra being in Marathon to the almost threatening email the guy had written to Mel. He would be careful not to let her out of his sight until he knew the salvor was out of Monroe County.

Sharing a dessert four ways was as domesticated as he cared to get, and he tapped his foot, waiting for the server to bring the bill. A blow to his shin stopped his foot from tapping, and he looked at Mel, who shot him a "don't mess with my party" look. He smiled an apology. Finally, her social needs were satisfied, and they left the restaurant. They hadn't spoken about Gross or the hard drive in the restaurant. The Keys had a coconut telegraph, which was several times faster than the best internet connection. With everyone always wanting to know where the bite was, eavesdropping could be a professional sport here.

They said their goodbyes, and Mac started toward the car. Mel headed him off at the driver's-side door and held her hand out. He dutifully dropped the keys into it and went to the passenger side. Even without the drinks, he would have surrendered them. After two trips to Homestead this week to dive with Kurt, he had exceeded his driving quota for the year.

He must have nodded off, as he woke with a start as they reached the dock. They left the car and walked to the boat. It was instantly apparent to Mac that it had been moved. Good habits made for good boaters, something Wood had beaten into both Mac and his daughter. This covered everything from maintenance to the way a line was tied to a cleat. Where many boaters simply crisscrossed the lines and finished with a half hitch, Mac had learned to place a full circle around the cleat first.

Looking around the lot, he saw Trufante's motorcycle parked near the bar. He started for the entrance, but decided there would be no point in interrogating a drunk Cajun. Tomorrow would be soon enough. Mel was already aboard and had the engine running when he hopped down from the dock. The unauthorized use of the boat only added to his premonition that something was wrong.

SIX

"FIND ME SOMETHING I CAN WORK WITH," BUGARRA yelled into the phone, then calmed himself. Even with the company plane, it had been early in the morning when he arrived back from Marathon, and on only a few hours' sleep, he knew his fuse was short—shorter than normal. The minute he set foot on dry land, he had emailed the Rat the pictures he had taken from Woodson's computer. He'd suspected there was nothing there, but that was no reason to back off the pressure on his minions. He hung up, sat back, sipped his coffee, and took several measured breaths to bring his blood pressure back to earth. The deep breathing didn't seem to work, and he wondered if it was too early to dump a shot of rum into the coffee. He went to the sideboard and opened the bottle, hesitating. After finding nothing at the island and without a response to his email, before actually confronting the woman, there was one play left, and due to the location, he put the rum aside. He was going to prison.

Raiford Prison was a long way from Sebastian on the Treasure Coast. He would have preferred to live elsewhere. He spent a good deal of time raising money in Miami, where he had a condo, but the resting spot of the 1715 fleet was where the treasure-hunting community lived—all except Gross, that was. Maybe he was smarter to stay away and take his chances finding hit-or-miss wrecks that might or might not pay off. But the remains of the fleet resting in the shallow waters outside of the Sebastian Inlet had the potential to be the next *Atocha*. Before finding the famous wreck, Mel Fisher had cut his teeth here.

He got up from the table and dumped the remaining coffee in the sink, then went upstairs and showered. Bypassing his normal dress, he chose something simple: khaki slacks and a plain button-down shirt. There was no need to taint his linen and silk in the prison.

The three-and-a-half-hour drive passed quietly. Too quietly for Bugarra. He scanned the talk radio shows, stopping to listen several times when he heard the news of a large hurricane heading toward Haiti. Though it was a long way away, Florida was in its sights. Without a weather system to shift it farther out to sea, it would be here in days. He remembered Hurricane Andrew, as it had made a dead-straight beeline toward Miami in '92, going from nothing to a devastating hurricane in four days. Unlike most people who relied on the water for their living, Bugarra welcomed a storm and the insurance money that followed.

After turning inland at St. Augustine, he followed the dead-straight road toward Green Cove Springs and the prison. When he saw the high-voltage electric lines that supplied power to the prison's infamous electric chair start to parallel the road, he knew he was close. The chair was now just one of several modes of death presented to the inmates like a death menu.

Several small green signs directed him to the visitors' entrance, where he parked and walked to the door. After almost an hour of screenings and waiting, he was finally buzzed through a solid steel door with a small safety-glass window and led to a room, where the guard entered a code. The electromagnetic lock buzzed open, and he saw the wreck of a man sitting nervously in the chair.

Slipstream had always looked like he was ridden hard and put up wet. The deck hand had been around since Bugarra had first begun his business. Now, after a record-setting plea deal, he would be the guest of the state for at least a few years. How he had finagled a manslaughter conviction out of the murders of Gross, his backer, Morehead, and the attempted murder of Gross's daughter, Maria, Bugarra had no idea. Maybe only by rolling over on Jim DeWitt, the state archeologist who had been his accomplice. DeWitt was a high-profile takedown for both the state, looking to incarcerate him on criminal charges, and the feds, who wanted him on tax evasion for taking his own share of the state's cut of the treasures found each year by salvors.

Bugarra had an axe to grind with DeWitt, but that would wait. Since his shell corporation had been listed on the Treasure Hunters payroll as "research" for the last decade, the former state archeologist would tell him everything he wanted to know. The problem with DeWitt was that he didn't know much beyond the information listed on the permit applications he processed. That in itself often led to gold for Bugarra, but the treasure-hunting community was at odds with the state, and unless a salvor had already found something, DeWitt, as their representative, would be left out of the loop. Slipstream had been at the finds when they took place.

"Nice of you to visit," Slipstream sneered, clearly enjoying Bugarra's discomfort, who was examining the plain metal chair before sitting in it.

Bugarra finally decided to burn the clothes he wore, and then sat. "How're the accommodations?"

"Fair to middling. You going to pull some strings and get me out of here?" Slipstream leaned across the table.

"If only I could, my friend. If only I could." There was no way, even if Bugarra did have the influence, that he would help Slipstream get released even a day early. In fact, he already had a plan in place to sabotage the parole hearings. Bugarra was quiet for second, imagining Maria Gross's dramatic appearance before the board.

"Well, what do you want, then?" Slipstream asked.

"I want to help you, of course. Maybe a deposit in your scrip account, or a donation to the warden's favorite charity in exchange for some conjugal visits." Bugarra wondered how much it would cost to pay someone to come up here and actually have sex with the man.

"Hard times." Slipstream smiled.

Bugarra knew he had to play it carefully here. Slipstream might be the only man alive that knew what Gross had been working on before his death. "I'll do what I can for you." He rose as if to leave.

"Wait."

He heard the waver in Slipstream's voice.

"You didn't come all the way here to buy me some cigarettes and get me laid."

"Of course not, but I will."

"I want something in writing," Slipstream started, and paused, as if trying to figure out how to outwit Bugarra. "In a safe deposit box."

Bugarra knew Slipstream was grasping for anything he could get. Having dealt in high-level negotiations for years, he knew Slipstream was shooting from the hip. The best thing to do was be patient and let him finish.

"And fifty thousand cash. And a cut."

"You want a cut, you produce." Bugarra watched as the broken man smiled, thinking he had outwitted him. He eased off. "Any information will help your cause here."

"You know Gross found the *Sumnter*. Got some gold and silver off her too, before—"

He paused. Bugarra watched as the gears tried to turn in Slipstream's head. While he waited, he wondered how you talked about someone you killed as if you hadn't. "And what might that be? There were rumors that Gross had been looking near the Dry Tortugas."

"Shit, he'd just disappear for a few days."

"Didn't take the boat?"

"Nope. Only found out because I followed him to the airport one time."

"And what was he doing?"

"Took one of those little puddle jumper things to Key West. That's as far as I was able to track him down. Maybe flying all that money to the Caymans or something."

Bugarra would be able to check Gross's passport, but doubted the man had left the U.S. In the salvage business, there were the dreamers and the pragmatists. Gross was definitely one of the former. He would hide his finds under his bed before he even thought to fly them out of the county.

"Why do you think he was looking around the Dry Tortugas?"

"Heard him talking to some dude. Sounded like they were doing some air recon. So, about that scrip and all?"

Bugarra knew, at least for now, this was all Slipstream had. If he did know something else, he wasn't aware he knew it, or his alcohol-pickled brain had forgotten it. In all likelihood, he had told Bugarra everything he knew. "I'll make a deposit on my way out." Bugarra could see the relief spread across Slipstream's face as he said goodbye and called for the guard.

"SOMEONE WAS HERE," Mac said.

"Yup, I didn't leave the computer on this program," Mel said.

"At least three beers missing from the refrigerator."

"Trufante," they both said at once.

"He'd take the beer, but the computer's not his thing," Mac said.

"Never know what that meathead is up to. I don't know why you put up with him."

"It was your dad who said, when trying to find help down here, that it was better to deal with the devil you knew than the one you didn't."

This was not the first time they'd had this conversation. In recent years, the lack of affordable housing had made finding good help even tougher. Now, many of the low- and mid-income earners lived on rundown boats, anchored anywhere they could set a hook and still commute to shore for work. One hurricane was going to shut off the mostly unskilled help market.

Thinking about the oncoming storm, he looked outside. There was no sign of anything yet, but that meant little.

"You hear anything?" Mac asked.

Mel clicked the hurricane symbol on the favorites bar and waited for Mike's Weather Page to load. "Looks like it's going to pass the Dominican Republic today. Still shows it coming this way. Upgraded to a category five."

He felt bad for the people in Ruth's path, but knew that living here, for all its benefits, also came with a large degree of chance. Mac stood behind Mel, studying the screen. He put his hands on her shoulders.

"It's coming," Mac said. He'd been watching storms a long time, and it didn't look like there was anything going to steer this one somewhere else. Beside that, the hurricane was huge—he imagined that if overlaid on the state of Florida, it would cover most of the peninsula. He'd been through enough storms to know exactly what to do and when to do it. His decision to pull the traps earlier looked like the right one after seeing the marine forecast.

"Two to fours building to three to fives tomorrow. We'll get the lobster traps in the morning and be done with it."

She nodded. "I've got some emails to deal with, and then I can take a look at the drive that TJ copied."

"Can you stick the drive in? I'll have a look at it on the boat," he said, having planned on going down to the trawler to check on some things. He wanted to look at the areas from the aerial pictures on the chartplotter, and see if there was any evidence of what Trufante had been up to. Calling him was an option, but it was too late in the day-after-getting- paid Cajun time for that. With his girlfriend, Pamela gone, the balance that had once countered each of their mercurial behaviors was missing, prob-ably in both their lives.

After a quick inspection, Mac determined that Trufante had not been aboard, and he went to the wheelhouse. Mac was old school, still remembering the Loran time-difference numbers from the pre-GPS era. He had adopted the technology slowly, but finally had been convinced to upgrade the elec-tronics to the twin-screen units in front of him when the boat was refitted last year. He had wavered at the cost, which was almost as much as the rebuilt Cummins that he'd put in. The large screens were identical, synced to display two different views. The satellite internet he had installed for Mel came in handy as he connected to the Wi-Fi extender in the house. In seconds, he had one of the aerial pictures from Gross's drive on the left screen, and on the right, he used the touchscreen to pan the chart to the same area. Once they were sized correctly, he could imagine the bottom below the water.

Finding wrecks was part divination, part research, and a

good dose of luck. You could study logs all day and know where the ships might have gone down, but the ever-changing sands and waters of the ocean were not compliant, and wrecks were often found a dozen miles from where they were recorded to have sunk. As Mac looked at the screens, he focused on an area called the Quicksands. It wasn't hard to imagine how easily a billion-dollar wreck could be hidden beneath the shifting sands.

SEVEN

FEELING AS IF HIS OFFICE WALLS WERE CLOSING IN ON HIM, Bugarra had gone home. Sitting by the pool, he opened his laptop, checked the news, and saw the headlines completely dominated by the approaching storm. It had a name and likely a killer now: Ruth. Having wreaked havoc on the Dominican Republic, the hurricane was still a category five with no expectation of weakening in the next twenty-four hours, when it would give Cuba a glancing blow. The models differed from there, but Florida was definitely in the cone of possibility.

His response, unlike most people who protected their property, was to email his insurance agent and increase his coverage. After grabbing a cup of coffee from the machine, he sat back down and started making a mental list of the things that insurance or the government couldn't fix. The fate of the handful of wreck sites in different stages of salvage was mostly out of his control. He would have his captains and divemasters take one more shot at the sites today, then allow his employees to take care of themselves. His benevolence would, of course, be misinterpreted as caring about them.

There was no controlling the storm, not that he really cared to. By late today, Florida would be a disaster area before Ruth even hit. A mass exodus of evacuees would be underway, and he found it slightly amusing that the state magnanimously waived the tolls on the highways allowing those faced with losing everything the opportunity to save ten bucks. Stores would be cleaned out, and by tomorrow the fighting would begin over what was left. He didn't really need a plan. With the company jet at his disposal, he could decide when and where to go at the last minute.

He started to think about how Ruth could be the perfect cover to deal with Woodson and Travis. With the residents out for themselves and law enforcement agencies either checking evacuation zones or heading for points north themselves, he could make his move without anyone noticing—or caring. He knew Travis by reputation and expected, with Wood as his mentor, that the apple wouldn't fall far from the tree. If Bugarra evacuated at all, it would be at the last minute.

Sending a crew south, against the grain of how the rest of the population was moving, would be easy. Bugarra picked up his phone, went to his favorites screen, and pressed one of the names.

"Got a job for you," he said when the call was picked up. He seldom was sent to voicemail.

"Hurricane's coming," the man said.

"Good for business. It needs to be done now." Bugarra went on to describe the location and layout of Mac's island. "Whatever it takes." The man agreed to put together a crew and leave immediately. Looking at his watch, Bugarra estimated it would take them about four hours to drive to Marathon, then another two to find a boat and reach the island.

Another glance at the spaghetti models and cone of probability, now permanent fixtures on every network feed, showed several storm tracks. Squinting to combine them into one, he divined that Ruth would hit the Middle Keys in about thirty-six hours—plenty of time to take care of business. With a footprint larger than the state, where it went next was a no-brainer, and he looked at the dot on the map at the end of the island chain that, for the time being, lay toward the southern section of the cone of death. It looked like, once again, Key West would be spared and might be the safest place in the state. Being close to the action was also a consideration as he called his pilot and arranged for the plane to be fueled and ready.

"FIND A WAY," Mac yelled into the phone, and hung up. Once again, Trufante had hit his last nerve. And once again, Mel pressed him to fire the Cajun.

"If it was that simple, I would have done it a long time ago."

"I know you have a soft spot for him, but—"

Mac wasn't going to let her start the same rant he had heard over and over. If he could replace Trufante, he would have done it long ago. Yeah, Trufante did stupid stuff and had a nose for trouble, but he generally could be trusted. "You grew up with my options. Can you honestly tell me any of them are any better?"

"I know, but still," she said.

"Natives are no good and the transients are worse." Wood used to say that the further down the island chain they came, the crazier they were. Either running away from something, someone, or, in many cases, themselves, the Keys and Key West in particular were a haven for the lost and lonely.

"After I skin him for coming out here last night, we're gonna pull the rest of the traps. That storm's getting too close for comfort." They had just checked the weather reports online, and it didn't look good.

"When are we evacuating?" Mel asked.

There was no fight about staying on the island. If the storm surge was anything over ten feet, there would be little left. Even Wood grudgingly had left when Wilma had come through in 2005. The house was built on the highest part of the island and could take a twelve-foot surge. It might make it, but the rest of the island would be wiped clean. The question was when and where to go.

"I'm not going to sit in traffic all the way to Georgia," Mac said.

"What's your plan, then?"

"Figured I'd take the trawler and tow the center console to the Tortugas."

"Gee, and if you're wrong?"

She had a point. "We'll see it coming. With the new engine, the boat can make thirty knots, Ruth's moving at fifteen. Just have to stay ahead of it." The math sounded simple, but he knew it wasn't all numbers. This hurricane was so big that the outer bands would chase him down like a marlin after a mullet. With high winds, torrential rains, and big seas, outrunning a hurricane wasn't as easy as it sounded. The boats were a concern, though, and he was willing to be uncomfortable and fight the building seas to save them.

"You go your way. I'm flying up to Atlanta to see my old roommate."

Mac breathed a sigh of relief. Mel leaving the state was going to make things a whole lot easier. He stepped behind her and saw the computer screen was open to the Silver Airways website. The small carrier had the most flights from Key West. "You want to schedule one, I'll run you down there."

"Today, Mac."

"We can leave as soon as I'm back. Be in Key West around five." He calculated the time it would take to pull and stack the traps. He could sell the catch in Key West, probably at enough of a premium to pay for the gas. The only problem was going to be Trufante.

"Last chance?" she asked and when he shook his head, Mel clicked a few keys. "Okay, booked. Six thirty out of Key West."

"Better get ready. The boy wonder should be here anytime now," Mac said, and kissed the top of her head. He left the house and headed for the beach, hoping Trufante had his transportation issues figured out. A half-hour later, Mac was getting antsy and thinking about heading out himself when he heard the whine of twin outboards. He shaded his eyes from the morning sun and looked out over the water. A minute later, he saw the boat and cursed Trufante under his breath. He had gotten a ride instead of borrowing a boat. Now Mac would have to figure out how to get rid of him later.

The thirty-foot boat fishtailed as the driver spun around the rock and coasted to a stop about a foot from the beach. Both men aboard had huge smiles.

"How's it going, Commander?" Mac said to the driver. He didn't know him by any other name.

"Got your man here for you. Said you were gonna pull the rest of your gear today."

"Got most of it the other day. Not worth leaving it out. What's the bait telling you?" Mac asked. How the ballyhoo were behaving was a good indicator of what was to come. They seemed to sense approaching weather faster than the meteorologists—and more accurately. Commander ran a network of bait fishermen. Though Mac didn't like him personally, he knew he had answers.

The flat bill of Commander's hat remained slightly askew as he spun it around to shade the sun. "Moving out. Stopped fishing yesterday. Ain't no market right now, and if we lose power, all the frozen stock I have is gonna go bad. They were starting to hold off the reef in the deeper water."

Mac knew that meant they were hunkering down somewhere the storm wouldn't affect them. "Appreciate you bringing him out."

"I could give you a hand, then run him back in."

Under most circumstances, Mac would have refused, knowing Commander would poach and sell his numbers, but with Mel watching the clock and an easy way of getting rid of Trufante standing in front of him, he accepted.

"Right on." Commander adjusted his hat again. "Tru, toss the man a line. Daylight's burning."

Mac tied the thirty-footer off to his center console and climbed aboard the trawler. Trufante ambled over, followed by Commander. The trio were soon underway, heading northwest toward Mac's traps.

Though he could have hauled the traps himself if it weren't so inefficient, Mac was pleasantly surprised how well the three men worked together. Trufante was obviously working harder with Commander aboard, hoping to impress him and get some work on the days that Mac didn't go out. Three hours later, the lobster were iced down and the traps stacked on the deck. The engine growled, clearly protesting the extra weight, and Mac goosed the throttle, trying to get the most out of the rebuilt eight-hundred-horsepower Cat C-18 as they headed back to the island.

"See that, Mac Travis? Look at that haul. We should partner up sometimes."

Mac knew that was Commander's MO. Collecting partners was profitable when they owned their own boats and gear, and had the knowledge to use them. Mac didn't bother answering and continued to steer toward home, then saw a flash coming from the island.

Instinctively, Mac knew it wasn't from the boats moored there. With the wind out of the southeast, they would be facing away from him. Whatever had caused the reflection was coming toward them. "Hey, look ahead and tell me if you see anything."

In order to eliminate the distortion from the windshield, Trufante and Commander both peered around either side of the wheelhouse. With a reputation that was apparently deserved for spotting birds from a mile away, Trufante saw it first.

"Another boat."

"What's it look like?" Mac asked. Reaching into the compartment below the wheel, he found the binoculars and handed them to Commander.

"Go-fast boat," Commander said. "I think mine could take it."

Mac didn't care about that. "Can you see who's aboard?"

"One guy, just hanging."

Mac sensed trouble and pushed down on the throttle, throwing both men from their feet.

"You expecting company? Maybe if you slow down, I can see what we're heading for," Commander said.

Mac knew the other man was right. At best, they would arrive only a minute or two earlier. Once the boat had settled, Commander raised the binoculars to his eyes. Mac waited patiently, stuck squinting through the scarred windshield to see.

"Dude's got a rifle," Commander said, handing the binoculars to Mac, but Trufante grabbed them. "What kind of friends you hangin' with, homie?"

EIGHT

Mac took the binoculars back from Trufante and studied the man sitting on the boat. The bulging muscles on his shaved chest told Mac two things: The man was a hired thug, and he wasn't a local. There weren't many gyms on US 1 and even the diehards had accepted that skin cancer was an unacceptable risk and had started wearing long-sleeved shirts. That was all Mac needed to know. The question was how to proceed.

"Take her around the back of the island," Mac told Commander, handing the boat off. He went forward into the cabin, thankful that Commander was along. Trufante was close to worthless in these situations—but he could shoot. Mac retrieved a shotgun from the rod rack mounted to the ceiling and brought it, along with an open box of ammunition, back to the wheelhouse.

"What's your preference?" he asked Trufante, who had a hurt look on his face, probably because Mac had asked Commander to run the boat. Trufante's teeth showed again, but it wasn't a smile, and he reached for the shotgun.

Growing up in the bayous of Louisiana, Trufante had learned a skill set foreign to most. Besides being able to shoot a snake's eye at a hundred yards, he could track, and had an uncanny sense of direction.

"Got your phone?" Mac asked as Trufante placed the shells in the chamber of the shotgun.

"Yup," Trufante answered.

Mac almost asked if the bill was paid, but knew the deck mates and fishermen would pay their cell phone bills before they bought food—though he wasn't sure about beer. The devices were their lifeline. He saw Commander's phone hanging from a clip on his belt.

"I need your number."

"Turning out to be a good day," Commander said. "Fishing with the legendary Mac Travis; now he wants my number like he's going to ask me on a date or something. Homies ain't gonna believe this."

Mac turned to him and waited. Commander spat out the digits as Mac entered them in his phone. He knew enough to see past the talk. A lot of the wannabes used tough talk when they were nervous. Commander was intent on the water ahead and was an experienced boater—he would be fine.

"Drop us by that point there," Mac said, pointing. "There's enough draft right to the beach, but you'll have to back out the same way you came in."

Commander nodded and steered a serpentine course toward the point—a straight course would have grounded them —and Mac watched as he read the water, staying in the white and blue areas where possible. There was no need to worry about Commander's skill.

"Y'all got another gun for the captain?" he asked.

"Spear gun with a power head is all I got left. Wasn't exactly looking for action when I left the dock."

"You hang with old Tru enough, you ought to be loaded for bear."

Trufante smiled at the mention of his name. "How you want to do this?"

"Take the old path in, then we'll split and circle the house," Mac said. "Unless it's an emergency, let's just see what's going on and meet up back here."

The plan changed when he heard a pistol shot.

WE'VE GOT her cornered in the house, the message read.

"Stand down, you moron," Bugarra yelled as he texted the same message to his man on the ground. The pilot, about to begin takeoff, looked back to see if he was all right, and Bugarra waved him off. Bugarra had a mental picture of the island in his head and didn't like what he saw. ACLU lawyer or not, her father was Wood, and she was likely armed. He remembered from his visit last night how the boundaries of the clearing where the house stood were meticulously maintained against the tropical growth that fought to infringe on it. The way the windows were placed, she would have a clear shot at anyone approaching. Almost like it had been designed for defense.

He cursed the hired help he had to use for this operation. All he wanted was Gross's research—and to recover it anonymously. These idiots were not the Marines. If one of their own was shot or injured, they would leave him behind in a heartbeat. It wouldn't be hard from there to get a confession out of the scum that would surely implicate him.

"Wheels up," Bugarra called. He thought about changing the flight plan to land at the Marathon airport, but decided against it. An unforeseen liability had developed over the years as he nurtured his larger-than-life persona: He could no longer be invisible. The plane bore the large company logo on its fuselage. Someone would have noted that he'd landed, then took off the day before yesterday, which gave him an alibi, but also prevented his return. Key West would have to be close enough.

"Roger, Mr. Bugarra. We've been cleared to taxi," the pilot said, reaching behind him and pulling the curtain across the aisle. Once Bugarra found whatever Gross had been after, he promised himself he was going to upgrade to a plane with a cockpit door. He felt helpless as the plane taxied to the runway.

"Update," he commanded to his message app once they were airborne. Though Siri wouldn't understand the anger in his voice, it felt better than typing the words. A few seconds later, the phone pinged.

The bitch is shooting at us.

Bugarra sat back and thought about the situation. He knew he had enough manpower on the ground to subdue the woman and find the drive, but Travis and his mate were wild cards. Keeping one man aboard the go-fast boat had been a reasonable precaution, but he knew from his visit that the entire island was exposed. He hadn't seen the backside, but a satellite image had shown a few streaks of blue and white were intermixed with a whole lot of brown. If Travis suspected anything and reached the island in time, he would come in from that angle.

"Just get the hell out!" he screamed in the phone.

Roger, came the reply.

Frustrated, he looked out the window at the water below. Flying from Sebastian, they had crossed the Everglades and were now over Florida Bay. Hitting an icon on his phone, Bugarra looked at the plane's position overlaid on a map. They were on a collision course with the island.

He went forward to the cockpit, brushed aside the curtain, and sat in the right-hand seat. Usually, he would have a copilot and, if he had guests, a flight attendant too, but the approaching storm had made it hard to find even a single pilot willing to fly.

Once situated, he consulted the map again and gave the pilot a course change.

Florida Bay was known as the backcountry for good reason. The myriad of small islands, channels, and shoals made it a smuggler's paradise. At one point in the eighties, Everglades City had been the smuggling capital of the world. Bales, known as square grouper, had been as common as pelicans, and Bugarra could only imagine the many wrecks lying in only a few feet of water below him. Soon after reaching Islamorada, the back country faded behind them and there was a large expanse of open gulf. Marathon passed to port, and he could see the long stretch of the Seven Mile Bridge. Big Pine was on the horizon. The island was different from the rest of the Keys, with its mass running north and south, rather than east and west. He directed the pilot toward the northern tip, where several islands could be seen beyond.

Even after being there, it was hard to find, and he had the pilot fly several circles over the islands. One had a well-designed compound on it, complete with bunkhouses, a boathouse, and a residence. Several people were on the ground, looking up at the plane as it made a low pass over the island.

After one more circle, he found it. "There." He pointed, and the pilot banked and descended. Bugarra could see the clearing, house, and shed now. There were three boats by the single piling that Travis used for a dock, one with one of his men aboard. When he saw the trawler beached on the backside of the island, he started to worry.

"You've got company," he yelled over the engine noise, then slammed his fist into the dashboard when the transcription on his phone came out garbled. Grabbing the phone in two hands, he tried to relax and type the message.

Looking down again, he could see what might have been paths, but the mangroves formed a canopy above them. There was no way to see what was happening on the ground without the risk of getting shot. He ordered the pilot to pull up and circle.

———————

MAC HEARD the plane overhead and slowed. There were only a few people he knew with these kinds of resources, and after Gross's death, Vince Bugarra was on the top of the short list. After hearing the shot, he and Trufante had hooked up and were making their way toward the main clearing. He grabbed the lanky Cajun by the shoulder and stopped him.

"They've got a lot of assets. We have to be careful." They worked their way to the edge of the clearing. Another shot was fired.

"Twenty-two—that's Mel's gun," Trufante said.

Mac heard the respect in his voice. The two of them might be constantly at odds, but they did respect each other's abilities. Mac turned away, sensing movement in the brush near the trail to the beach. Suddenly, two men were visible, running down the path.

"Ol' Mel scared them off," Trufante said proudly.

Mac suspected it was the plane flying above the island that had alerted the men on the ground that the trawler was beached on the backside of the island. A minute later, Mac heard one engine start and a second later, another. He relaxed when he saw the text from Commander that the strange boat, with three men aboard, was heading toward Marathon.

"Mel," he called out.

She appeared on the wraparound porch, still holding the gun.

"It's good. They're gone." He rose and walked into the clearing.

"Damn, girl, scared them off with that shot I taught ya." Trufante smiled at her.

"I got a bad feeling about this, Mac," she said, ignoring the backhand compliment. "We should get out of here before they come back."

Mac wasn't going to argue, and texted Commander to come around to the other side of the island. Mel came down the stairs with the gun still extended in front of her. "We'll shutter the house and go," he said, seeing the expression on her pale face.

Fortunately, with all the windows being accessible from the covered porch, the shutter installation took less than an hour. Trufante and Commander might be good on the water, but they were worthless on land, and drank beers while Mac and Mel finished securing the house. Knowing many tasks were easier to accomplish when you did them yourself and didn't have to give directions, Mac encouraged them.

Finally, the house and shed were locked and shuttered. Mac disconnected the solar array. The valves on the propane bottles had been closed and the tanks were now secure in the shed. Mel came down the stairs with two duffle bags and a backpack with her computer. Mac recognized one of the bags as his.

"Ready?" He took the bags from her.

"I was just starting to get to like it here. Hope it blows into open water."

That was the best-case scenario. Mac led her to the boats and, reaching over the gunwales of the trawler, placed the bags on deck. He waded back to the center console and, using a hundred-foot line that was stowed aboard, made a bridle and attached the end to the bow cleat. Mel was already aboard the trawler and took the line, which she secured to one of the stern cleats, leaving only ten feet between the boats. She dumped the remainder on the deck in a loose coil. Once they were clear of the channel, they would properly attach the bridle.

Mac was about to thank Commander and say goodbye to Trufante when his phone rang. He could tell right away, when Trufante's teeth disappeared, that it was trouble. The conversation was one-sided, and Trufante ended it with the only word he had said: Okay.

"That was Pamela. I'm going with you," he said, stretching one of his long legs over the gunwale and hoisting himself on deck. The twin engines on Commander's boat fired before Mac had time to react.

"See ya on the other side, Travis," Commander called, and sped out of the channel.

NINE

Key West's reputation for being the capital of weird was often understated. Throw in a category-five hurricane a day away and it very much resembled what Hunter S. Thompson had said about Las Vegas: *When the going gets weird, the weird turn pro.* Weaving through the boat traffic in the harbor, Mac called the dockmaster on the VHF and got a surprised response when he asked for a slip.

A steady stream of boats exited the harbor, mainly larger oceangoing vessels capable of riding out the storm. There were more theories about how to secure a boat to survive a hurricane than there was time to consider them. The best solution was not to be in one, and as Mac observed the line of boats heading out to sea, he knew he might be right behind them if his estimation of Ruth changed.

Mac watched as people scurried around the docks, moving back and forth in a controlled panic, knowing that with one change in the forecast models, the scene would turn into chaos. Some boats were being rafted together with a spider web of lines. Others were tied loosely to the dock with enough slack to allow the boat to go where the storm surge took it. Only time would tell which was correct, but after riding out several tropical storms and hurricanes over his three decades here, Mac knew that chance played as large a factor as preparation.

Holding his phone to his ear, Trufante nervously paced the back deck. Mac noticed him waver several times and wondered how many beers he'd had on the way down, figuring it was at least a six-pack ride. Mel sat across from him with her face buried in her phone as well.

"Going to need some help here," Mac called out to them. The dockmaster had assigned Mac a slip toward the corner of the marina after he had refused several others. After surveying the location, he thought it was as protected as there was available, and headed to the fuel dock with the center console still in tow. Gassing up in Key West was a necessary expense. With the island secure, he wanted the boats ready for anything, and that meant filling the fuel and water tanks.

Pumping two hundred gallons exceeded Trufante's patience level, and with the phone still to his ear, he went over to Mac, who was filling the freshwater tank.

"Gotta go, man. Pamela's freaked."

Mac knew exactly what Tru was dealing with. After finding Pamela dragging a suitcase around Duval Street several years ago, the couple had been inseparable, at least until the last fight. Pamela was an enigma that they couldn't figure out. Mel had run, or tried to run, a background check on her, not so much to look out for Trufante as to protect Mac. It had come up blank, unusual, since she had used Pamela's credit card to start the trace. All they knew was that she received money on the first of every month, and that the couple burned through it by the third week—at least, that was when Trufante started bugging Mac for work.

Fear wasn't what Mac felt when he saw her, but she seemed to have the same magnetic force that attracted trouble as the

Cajun, and when they were together, with double the energy, the trouble was multiplied.

"Go on, but best keep your phone close. This storm keeps coming. I plan on heading for the Yucatan," Mac told him as Trufante hopped onto the dock and started loping toward town. Mel gave him a look that said they should dump Trufante now, but Mac wasn't ready to abandon him yet.

After topping off the tanks, Mac tossed the lines onto the fuel dock and headed across the marina to the slip.

Mel looped the forward lines over the pilings as the boat coasted past, and after applying enough tension to halt the progress of the boat, she went to the stern and jumped onto the dock, catching the lines as Mac tossed them to her. Mac wasn't overly concerned at this point about how the boat was secured. The calculation was already done, and he knew exactly where he stood. The trawler's two gas tanks held a combined three hundred gallons of fuel. Even running fast, that was almost two hundred miles of range. Once Ruth committed to its course, he had about an eight-hour window to get to safety.

"We're in a good spot if you want to stay," Mac said, as Mel pulled her bag out of the cabin.

"I've wanted to visit some friends anyway. This is as good a time as any."

Mac knew that Trufante and Pamela played a part in her decision, and he couldn't blame her. He just wasn't the guy to hop on a plane to avoid danger. Running toward the bullets was how he had always rolled, and although he had a few scars to show for it, overall, it had proven a good tactic. "I'll take you to the airport."

"You don't need to," Mel said, tossing her bag on the dock.

Mac knew she didn't need him to go, but with Ruth bearing down on them, he didn't want this to be the way they said goodbye. "I want to."

"Suit yourself." She stepped onto the gunwale and then down to the dock. "But I gotta go."

Mac checked his watch and realized he had cut it closer than he'd wanted. Her flight left in less than an hour. Though it was only a few miles as the crow flew, the streets of Key West were manic. Typically, it was a battle between the vehicles, bicycles, scooters, and golf carts—now it was all-out war. As he looked out on Caroline Street, he was worried that they wouldn't make it in time.

Brake lights and horns of all varieties gave a sense of urgency the laid-back island didn't often have. Bicycles and scooters wove through the gridlocked vehicles. That would be the only mode of transportation that might have a chance of success. Just as he thought it, a bicycle-powered rickshaw pulled up to the curb and dropped off its passengers.

"That looks like the only way we're going to make it," Mac said.

Mel went toward the driver, then turned away. Mac approached her and saw what had stopped her.

"We don't have a choice if you want to make it," he said.

"Riding out a cat five with Tru might be better."

"Your call," he said.

"Mac Travis, and with the lovely lady." The driver had seen them.

"Billy." Mac spat out the word as if it was poison.

Billy eyed the bag. "Billy Bones at your service."

Mac looked at Billy, wondering how he was still alive. The last time Mac had seen Billy, he had thrown the man out of a boat twenty miles from shore. He guessed Billy must have come from the same feline gene pool as the Cajun—they both had nine lives. "You want to make the plane, we don't have a choice."

Mac could see her weighing the pros and cons. "Can you get us across the island without doing something stupid?"

"You misjudge me," Billy said.

"Hardly," Mel said. She had made up her mind and climbed into the bench seat behind the driver.

Mac shook his head, went around to the other side, and climbed in. "The airport," he said. "No detours."

The tails of Billy Bones' unbuttoned Hawaiian shirt floated back toward them as he pulled into traffic. Mac was grateful he was seated in front of them until Billy spoke. Without an engine, the cab was surprisingly quiet.

"What brings you to Key West?" Billy asked.

It might be the same line that he used on every other tourist, but Mac knew he meant it differently. "Just pedal, Billy."

"Tru down here with y'all? I seen Pamela around. Thought about making a move on her, but I wouldn't do that to my buddy."

Mac knew that wasn't the case and was sure Billy had tried and failed with her. "He's around," Mac said. Bones wove the rickshaw through the narrow gaps between the cars and sidewalks, receiving several curses and horns as he moved through the backup.

"Whole damned island's like this. Hurricane adds a little spice, don't you think?"

Mac wondered about why the wannabe gangster was driving a rickshaw. Billy Bones was typical of a class of the population here. Originally from New Jersey or somewhere similar up north, he'd followed the only road through the Keys to the end of US 1. Wood had a theory that, like marbles rolling downhill, the crazies landed at the bottom—Key West. Billy, like many others, had run out of money in Marathon. Wood hired him, but the man was work-averse and had lasted one memorable week before he pawned one of Wood's compressors.

That gave Bones enough money to finish his pilgrimage to the pit of despair, or the capital of cool, depending on how you looked at it. Wood had let him go—knowing once they reached the end of US 1, they rarely came back.

"What's the deal with you driving one of these?" Mac asked. He shied away from Mel's piercing glance. Billy seemed to turn up in the wrong place at the wrong time. Mac wanted to know what he was up to.

"Shit, Mac. I'm a business owner. Got me a half-dozen of these bad boys. Just running one today because the labor force is all freaked out about the storm."

Mac knew the licenses were limited and expensive. Billy had to have pulled a scam to get one. "How'd you work your way into this?"

"Met this girl down at the city."

That explained as much as Mac wanted to know. In typical fashion, Billy was sponging off someone. "Good for you." Mac glanced at his watch, figuring they would get there right when the plane started boarding. They had made good time crossing the island, and he hoped, as Billy turned left on South Roosevelt, that the conversation was over. The noise from the busier street helped, as did the phone call that Billy got just before turning into the airport. Mac looked at Mel, willing her to keep her head buried in her phone, because there was no doubt it was Trufante on the line.

Trouble multiplied exponentially, and now with Trufante, Billy Bones, and Pamela all talking, Mac breathed a sigh of relief as Billy pulled up to the departure area. With fifteen minutes to spare, Mel would have to rush through security, but she would make the flight. "Wait here," Mac told Billy, and walked her into the terminal.

"It's not too late to come with me," Mel said.

"You know I can't do that with the boats here and all."

"*And all* better not be Trufante and Billy Bones. Stay clear of them, Mac." She reached for him.

Mac watched her through the glass partition until she had cleared security. After one last wave, she disappeared into the departure terminal. Mac waited for another minute, then turned toward the street and, feeling like a lonely salmon heading upstream against the fleeing islanders, walked out of the terminal, knowing he was going the wrong way.

A flash caught his eye just before he stepped back into the rickshaw, and he followed the taxiing plane as it spun and stopped at the FBO terminal. "How much, Bones?"

"Shoot, Travis. This one's on the house."

"No. I'll pay you." The last thing Mac wanted was to owe Billy anything—especially a favor.

"Forty'll do it."

Mac fished in his wallet and pulled out two twenties. He handed them to Billy and walked away. The plane had come to a stop, and he watched as Buck Reilly climbed out of the cockpit.

TEN

When Vince Bugarra travelled, he preferred the penthouse suite. The staff at the Casa Marina Hotel knew him on sight, and though they weren't expecting him, and there were more people checking out than checking in he got his usual VIP treatment. In fact, he was the only person at the registration desk. Fleeing guests glanced over at him as they moved quickly by, consumed with the single-minded task of getting off the rock before the hurricane hit. Bugarra caught several staring, asking themselves why someone would be checking in with the storm coming this way.

"Mr. Bugarra," the clerk said. "I didn't see a reservation? Perhaps we've made a mistake."

"No, I didn't make one, but ..." He looked around the lobby. "It looks like you might have some room."

"Your usual suite, sir?"

Bugarra paused for a moment. His usual was on the top floor. It offered sea breezes and views. Both he figured would be detrimental now. "No, I think something facing inland on a middle floor." He wanted protection if he was to ride the storm out here. An inland room would offer slightly better protection than a waterfront, and the middle floor would be above the storm surge and below the beating the top floor would receive. The clerk handed him a plastic card.

"You have any real keys?"

The clerk gave him a look like he had already answered this question more times than he cared to. "The locks all have battery backups. You should be fine in the event of a power outage. Do you have any bags?"

Bugarra nodded and took the card. "It'll be transferred from the plane. I just have this carry-on for now." The small bag sat at his feet. Aboard the plane was all manner of surveillance equipment—for underwater and above.

"Just let us know if there is anything we can do to make your stay more comfortable."

Bugarra thanked the man and headed toward the elevator. The only thing that would make him comfortable now was to recover Gross's research and get out of here before the power went out.

He opened the door and turned up his nose at the accommodations. The single room had the standard king bed and several pieces of furniture, with a bathroom off to the side. It brought him back to the old days, when he had just started out and stayed in rooms like this in high-dollar hotels to give the illusion he was doing well, often smuggling in a hot pot and ramen noodles.

After dropping his bag on the bed, he went out to the balcony. It wasn't an ocean view, but the immaculately groomed grounds were far from an eyesore. Several workers were trimming some of the larger trees, a sensible precaution if hurricane-force winds hit. He pulled out his phone and pressed a button on his favorites' screen.

"Are you in place?" he asked when the man answered.

"Yeah, pulled into the harbor about half an hour ago. Travis is here with the trawler and his center console. Looks like he's going to ride it out here."

"Any sign of the woman?"

"They both got into one of those bicycle rickshaw contraptions a little while ago. Traffic is a freakin' mess. We tried to follow on foot, but lost them."

Bugarra had noticed the traffic was heavier than normal on the short drive over from the airport, but he wasn't near the business district. "What about the deckhand?"

"He took off earlier."

"Find him." He paused. "He'll be in a bar," Bugarra said, then hung up. There were about two bars per capita here, but the search would be easier than finding Travis. He would take that task on himself.

"HEY, MAC." Buck lifted his head from the engine and came down the ladder, wiping his hands on a rag. "My partner says there's a bad cylinder."

"If it was a boat, I could help you out," Mac said. "What's going on around here? Place is crazy."

"We've been flying folks out of here nonstop for the last few days."

"I was hoping on checking out a few sites by the Quicksands," Mac said. When he mentioned the Quicksands, an area off the Marquesas Keys where Mel Fisher had found the *Atocha*, he could see the look in Buck's eyes. Where a second ago, he had been focused on the engine, now his attention was riveted on Mac.

"Any other time," Buck said.

Mac could hear the regret in his voice. "No worries."

"Forget about the charters and Ruth—if the cylinder was good, I'd fly into a cat five in a heartbeat if you have good intel."

"Get your engine fixed and let's connect after the storm," Mac said, extending his hand.

Buck grabbed it. "You're on."

For the first time in a week, Mac had no immediate agenda. He'd spent several days up in Miami with Kurt Hunter finding the *Sumter*, then came the start of stone crab season, and now the hurricane. With a small window before Ruth made landfall, he decided to have a look for himself.

Mac walked out the gate of the FBO, past the trailer that housed the seaplane operation that flew to the Dry Tortugas, and crossed the parking lot to the main terminal. Once there, he found a cab and instructed the pink-haired driver to take him to the marina.

The air conditioning was a relief, but the traffic looked like it had gotten worse. The driver, thankfully, stayed to herself, and Mac, grateful for the cool air and quiet, opened the Google Earth app on his phone and scrolled to the Quicksands. The undulating bottom of the Quicksands rendered marine charts close to worthless in the area. Their only real use was to point out a few channels that crisscrossed the shallow flats. As the name implied, the shifting sands ate boats. For now, the satellite view was the best for his purposes, but he also knew that when whatever Gross had been looking for sank, the bottom was likely very different than it was now. Mac knew he was just dreaming. Without even knowing what wreck he was searching for, finding that single sign of man in a hundred square miles of shifting sand had worse odds than an injured pinfish eluding a tarpon.

Mac had been there before. When the lobstering was slow in his usual spots around Marathon, he knew he could count on finding them west of the Marquesas. It was a ways to go, but he'd never come back empty-handed. With the center console fueled up, he had the range to make the trip. What worried him was he had no specific coordinates; it would have been helpful to have Buck fly him over the area. From an easy cruising altitude of five hundred feet, he would have been able to see the bottom.

The lure of the water and what might lie beneath it was strong, but Mac knew it was a fool's errand to run out there without a real destination. The news was on the cab's radio, and he heard that the public safety agencies all had plans to shut down soon. Getting stuck out in a squall was risky, never mind a full-fledged cat-five hurricane. There was another way, though.

The traffic southbound on Roosevelt had been light, but once the driver turned right to cut across the island, they came to a standstill. "Any way around this?"

"Just been here a month, man," the young woman said.

Mac recognized a Texas accent. With nothing to do except wait for the traffic to thin, he suggested a route around the cemetery. It was longer, but all side streets.

"You have plans for the hurricane?" she asked.

Mac wondered if she knew how serious this could be. "Got my boat. I'll see how Ruth tracks over the next day and decide." He paused for a second and then, uncharacteristically, asked if she had a plan.

"I've got some friends. We got candles, water, and a case of rum." She laughed.

He thought for a minute before responding. "You really ought to evacuate."

"Living the dream one day at a time doesn't include evacuation."

The idyllic Key West attitude was going to get people killed. "Look, take my number, at least. If you get scared, call." He cringed when he said it, but there was something about the lost expression on the girl's face that made him feel something. There was a good chance she would delete it, thinking he was a creeper or something, but she called out the numbers as he dialed. Once the call went through, he disconnected, but they both had each other's number in their recent call logs.

They were passing through a residential area now, and Mac watched as people finished boarding up their homes and packing their cars.

US 1 was two lanes through much of the hundred-twenty-mile stretch to Florida City. If it wasn't already, it would soon be a parking lot. Ditto for the three main routes out of Miami. His skin was already crawling. It would be a relief to get out of the car and back aboard his boat. Rough seas he could deal with; traffic was another story.

"What's your name?" Mac asked the girl.

"Sonya, but they call me Sonar," she said, turning around to face him.

The smile was genuine. "Look, Sonar. You and your friends need to get out of here. Please."

"If it'll keep you happy, we'll look at the weather in the morning. Tonight, there's a bunch of hurricane parties, first time for me. It's going to be awesome."

Mac knew the type. After running from their boring lives to live the dream, they would be all in for a while, then the veneer would start to crack. Most would do all they could to convince themselves it was still paradise, but for many, malaise set in. Mel had unearthed a little-known fact that the suicide rate in Monroe County was twice as high as the state average, and just behind Las Vegas for the top spot in the country.

They reached the dock, and he paid the fare, leaving a tip that would buy enough gas to reach the Georgia border. "Please think about it," he said, as he left the cab.

Mac stood by the statue of the fisherman in the turnaround

between Turtle Kraals and the Half Shell Oyster Bar. His stomach growled, and he looked through the open shutters of the Half Shell. Normally their happy hour was busy, but the place was less than half-full. Wanting some food and an update on Ruth, he went in and sat at the bar.

Sipping a beer and waiting for his steak sandwich, he watched the big screens behind the bar. Usually, nonstop sports played on them, but today it was all weather. Two Miami stations and the Weather Channel were featured. All three showed the cone of death. One of the local stations switched to an animated graphic showing what a ten-foot storm surge could do to a house. The other showed an aerial view of a congested highway. The northbound lanes were at a dead stop.

The Weather Channel interested him more, and he asked the bartender to turn up the sound. No matter your reason for being on the water, if you were going to make your living on it, you needed to learn how to read weather. That meant more than clouds and swells, but the technical stuff as well. Mac studied the charts on the screen, making his own projections about the path of the storm. It was now brushing the eastern tip of Cuba; his prediction that the Keys were going to be dead center matched that of the experts. The only question was exactly where the eye would cross. A storm this size had a forty-mile eye. That was where you didn't want to be. There would be death and destruction far outside the center, but the eye wall brought devastation. He squinted at the TV. His guess was Big Pine Key. His and Jesse McDermitt's islands were just to the northeast, near dead center of the projected path.

ELEVEN

FROM THE SHADOW MOVING ACROSS THE CABIN, BUGARRA guessed Travis was aboard and, with his deckhand at large, he was probably alone. The Rat had confirmed that Melanie Woodson had flown out earlier today. Standing in the darkness on the dock across from Travis's boat, Bugarra continued to watch, but it was getting late. He was about to give up when he saw the light go out.

Most endeavors required patience. To be successful in the treasure and salvage business, it was especially necessary. Besides the inherent difficulty of locating a centuries-old wreck lost on the ocean floor, there were many other obstacles. Weather, permits, and equipment malfunctions were just the short list. The successful salvors spent as much time filling out paperwork, researching, and repairing as searching. If you were after a Spanish galleon, it would be necessary to spend as much time in the *Archivo General de Indias* in Seville as underwater.

Bugarra had people for that—or, actually, he had people to steal that. He knew finding a five-hundred-year-old galleon was close to impossible. Dealing with the governments of the countries in whose waters it might lie only added to the difficulty—

including the U.S. Bugarra was interested in the permits more than the actual wreck, for those gave him permission to raise money. At that point, finding the wreck itself became secondary.

Movement on the boat brought him back to the present, and a second later, Travis appeared on deck. He stepped onto the gunwale and then the dock. After checking the lines and shore power, he started toward the street. Bugarra was surprised to see Travis head down the boardwalk, which passed a dozen bars before terminating on Duval Street. From what Bugarra knew about the recluse, this was out of character, but hurricanes did that to people. More interested in what he might find aboard the trawler than where Travis was going to drown his sorrows, Bugarra waited until Travis was out of sight before backtracking to the pier where the trawler was docked.

Careful to make as little noise as possible, he climbed aboard, waited for the boat to stop rocking, and moved toward the open wheelhouse. Forward was the small cabin, which he checked before returning to the helm. He was surprised to see the pair of screens cut into the dash. Like his mentor, Wood, Travis had the reputation of being old school. The electronics Bugarra was looking at were clearly not.

Popping off the small cover on the front of the right-hand unit, he checked for a microSD card. The slot was empty, as was the unit's twin. Bugarra hadn't expected it to be that easy, anyway. Travis was both a salvor and commercial fisherman; both trades were fanatical about protecting their numbers.

After checking the helm area, Bugarra moved to the cabin, hoping to find a computer. There was nothing other than a few charging cables. Discouraged, he did a quick check of the compartments and holds, but wasn't surprised when he came up empty. Boats like this often had several lives before the current owner. The older boats, which had been around in the eighties and nineties, had often been used for smuggling. Secret compartments were sometimes built into the hull and engine room, so well concealed they could pass inspection if the ship was stopped by the DEA, or now, ICE. If Travis had hidden the drive in one of them, it would take a more thorough search than Bugarra had time for. The better possibility was that Melanie Woodson had it with her. He would make a call to an associate in Atlanta when he got back to his room.

He carefully replaced everything he had touched, then exited the boat. Blending in was easy. The docks—in fact, the entire island—were on high alert, which meant its population was out and about. People were everywhere, the traffic was still snarled and not heading in the direction of Duval Street, as it usually was at this time of night.

Staying to the shadows, he left the dock and started down the boardwalk. Most salvors were early risers, wanting to get out on the water while it was most calm. Bugarra was a night owl, both by nature and his preference to raise funds rather than dive. While many of his contemporaries would be getting ready for bed, he was ready to go out.

For a destination already known for being wild, the knob had been turned to high, as the hurricane was pushing some kind of hormone-induced craziness ahead of it. Looking into the bars he passed, he saw a level of insanity that could only be beneficial. Thinking Travis's deckhand was somewhere in the middle of it, Bugarra started checking inside the bars as he went. The Cajun likely knew nothing about Gross's research, but Travis liked him. He could be used as a pawn.

MAC SHOOK his head as he passed bar after bar, all full of pre-hurricane hysteria, music blaring at unbearable levels.

Through open doors, he could see women, sometimes topless, dancing on bar-tops. Moving quickly, he kept his head down and continued on his way.

The fever pitch surrounding him dropped a noticeable notch or two when he left Duval Street and turned on to White-head. From there, he entered a small alley. Opening a colorfully painted gate that led up a landscaped path to a classic Key West Victorian house, he started up the walk to the entry. Even in the low light, Mac could see the property had been restored, although not as meticulously as some of the others. The house looked heavy, bearing the weight of its years, and it was evident from the way the gingerbread reflected the light that it had been repainted without stripping the previous layer, resulting in an uneven look. Mac knocked on the door, noticing the landscape was overgrown while he waited for an answer.

"Mac freaking Travis. Took a hurricane to bring you down here." An older man moved out of the way, allowing Mac to enter.

Mac shook his hand. "Ned. Still alive, I see." The old man had worked with Wood back in the eighties and nineties. He and Wood had made an interesting pair, but they got along and had several successes as partners. Where Wood had been the "get out there and do it" guy, Ned was an academic. It was a typical case of opposites attracting.

"What are you drinking?" Ned asked. "I know you're not here to reminisce with an old man. Let me pour you something and we'll get right to it."

Mac asked for a scotch neat and started to relax. Small talk, even with someone he was close to and trusted, was not some-thing he was good at. Ned directed him to a corner room with French doors and a transom off the main hallway. The walls were lined with books, and instead of a desk, there were several tables in the middle of the room. Each had charts or books stacked on them. It was more like a library than an office. Going to the closest table, Mac looked down on a chart so old it belonged in a museum.

"Seventeenth century," Ned said, handing Mac a half-full glass.

Mac toasted and took a sip. There were several things he could count on Ned for: one was good information, the other good scotch. He took another sip.

"Private blend from some distant cousin. Family sometimes has its perks. But you're not here to discuss my lineage. What do you have?"

Mac took the flash drive from his pocket. It felt like a weight was removed from him when Ned took it. He held it carefully, like it was an old relic.

"Let's have a look."

Mac thought it might not just be himself who wanted to avoid small talk. Ned quickly led Mac to a table with a large monitor set in the corner of the room, pulling out two chairs. Reaching behind the screen, he inserted the drive and waited while the computer came to life.

After pulling a pair of thick reading glasses from his pocket, he started to work the keyboard. Mac was surprised at Ned's aptitude with the computer as he skimmed through screens of data that Mac had no idea how to access.

"Got years of research on here. Scanned documents from Seville, charts and spreadsheets loaded with data from their searches with a magnetometer. I'd be happy to sit here all night and look through this, but I'm guessing you have something more specific in mind."

Ned knew Mac too well. He leaned forward and almost whispered, "Civil War era."

"Really? There's dozens of galleons out there loaded with treasure, and you want some old hunk from the Civil War?"

"I do." Mac took a sip of his drink. "It appears to be what Gross was into. A buddy of mine who works for the park service came across the data while investigating his murder."

"Bastards. I heard about that. Hope Slipstream and DeWitt have a nice stay in Raiford." Ned turned back to the computer and scrolled through several more screens. "Sure is a lot about Lafitte on here."

"Interesting, but from my recollection, that was earlier than the Civil War. More like the War of 1812," Mac said, remembering the history of Lafitte saving New Orleans. He was quiet for a minute. "You know we found the *Sumter* up there in the park—or, rather, Gross found her."

Ned got up, walked to a shelf across from the window, and came back with a coffee-table-sized book. He went right to the index, found the entry, and flipped backward until he found the page. "Nice find." Ned sat back down and studied the picture and history of the ship.

"What's so special about these wrecks when there's still billions in Spanish gold out there?"

"Gross was broke. He was after anything he could get a dollar from," Mac said.

"That's a tactic, not a strategy," Ned said. "You have to understand the man. You met him, right?"

"Briefly." Mac recalled meeting Gross during a week-long excursion on the 1733 fleet off Islamorada.

"And what did you think?"

Mac sipped his drink before answering. "Principled, passionate ... people change."

"They do, but not him. Gill Gross was one of the few who could be trusted in this damned business. If he was going after nineteenth-century wrecks, it was only to raise enough money to find something big."

Mac was relieved to hear Ned's explanation. He wanted to

think well of Gross. "Okay, I'll buy that. He took a bunch of aerial shots of the Quicksands."

"Now you're talking," Ned said, diving back into the computer. A few minutes and dozens of screens later, he pulled up an image that looked familiar.

Mac stared at the horseshoe-shaped atoll known as the Marquesas Keys and the waters to the west. "The *Atocha* was found near there."

"And you think that's the only galleon stuck in those sands?"

"WE NEED TO MAKE A PLAN," Justine told Kurt.

After working the swing shift at the Miami-Dade crime lab, she would often find him asleep when she got home. At least when they stayed at the same place. Newly married, they continued to maintain two residences. Kurt had a park service-issued house on Adams Key in Biscayne National Park. Justine had her apartment in Miami. It was something they needed to work on, but, needing both incomes, two houses were also a necessity. A commute that entailed an eight-mile boat trip plus an hour drive was a little too much to do every day.

"I'm going paddling in the morning. Then, whether Martinez makes a decision or not, we're getting out." She had woken him to deliver the proclamation. Kurt's boss was an unrelenting ass, pure bureaucrat. She'd been a teenager when Andrew had come through Miami in 1992. The memories had stayed with her. That quickly developing storm had taken only four days to grow from nothing to a category-four storm. This one looked equally intense as it sped toward Florida. Most of the projections had Miami well within the danger zone. Miami-Dade had released all nonessential personnel as of midnight. For the first time being called "nonessential" worked for her.

Kurt rolled over in bed and faced her. "I'll go down and button up the house tomorrow morning and we'll get out. I need to see if Jane has a plan for Allie."

The mention of Kurt's ex didn't faze her. She thought of Kurt's daughter, Allie, as her own. "It's almost the weekend, and the schools are closed. We should have her."

"Just need to clear it with Jane."

Justine kissed him on the forehead, turned off the light, and went to the bathroom. After a quick shower, she hopped in bed, dreaming not of her husband lying next to her, or even the approaching storm. The surf claimed her dreams. The Atlantic rarely had the big, long-period swells more common to the Pacific—unless there was a storm coming.

TWELVE

Trufante stumbled into Sloppy Joe's and saw Pamela standing high above the crowd. It wasn't her five-ten height, but the platform placed for the servers that she stood on. He hummed the melody to "Honky Tonk Women," adding "Key West" in place of "Memphis." He'd been cruising Duval Street for several hours looking for her. Staggering as he entered the iconic bar, he belted out the song loud enough for her to hear it..

Tru had been worried about seeing her and had stopped at several bars along the way for some liquid courage. "Baby?" he called over the sound of the bleached-blond cowboy-hat-wearing singer.

Pamela looked down from her perch at the service station. She smiled, and that was enough to set him diving through the crowd in her direction. He was tossed back and forth between the patrons, but, feeling no pain, continued toward her. Pushing his thin frame past the standing-room-only crowd at the bar, he eased up next to her.

"YOU'RE FREAKING DRUNK," she yelled, loud enough to turn most heads at the bar. Instead of hugging him , she grabbed the tray of drinks and stepped down to the floor. "I ask for help and you show up hammered!" Turning the other way, she moved toward the stage. Where Trufante had to battle his way through the crowd, the sea parted for her, and she started handing out drinks to a table of rowdy tourists.

Undeterred, Trufante followed. Pamela finished with the first table and turned to take orders from a group of coeds. If the fire marshal were to review the seating plan when the bar opened in the morning, there would be plenty of aisle room, but the place was close to capacity and the furniture had rearranged itself to accommodate the crowd. Someone shoved Tru, and he bumped into two men, both with buzzcuts, standing by a column. One pushed him into the table Pamela had just served.

They shoved him back like a bumper in a pinball game. A pair of men with SECURITY stenciled on their black shirts approached, but the crowd had closed in on the action.

"Get out," Pamela yelled.

The crowd quieted as she stormed toward the lanky Cajun, just as the singer called out, "Who out there's got a birthday today?"

Trufante's sixth sense for both survival and free shit kicked in as he was temporarily distracted.

"Come on now, who's thirty today?" the singer said, strumming a few chords to build the tension.

He had the attention of the crowd. It was commonplace to see some birthday boobs, and they sensed an opportunity. There were a few catcalls, but no takers.

"Forty?" He strummed a blues riff on his guitar.

Sensing there would be no show, the crowd turned back to the Trufante and Pamela drama. She was just a few feet from him.

"Fifty? Come on now." The singer wasn't giving up.

Pamela took a step closer. Trufante looked past her to the

buzzcuts, who had decided to back her up. "Yo, yo, yo, I'm fifty!" he yelled.

"Hot damn, my man. Come on up here," the singer called out, and started strumming "Happy Birthday." With yet another distraction, the crowd started raucously singing along.

A path opened as Trufante made his way to the stage. He glanced back before stepping up next to the singer and saw that Pamela had turned the other way and gone back to work. The security crew were hovering, but, being Key Weird veterans, they'd seen it all, and were willing to let things play out. The two men moved back to their column, their muscular frames working again on holding up the roof.

There was little chance the singer truly believed it was Trufante's birthday, but his business was entertainment, and all eyes were on the Cajun as he double-timed the short flight of stairs to the stage. The last chorus of "Happy Birthday" ended as he approached the singer. Heckles mixed with loud applause as Trufante shook the singer's hand.

"My man is fifty," he said into the microphone, and strummed a few bars on his guitar. "You here alone, buddy?"

Trufante scanned the room looking for Pamela, but didn't see her.

"Who wants to make this a special birthday for our friend here?"

Trufante forgot all about Pamela when two twenty-some-things jumped up, their braless boobs nearly falling out of their tops..

"Lovely ladies, come on up," the singer called out, and picked a quick riff as they made their way through the crowd.

Trufante watched them approach, gauging their intent as well as their state of inebriation. He mentally calculated that the C-notes still left in his pocket from the lobster haul would cover any possibilities. The women walked up on stage, looked at each other, and lifted their shirts. The crowd erupted in a cheer, and Trufante placed a long arm around each of them.

"What're y'all's names?" the singer asked. He was clearly more interested in them than the birthday boy.

"Sadie," the first one said, shyly.

"Dannie," the second said more enthusiastically, while raising the front of her shirt again.

The singer started playing the Jimmy Buffet favorite "*Why Don't We Get Drunk*" while the trio paraded around the stage. When they headed down the stairs, Trufante went on high alert. With an irate Pamela and the two buzzcuts by the column glaring at him, he steered the girls toward a hallway that led to the bathrooms and the side entry to Joe's Tap Room. Looking back, he saw the two men coming toward him.

"I know a place we can have some fun," he said to the girls, steering them past the small bar and out the side door. He stepped onto Greene Street and, grabbing Sadie and Dannie's hands, headed back toward Duval.

BUGARRA HEARD catcalls and applause through the open shutters of Sloppy Joe's and stopped. Above the crowd, he saw Trufante with his arm around two women on the elevated stage. Entering the bar, Bugarra started toward them, but was stalled in traffic when one of the girls lifted the front of her shirt. The crowd tightened around him, leaving him stuck near the main bar, able to only watch as Trufante and the women took off through the side door. Backtracking, he easily made it to Duval Street and froze when he saw them round the corner. Thinking it better to follow and see what they were up to, he slid into the gift shop and waited for them to pass. Standing by a rack of t-shirts, he flipped through them as if looking for his size while he watched the trio walk past. Just as he was about to follow, he saw two men following Tru and the women. Allowing the two men to pass, he stepped onto the sidewalk, carefully avoiding the Solo-cup-wielding tourists weaving in and out of the shops, and followed.

Standing six inches over six feet, Trufante was easy to spot as he crossed the street. The two men were still behind him. Bugarra picked up his pace as he jaywalked across Duval, trying to reach the men before they could catch up to the Cajun. From the look of them, they weren't long-lost buddies, and Bugarra needed Trufante in one piece.

"Hey, buddy," Bugarra called out at the men.

The larger of the pair turned. "Who the hell are you calling buddy?" he said.

A large man himself, Bugarra was no match for even the single man, let alone his partner. But he didn't intend to fight. Pulling out his wallet, he showed a flash of green. The man's attitude changed.

"Something we can help you with?"

Bugarra breathed out. "Vince Bugarra," he said, extending his hand. "Looks like you and me"—he paused, careful to parse his words—"might be interested in the same man."

"That fruit-loop-looking cowboy?" the man asked. "Damned sure ain't his birthday." He shook Bugarra's hand. "I'm David Culbreath, and this is Rusty Faulkenberry."

"Right. I'm sure it's not."

The men stood facing Bugarra, who still held his wallet in his hand. Realizing it, he pulled out two hundred-dollar bills and handed one to each man. "I'd like to have a conversation with him. Private, if you know what I mean." Bugarra looked down the block and saw the trio walk into the alley leading to the Hog's Breath Saloon.

"Why don't you go bring him around back for me?"

The bills had already disappeared, and the men nodded. They strode to the corner and turned left. Bugarra followed at a distance, waiting outside the open-air entrance. After six o'clock, just about every bar had entertainment, and he listened to the singer to his right as he watched the men approach Trufante at the bar. He wasn't sure what to expect, but what he saw wasn't it. The two women were all over the men, and Trufante was shaking their hands while calling to the bartender. Seconds later, shot glasses were placed on the bar and filled. The group toasted and drank. Bugarra needed a new plan as he watched his two hundred dollars slide down their throats.

TRUFANTE LIVED BY HIS GUT, his instincts being the only reason he was still alive. He'd essentially been on the run since 2005, when another hurricane, this one named Katrina, had leveled New Orleans. He had no idea how many lawsuits his old concrete-contracting company's name, or much less his name personally, appeared on. His instincts told him the good days there were over. There would surely be investigations, and it wouldn't matter how much he had paid off to administrators and inspectors—someone would talk. He'd run then, taking the last of the cash left in his safe and buying a sailboat. The Gulf Coast was an easy place to disappear, and he had, slowly working his way via sea instead of the highway to the end of US 1.

Now, his instincts told him another hurricane was about to change his life. This time there was little to lose, and when he saw Bugarra lurking at the entrance to the bar, he realized there might be something to gain. Mac had something, Trufante was sure of it, and whatever it was, Bugarra wanted it badly enough to have paid Trufante to take him out to Wood's island the other night—and now Bugarra was following him.

First, Trufante had to deal with the buzzcuts. He had ammunition now, and whispered to Sadie and Dannie what he wanted. They looked at the men and gave each other a *what the hell* shrug. Seconds later, with the women caressing their muscles, the men had forgotten what they were here for, and Trufante reached into his pocket and slid a hundred across the bar. The bartender brought another round. When one of the men spilled his shot, Tru sacrificed his own, sliding it to the man and at the same time jerking his phone out of the way, reaching up and setting it in the gutter running around the perimeter of the roof of the open-air bar. With his height, he could easily reach it, and it would be safe there.

With the threat mitigated, it was time to see what Bugarra wanted, and Trufante ordered another round of shots. He had an innate respect for cons and crooks. While he could easily manipulate the general population, Bugarra was a worthy opponent. Besides having no easy back exit here, Trufante figured the best way to handle him was face to face.

"Y'all have another round," he said, waving to the shots the bartender was placing on the bar. "I got a little business, then we'll have some real fun."

With a hand on each girl's shoulder, he eased them back toward him. "Y'all hang tight. I've got big plans for you girls," he whispered to them. They giggled, and he started for the entrance. Looking back, he realized he would have another problem when he got back. Three men with two women were not good numbers. He'd deal with that right after Bugarra.

"Vince Bugarra," he called out just as the treasure hunter had turned away. "Surprised to see you here. Riding out the storm in the city of weird?"

THIRTEEN

DUVAL STREET WENT FROM ITS CURRENT FRENZY TO DEAD stop as all eyes were glued to the TVs above the bars. Bikes and golf carts pulled off to the side, the drivers wondering what was happening, leaving only the fleeing vehicles gridlocked on the streets. Mac walked to the closest bar and, standing next to a handful of people, stared at the screen.

Ruth remained at category-five strength, and Key West changed from a hurricane watch to a warning. Not a subtle difference. The former meant that there was a possibility of hurricane-force winds; the latter made the chance a reality. Key West was going to get a hurricane. For a city that had somehow managed over many years to remain unscathed by the storms that generally passed through the middle and upper Keys, this was big.

Mac squinted to see the screen, then turned away, pulled out his phone, and opened the Mike's Weather Page app. The cone of probability had been easy to see on the TV; the time of estimated landfall had not. Here he could see the different models that were starting to come together into a solid line instead of the spaghetti they had looked like earlier. Most now forecast Ruth to make landfall somewhere between Key West and Miami. Another view showed the times overlaid on the projected path. With landfall forecast for less than twenty-four hours away, it was time for Key West to wake up and prepare.

In the space of several minutes, the city had turned from jubilant hope to deadly certainty. People streamed out of the bars to evacuate or prepare. Mac thought about Sonya, the cab driver, hoping that she had the sense to leave. He already had his plan. The Yucatan Peninsula was an easy trip and opposite the path of the storm. Staying to the less crowded side streets, he made his way back to the marina. He was also happy Mel was safe.

The boaters were clearly more prepared than the residents. As Mac walked to his boat, he figured that half the slips were already empty and the boats that remained were tied off, ready to ride out the storm. He boarded the trawler and went immediately to the pantry, where he inventoried the supplies. There was enough food and water for three or four days, which would be plenty to reach a safe port. Back on deck, he sat on the gunwale and texted Trufante and Ned, telling them to be aboard at six a.m. That would give them a good eight-hour head start on the storm. Running at thirty knots, that would put him 240 miles in the opposite direction. The rough seas wouldn't be comfortable, but they would be safe.

A babysitter he wasn't. With notice given, it would be up to Trufante and Ned to make their own decisions about leaving. Now, with a deadline looming, Mac knew that sleep would elude him, and opened the cover to the engine. It was time for a regular service anyway, and with a run across open water imminent, he decided to change the filters now. Cursing the designers who made access to the engine harder than it needed to be, he had already skinned two knuckles when he heard his phone. Mel wasn't into the touchy-feely thing, but she had programmed her own ringtone into his phone with an "answer it or else" threat. Mac climbed onto the deck, wiped his hands on a rag, and answered.

"You have a plan?" Mel asked.

"Out of here at six a.m. Gonna take Ned and Trufante if he shows."

"I'm glad about Ned. That old Conch would ride it out for sure."

"Went over to see him earlier."

"Anything interesting?"

Mac looked around, relieved that Mel was safe in Atlanta. While Key West was in the midst of preparations, for the unaffected parts of the country, this was like a spectator sport. Knowing the world would still exist once Ruth passed, he decided to indulge her.

"It appears that Gross was doing only the minimum amount of work on the galleons to keep his backers happy. Most of his recent research was centered around the years before and the early part of the Civil War."

"Like the *Sumnter*?"

"Yeah." Mac got up and went past the wheelhouse to the galley, where he grabbed a beer out of the refrigerator. He made a note to hide the rest of them, along with whatever other alcohol was aboard. With the possibility of spending the better part of a week confined with Trufante, it was a necessary precaution.

"Anything I can do from here?" Mel asked.

"During that time period, New Orleans was the center of the world as far as the gulf was concerned. I'll email you what I have if you want to do some research."

"Might be a good idea. Looks like the outer bands of the storm might reach Atlanta. New Orleans looks like it's in the clear. Maybe I'll head over there."

"Cool. I'll check in when I can."

"Mac, please don't let Trufante—"

He didn't want her to finish her sentence. "Sort the files by date. That should give you what he was working on recently."

They disconnected, and he sensed that she was happy. He knew her well, and despite the hardships Ruth brought there would be a little *schadenfreude*. The storm was big enough to cover the entire state of Florida. One of the consequences from its rainfall was that the sugar crop would likely be destroyed. That was all good, but the fertilizer and chemical-laden water had to go somewhere, and Mac expected the opened flood gates would be pouring chemicals into the Atlantic and gulf. Mel would have plenty of ammunition for her battle after it was over, but for now, what was coming was inevitable. Mac figured she could use the break from her fight with Big Sugar.

With the filters changed, Mac started the engine and checked the hoses and electrical connections. After inspecting for leaks, he went to the helm to make sure the oil pressure and temperature were all within their parameters. Everything seemed to check out, and, satisfied, he closed the hatch.

When he shut down the engines, a strange silence fell over the marina. In comparison, the streets, just a few feet away, were awash in activity. Mac sat on the gunwale drinking his beer and trying to figure out how to proceed with the information he had.

Considering what Gross knew about the current political climate, both within the state and internationally, it was no surprise that the salvor had shied away from the Spanish galleons. Mel Fisher had spent millions in legal fees to protect his claim to the *Atocha*. Despite his victory, the field had tilted against salvors in recent years. In the past, salvors had been sponsored by kings—the most notable being William Phipps and his 1600s search and recovery of the *Concepcion*'s treasure, sponsored by the king of England. Those days were far removed, and now it was a private enterprise, but even that was burdened by government intervention.

In return for their research, patience, and money, today's treasure hunters were rewarded with state oversight and legal battles. Recently France had won a landmark decision ensuring that the contents of her ships wrecked off the Florida coast and found by a private firm remained her property. In short, though it might be glamorous to discover a long-lost galleon, it was far more profitable to find more recent wrecks.

Not that they were easier to find. The Spanish were fanatics about documenting everything. The archives in Seville were jammed full of manifests and firsthand accounts. On the other hand, wrecks, especially in the gulf, were shrouded in secrecy. There were no records—but there was treasure. As the last deepwater port in the Confederacy, New Orleans had seen its share of gold leaving the southern states, to be stashed in the Bahamas or traded for goods.

Treasure from the later wrecks was also less problematic to cash in. An eighteenth-century Spanish coin was considerably more valuable than just its metal content—but try and unload it. Mac and Wood had found some and knew that selling was near impossible. Melting down history for cash was not something that Mac was willing to do. He still kept a jar full of coins at the house.

Technically, the Division of Historical Resources classified anything over fifty years old as of archeological significance, so that would include the Civil War-era wrecks. But without the romantic or historical value of the coins and artifacts, there was no conflict in melting them down and cashing them in.

Melancholy settled over Mac. He went down to the galley and grabbed another beer, but before he could take a sip, his phone rang again. It wasn't Mel's ring, and he almost didn't answer, but he thought about Sonya and glanced at the screen. Seeing a local area code, he decided that, with Ruth coming, he owed it to the select few who knew his number to answer.

When he heard the woman's voice on the other end of the line, he instantly regretted that decision.

"Mac, you've got to help me."

Pamela's voice came through the phone. If Trufante was Mel's nemesis, Pamela was Mac's. He was quiet, not knowing what to say. He never did with her.

"Mac, Tru was here all drunked up and I kind of blew him off. Now with the storm coming and everything, I'm worried for him."

Mac wondered why she wasn't worried for herself. He drank the rest of his beer in one large gulp and crushed the can in frustration. It looked like Mel's worst-case scenario had come to fruition. Now, the question was what to do about it. Pamela was still talking, but he ignored her babble and thought. Sending Billy Bones to pick her up crossed his mind, but that would only complicate things even more. No, he would have to go to her.

"Where are you?"

"Sloppy Joe's. I work here."

Now that was an interesting twist. Pamela and work didn't often go together. He was quiet for another minute while she rattled on about how great the job was. After running every possible option through his mind, he knew he would have to help her. As much as Mel didn't like Tru and he had his issues with Pamela, they still fell into the family category. As dysfunctional as it was, he would help.

"Hang out by the door. I'll be there in fifteen minutes."

"Thank you, Mac," she said.

He could hear the relief in her voice, and it might have been the most sincere thing she had ever said. Dismissing that thought, Mac locked up the cabin and headed back toward Duval Street. One step on solid ground brought him into the pre-storm frenzy. While most of the bars had closed, and the employees were hard at work boarding windows, several open-air spots continued to serve and were still busy. There was no point shutting down if there was no way to secure their properties.

After almost being run over by two cars loaded to the max with personal belongings, Mac backtracked to the boardwalk. Reaching Front Street, he turned left on Duval and walked toward Sloppy Joe's. Checking out the preparations as he went, he noticed only about a quarter of the businesses were prepared. The others were left to the mercy of the storm.

The usually open shutters of Sloppy Joe's were closed, giving the place a different look. Mac walked to the entrance. The door was open, but a bouncer stopped him.

"I'm looking for Pamela," Mac said, hoping somewhere in the back of his mind that the man wasn't judging him.

"Hold on."

"Mac." Pamela came forward and reached for him.

He instinctively shied away, but saw the panic in her eyes and accepted her embrace. "You ready?"

"Ready for what?"

And the ball started rolling downhill. The only question now was how many lives would be endangered by what was coming next.

"We have to find Tru," she said.

As she moved toward the door, he saw her face. It was clear from the damage to her makeup that she'd been crying, and he caved in.

"Where do you think he went?"

FOURTEEN

Justine was about to climb through the roof. Adams Key, the small island in the string of barrier islands separating the bay waters of the Biscayne National Park from the Atlantic, was secure. Kurt's only neighbors on the island, Becky and Ray, their little boy, and Zero their dog, had already left to evacuate to her parents' place in Alabama.

"We can't wait for that needle-nosed boss of yours to make a decision. Ruth's coming fast and strong. Remember what happened to this place after Andrew."

Kurt put a screw in the last shutter, wondering what the storm would do. Having lived in California until a year and a half ago, this was all new to him. Kurt hadn't been in Miami in 1992 to see the devastation, but knew the eye of the storm had passed directly over the island he now lived on, erasing, among other things, the remains of the infamous Coco Lobo Club.

"You're right. A lot of the projections show it turning north." Just as he said it, the text message signal on his work phone went off. *Temporarily reassigned to Ft. Jefferson.* He read the message out loud.

"I can live with the Dry Tortugas for a few days," Justine said. "But what about Allie?"

"I texted Jane this morning." He looked down and checked the screen, then called her number.

Justine had never had children, but in the year and a half that she had been with Kurt, Allie, his sixteen-year-old daughter, had become like her own.

"With the way this storm's looking, south is better than north. Jane would probably evacuate to her sister's in Orlando."

"They're gonna get hit, too," Justine said.

Jane came on the line. Kurt pleaded his case to his ex-wife. From the conversation, Justine could tell she was nervous about the storm and her plan, then got the sense that Kurt was going to ask her to come with them and adamantly shook her head. There had to be a cut-off point in their lives. If Jane were in dire straits, with nowhere to go, Justine would help, of course, but Jane did have her sister. Finally, Kurt smiled. Jane had agreed to have Allie ready.

"We're out of here," Kurt said, wiping the sweat from his brow. The park service-issue stilt house was well-built and air-conditioned, but he had shut off all the breakers to stop any surges when power was restored. There was no question it would go out.

They took one last look around and locked the house. Justine smiled at Kurt, who, remembering a piece of advice from his more seasoned neighbor, had a piece of duct tape ready to place over the keyhole.

A strange feeling came over her as she walked down the stairs from the stilt house and across the concrete path to the dock. They both knew there was a good chance the island wouldn't look like this when they returned.

Justine felt his anxiety and grasped his hand. "I heard the roads are a mess," she said, looking out at the calm seas.

"I was thinking the same thing. We can run up the coast and leave the boat by your place." Kurt started the single hundred-fifty horsepower engine of the park service center console, and Justine freed the lines.

"Once we get Allie, it should be an easy drive south, but how do we get from Key West to the Dry Tortugas?"

They were up on plane now, and the bay boat cruised easily at twenty-four knots over the small waves. Justine pulled out her phone and started searching for an answer. While she searched, Kurt plotted a course to the Miami River.

Originally from Northern California, Kurt had been new to boating when he was relocated to the park in what seemed a kind of a federal employee witness-protection program. He had been assigned here after stumbling across the largest pot grow to date ever found on federal land in the Plumas Wilderness, where he had been working as a special agent. Running a boat at night had at first been intimidating, but he had learned to trust his instincts — and the chartplotter.

With the boat up on plane, Justine saw the smile on his face as he adjusted the tilt of the motor and watched the speed increase, smiling too.

Less than an hour later, they entered the mouth of the river. Usually busy with all manner of boat traffic, from water taxis to cruise ships and freighters, the Intracoastal Waterway was deserted except for a lone cruise ship departing from the port on Dodge Island. After entering the river, Kurt slowed and ran past the million-dollar homes near the bay. As they approached the airport, industrial buildings and boatyards were more prevalent. Justine directed him to the dock used by Miami-Dade, hoping it would be deserted. It was, and Kurt pulled up and tied off the boat.

"Best we can do," Kurt said as he added a forward and aft spring line.

"I have an Uber en route. Should be a few minutes," Justine said.

They left the boat, and again Justine had the feeling that when they returned, things would look different. The gate to the street was locked, forcing them to climb over the chain-link fence. The Uber driver pulled up just as they dropped to the ground, and she wondered if he would reject them for shady behavior. With half the county evacuated, it must have been a slow night, and the driver waved them over. Within minutes, they were at her apartment, and, a half-hour later, in front of Jane's house.

Kurt texted Allie, who responded that she needed a few more minutes, an annoying habit she had recently acquired.

"Any luck on transport to Fort Jefferson?" Kurt asked.

"Two ways. There's a ferry and a seaplane service."

Allie must have heard "seaplane," as she opened the door, and the choice was made, provided the planes were still running. As Kurt pulled out of Jane's driveway, Justine made the call, surprised when someone answered, and a few minutes later, she had made arrangements.

"Seems the park service uses them all the time. Pilot's name is Gary. He said he's taking the plane down in the morning to escape the storm."

"Awesome," Allie said, burying her head in her phone.

Kurt glanced back at her. "Let's leave this off Facebook, okay?"

"Dad ..."

Kurt didn't engage her, and Justine started asking questions about what Allie's friends were doing for Ruth. Justine had surmised that there was a possible boyfriend, and as Kurt drove toward I-95, he listened as Justine skillfully steered the conversation. As they had suspected, the southbound lanes were deserted, while the northbound were practically stopped.

"With that traffic, Ruth'll be here before those cars reach West Palm," Justine said.

"I hope Mom gets going soon," Allie said.

"Maybe you should text her that the traffic is heavy," Kurt said as he accelerated into the middle lane. In record time, they were past Miami and about to enter the Keys.

BUGARRA WINCED when he saw the lanky Cajun stride toward him. The two men might have weighed the same, but he felt small as Trufante towered over his stocky frame by half a foot.

"Party is on out here tonight," Bugarra said, wondering what Trufante wanted with him.

"You put those boys on me?"

"Why would I do that? Just out here enjoying the pre-storm festivities."

"Didn't take you for much of a Duval Street kind of guy."

Bugarra started to back away, stepping to the side. With his long legs, Trufante reclaimed the ground in one stride. "I know you're after whatever Mac has, and I mean to tell you that I don't know anything about it. Now, about all I can do for you is maybe get you laid with one of those hot babes."

Bugarra had seen the two women. He was alone here, and with no leads, he thought a little distraction might settle his nerves. Besides, he could keep an eye on Trufante at the same time, hoping eventually he would be lead to Travis. Hitting the wall in the search for Gross's data made the Cajun a possible ally as well.

"Might have a business proposition for you. How 'bout we go have a drink?" Bugarra said, leading the way back into the bar. He'd had his share of confrontations searching for lost riches. It was unavoidable with greedy bureaucrats, sleazy scammers, and competitors all after the same thing. Experience had taught him that with his personality, running toward the fire was usually the best course. Bugarra sucked up his chest and prepared to assume the larger-than-life persona he was famous for. Sometimes it was work, but when he saw the two women, he smiled.

"A round for my friends," he called out as he reached the bar.

"Now you're talking," Trufante said, sliding between the women. "Got us a new daddy now, ladies."

The shots were placed on the bar, and as the group tossed them down, Bugarra glanced up at the TV and reached into his pocket for his phone. His insurance agent was high on his favorites list, and he pressed the call button. "Be right back," he said, and stepped away.

The inside of the Hog's Breath was quiet, with several employees securing what they could. If the storm came through here, the outside bar was a lost cause, but they might save something. It was still too loud to hear, and Bugarra moved to the corner closest to the street.

"Vince, Rick here."

"Maybe we ought to set an appointment for early next week to review." There was sure to be damage to Bugarra's fleet, whether from Ruth or not. Several boats were aging and ready to be replaced. This would be as good a time as any.

He had turned away from the bar while talking, and was surprised to see Mac Travis walking across the street with a tall blonde. Stepping back to use one of the small palm trees for cover, Bugarra watched as the couple walked into Irish Kevin's. Known for its loud music and rowdy atmosphere, this was not a place that Bugarra would expect to find Travis. A minute later, they walked out and entered the bar next door. They were clearly looking for someone, and Bugarra thought he knew who it was. Before he could decide what to do about it, a rickshaw pulled up next to them and stopped. He couldn't see Travis or the woman, but he could see the driver. Another ghost from the past had reappeared.

The last thing Bugarra needed was to be seen with Trufante by either Billy Bones or Travis. There were a lot of moving pieces in this puzzle, and he needed to step back to observe. Turning away from the street, he re-entered the Hog's Breath. On the way to the bar, he bumped into the two men he had paid. They must have done some math and realized that, with the arrival of Bugarra and his wallet, they didn't stand a chance with the women. Trufante was still at the bar, and Bugarra approached, trying to think of a way to pry the women away.

"There's the man," Trufante said, wrapping a long arm around Bugarra.

The Cajun drawl stung Bugarra's ears like an insect bite. After ordering one more round of shots, mainly for him this time, Bugarra needed to make Trufante an offer that was too good to refuse. Pulling him away from the women, Bugarra faced Trufante and looked him squarely in the eye. Bugarra could tell Trufante was intimidated by the way the taller man's eyes darted away. "Travis has something that belongs to Gill Gross's family. I'd pay well to return it."

Trufante's gaze met Bugarra's for a second—enough to tell him the Cajun was bought. Regretting that it was too risky to stay and seduce one or both of the women, he said goodnight and slid out the entrance. The rickshaw was still across the street, and Bugarra was able to make it to Front Street without Travis seeing him. Standing on the corner of Duval and Front, he watched and waited.

FIFTEEN

"If this ain't the odd couple," Billy Bones called from his bicycle-drawn rickshaw.

Mac was starting to worry. They'd covered half the bars that remained open on Duval Street and there was still no sign of Trufante. That left a lot more territory, but it was getting late, and in the company of the two women, he could be anywhere. Mac could tell from looking at Pamela that, though she wouldn't admit it, the thought of Trufante with another woman was something that had her upset.

"We need to find him," Pamela said. "I just know he's in trouble."

Mac thought it strange how the threat of Ruth was bringing out repressed issues with people. Pamela had left the Cajun and moved to Key West several months ago. Mac knew she was about as stable as a suitcase missing a wheel, which was how Trufante had found her, so her behavior was no surprise to him. By enlisting Billy and his rickshaw, they could cover a lot more ground than on foot, but there was always a downside to working with him. Right now, with the window before Ruth hitting closing quickly, Mac knew he had to do something.

"All right," Mac said, casting a scowl in Billy's direction meant to impress the seriousness of the matter. "We need to find Tru. Can you help?"

"Right on," Billy said. "Business has ground to a halt, if you know what I mean."

Mac looked past him at the bumper-to-bumper traffic on Duval Street. Unless you were purposely cruising the street, most motorists generally avoided Duval. With half the bars and businesses already shuttered there, he guessed the other streets must be really bad.

"You've got my number," Mac said, walking away. Pamela followed behind him.

"I'm getting really worried," Pamela said, as they entered Willie T's. "I keep calling his phone, but it's going to voicemail."

The stage was empty, and there were only a half-dozen people sitting at the bar. Mac and Pamela walked in and out. With only a few bars on this side of the street left, and none that Trufante would likely hang out in, they crossed to the south side and started walking back to Front Street. The Bull and Whistle was shuttered, as was Margaritaville—not that Trufante would be caught dead in Buffett's tourist trap.

Mac could tell that Pamela was getting more anxious as they neared the Hog's Breath and Front Street. The singer there was just finishing up, and the bar was near empty with no sign of Trufante. Mac looked back toward the street and saw a rickshaw turn south on Caroline.

"That's the last of them," Mac said.

Pamela slouched against the wall of a brick building. "We've got to find him."

"You know Tru," Mac said, trying to reassure her. If it were anyone else, he might have put his arm around her for comfort. He kept his distance. It certainly wasn't because of her looks. He and Mel had often wondered what she was doing with

Trufante when she clearly could have found a sugar daddy. Money didn't seem to be an issue, though, and from what they'd seen, as the end of a month neared, she was generally slinging her credit card around like the bill of a hooked marlin. It definitely wasn't money that drove her.

"I texted him before that I'm heading out at six a.m. He'll be at the boat."

Mac's earlier adrenaline rush had long passed, and he was ready to crash. There was no telling what tomorrow would bring, and a few hours of sleep was a good idea. With his bunk now in the forefront of his mind, he knew the only way he was going to see it was to take her with him. "Come on back to the boat. You can sleep aboard. He's bound to show."

Tears streamed down her face as she followed him back to the marina. Mac had watched her try his phone several times while they were checking the bars, and she tried once again before stepping aboard, but shook her head and disconnected without leaving a message.

"You have anything to drink?" she asked, lifting a long leg over the gunwale.

Mac was surprised she'd stayed sober during their search. They must have canvassed two dozen bars, and she hadn't had a drink. Remembering that he still needed to hide the alcohol before Tru came aboard, he offered her a beer.

"Anything with more power?" she asked. "Beer makes me fat."

There was a good bottle of rum; he retrieved it and poured several fingers for her, figuring the best way for him to get some sleep was to knock her out. She took the glass and downed it in two gulps, then handed it back to him. Mac poured an equal amount in and watched as she sat back and sipped it.

The alcohol had an immediate effect. He could see it in her eyes. Instead of her previous focus when they were searching for Trufante, something he thought unusual for her, she now had a faraway, dreamy look. Hoping that was the first sign that she was going to crash, he sat in the captain's chair at the helm and checked his phone.

There were two messages. He was relieved by both. The first was from Ned, that he had accepted Mac's offer and would be aboard at six. The second was from Mel, saying that she was leaving for New Orleans in the morning. After seeing the cone of probability widen as the storm grew and strengthened, Atlanta would likely be facing some weather, too, as the hurricane moved overland.

Pamela perked up suddenly and leaned forward. "Why do you just call your boat "my boat"?"

If this was a trap, Mac couldn't figure it out. "Because that's what it is."

"A boat needs a name. They have souls, you know."

The only "sole" that Mac knew on a boat was the cabin floor. There was no point in fighting her, and he let it go.

"Really, you seem to have bad luck. If you named her, that could change."

She was right about that, but he and Mel usually blamed their misfortunes on Trufante. "Go ahead and name her, then. We've got a big day tomorrow. I'm going to try and get some sleep."

"You're like a ghost, Mac Travis. Ghost should be in the name. Maybe that'll help you be invisible and elude some of the trouble that finds you."

Mac wasn't a superstitious guy. He didn't go for the voodoo-like rituals some fishermen used, or pray to the gods for a better catch. Maybe it was the low pressure from the approaching storm, but something came over him, and she didn't seem so crazy.

Boats had been his life for almost thirty years. They were

work boats, mainly—Wood's old skiff, which had been lost during a storm a few years ago, and the center console Mac used now to run back and forth to Marathon were the only pleasure-type boats he had owned. He had always just called them what they were: "the skiff" *or* "the center console."

"Ghost, huh?" The words left his mouth before he could stop them.

Pamela seemed to go into a trance. Rocking back and forth, she started muttering phrases he couldn't make out. He was about to leave her and head to bed when she said the same thing several times, then louder and clear enough for him to hear.

"Ghost Runner."

Mac wasn't often blown away, but the coming winds couldn't have hit him in the face harder than the new name for his boat. It just seemed right. Before he could say anything, she opened her eyes, sat up, and drank more rum. The urgency in her eyes returned.

"We have to do it now. There's not a moment to waste," she said.

"What? Leave? Tru will show up in the morning."

"No, not him. We have to name the boat before Ruth gets here."

If there was ever a time to be superstitious, it was in the face of a category-five hurricane. Especially with Trufante missing, Mac would need all the help he could get. "How do we do that?"

"Well, first you fill my glass." She held the empty glass out to him.

Mac dumped the rest of the rum in it. If she really did have some kind of secret powers, the alcohol seemed to bring them out.

"You have a marker?"

While Mac rummaged through a drawer in the helm, he

watched her out of the corner of his eye. She finished the drink and started to rock back and forth again. Finally, he found the broad-tip Sharpie that he used to label gear. Pulling the lid off, he drew a short line on his hand to see if it worked.

Pamela took the marker from his hand and crossed to the transom. Opening the small door, she stepped onto the dive platform and squatted.

Mac kept his distance, feeling strangely comfortable with what was happening. He stood back and waited, a little anxious, but at the same time, peaceful. Finally, she stood up.

"Done."

Mac remained where he was, almost scared to look. Though he had never done it, he knew putting a name on a boat was a big deal.

"You gonna look?" she asked, coming back through the transom door.

Mac pushed off the gunwale and went aft. It was one thing to let her name his boat, but he wasn't sure if lettering was in her wheelhouse. Finally, he resigned himself, knowing it would wear off eventually. He leaned over and saw the name.

"*Ghost Runner*," he said, testing the words on his tongue. The lettering was simple but good. He said the name again. It too was good.

Whether the black cloud that sometimes followed him would be lifted remained to be seen, but as he thanked her and said goodnight, a strange feeling of peace followed him as he went below and lay down on the bunk.

ALONE WITH THE TWO WOMEN, Trufante had to make a decision. He was mulling the possibilities when he saw Billy Bones walk into the bar.

"Yo, Tru!" Billy walked up to Trufante, grabbed his hand, and tried a man hug.

Trufante resisted. He knew Billy was one or two more degrees of trouble than he himself was.

"What do we have here? Hello, ladies." Billy turned his attention to the two women. "You gonna introduce Billy Bones to your friends?"

"What brings you here, Billy?" Trufante knew that there was always a reason when Billy came around.

"Shoot, I'm lookin' out for you. Seen old Mac Travis and Pamela a bit ago. Said you were down here too. Maybe lookin' for a little hurricane party action." He turned his attention back to the women.

The thought of Mac and Pamela together, especially after she had rebuffed him earlier, burned Trufante and left his mouth dry. The only way to cure it was taking another shot. He ordered a round and toasted Billy. "Sadie and Dannie, meet Billy Bones."

Billy downed the shot and smiled. "And welcome to hurricane season in Key West."

SIXTEEN

THERE COMES A TIME FOR EVERY PERSON WHEN ALCOHOL affects decision making. Everyone is different, and many can stop before they get in trouble. Trufante had passed the point of no return two shots ago. Not that he cared. It seemed that no amount of alcohol could take the sting out of Pamela's rejection. He knew deep down that if he wanted her back, this was not the way to go about it. Adding Billy to the party was one more bad decision fueled by the alcohol.

Trufante sipped a beer, taking a break from the shots to let his buzz even out. His decision making might have crossed the border, but he knew how to function with an above-normal blood-alcohol content. The main rule was, once you were where you needed to be, maintain, don't over-fuel, and that meant backing off some. Water was a natural option—except for being a party killer. Once one person asked for a glass, everyone else generally followed, and the party was over. Beer was a safer option and complied with the age-old drinker's adage: *liquor before beer—all clear.*

A quick glance at Sadie and Dannie showed they were still having a good time, and he looked over at Billy. Despite his failures, the New Jersey wannabe gangster always bounced back and still had his swagger. Trufante could tell from his dress and grooming that Billy was on an upswing. The guy was like a seesaw, swinging from looking like a destitute con-man to an almost presentable one. Some women had what they called *gaydar*, the uncanny ability to spot gay men; Trufante could sniff out a con from a mile away.

"You're looking good, Billy. What'cha been up to?" Trufante took a long pull on his beer. It was Billy's turn to buy shots.

"Cornered the market on those rickshaw things. You know they only have twenty of those suckers on this rock."

"Good money?" Trufante asked, hoping to guilt Billy into buying a round.

"Shit, I got a babe down at the city. Owed me one and rigged the lottery so I'd get a permit. Still gotta work, but I got me a stable and keep the thing going 24/7."

That answered Trufante's question, and he put his arm around the tightwad. "Must be busy with the storm coming and all."

"Shit. I even gave Mac and Mel a ride to the airport."

Trufante smiled for the first time in an hour, thinking about how desperate Mac must have been to get in the back of Billy's ride. "Things are going so well, maybe you could buy a round or two."

"I'll one-up you on that. Got me some of the magic marching powder. Share those ladies and I'll turn y'all on."

"Now that'll keep the party going." Trufante moved between the woman and asked if they'd like a bump. Both faces lit up, and he figured the party could last until Ruth had moved on. The promise of the drug added a level of friskiness to the already flirtatious women. Dannie grabbed Tru's hand, and Sadie put her arm around Billy. The women steered them to the street and into an alley. After fueling up, they joined a mass of people heading toward Mallory Square.

"What y'all got going on?" Trufante asked a green-haired woman walking next to him.

"It's a vigil, man," she replied. "We're gonna ride out the storm."

Trufante knew both idiocy and a party when he saw it. This looked like the latter until it turned into the former. By then, he'd figure something out. Reaching into his pocket for his phone, it was missing. Thinking back, he knew where it was, but with the bodies pressing him forward, he figured he'd get it later.

His intent was to check on Ruth's progress. Party or no, he was not going to be stuck on the exposed pavement of Mallory Square when the hurricane hit. Looking up, he noticed lines of high clouds backlit by the moon already making their way across the island. Hoping they were the outer bands and the storm was going to move north and east, he followed the group, carefully watching Billy and his stash.

They reached the end of Duval, and the crowd funneled to the left into the open square. Famous for its sunset celebrations and street performers, Mallory Square had a different feel now with the wind gusting and white-capped waves breaking over the seawall. Instead of following the group, Trufante grabbed Billy, Dannie, and Sadie, and led them to the right. He found an alley vacant, except for one of the feral cats that roamed the island, and pulled them into the shadows.

A few minutes later, with numb lips and jaws grinding, they joined the party in the square. From his vantage point, Trufante could see the crowd, and estimated there were two hundred people here. He recognized several bartenders and accepted a drink from a bottle that was being passed around. Several performers had set up their gear, not in an attempt to make money, but to enhance the already jubilant atmosphere. The smell of weed swirling around the square on the increasing wind brought a smile to Trufante's face, and he sought out the joint, but before he partook, he knew he better check the storm. This was going to be one hell of a party until it hit.

Dannie had apparently chosen him and had her arm intertwined with his. Sadie was likewise attached to Billy. "You got a phone on you?" Trufante asked, not sure where she could be hiding it.

Watching as she reached into her large cleavage, Trufante was mesmerized as he saw the top of her phone emerge.

"What else ya got in there?" he asked.

"Hmm. Maybe another blast of that powder and I'll let you find out."

It was almost enough to distract Trufante, but a wind gust brought him back to reality. He took the phone and scanned the apps, finally clicking on a web browser and entering the National Oceanic and Atmospheric Administration website. As he did so, he thought nothing of it, but not that long ago fishermen were considered Luddites. Now, they were quite the opposite. He skimmed the site and found the advisory, which, as with most weather forecasts, was fudged ten ways to hell. Instead of relying on the gloom-and-doom forecast, he opened the radar screen and studied the display.

Louisiana had its share of the devastating storms, and as Trufante watched the repeating loop on the screen, he remembered Katrina. This storm was bigger and badder, but from the location and movement, he surmised that Key West was relatively safe. Ruth was moving fairly quickly and looked to make landfall around Marathon. With the stronger bands to the north and east, Key West would escape most of its wrath.

Satisfied that the party would continue, he remembered Dannie's offer and put his arm around Billy's shoulder. "Girls are ready for some action if you light them up again."

"I got something way better if you're ready to ditch this place," Billy replied.

Trufante looked around the square. After an hour, the momentum of the party had started to fade. Looking up, he saw the cloud cover had thickened, and although it was dark, the moon was having a harder time breaking through these clouds. From the look of them, they held rain.

"What'cha got?"

"Got a buddy with some X."

That got Trufante's attention. "He gonna be around tonight?"

Billy pulled out his phone and scrolled through his contacts. He found what he was looking for and, a few seconds later, was deep into negotiations. "We're cool. Got to go to the dude's house, though."

Trufante shrugged as the first drop of rain hit his receding hairline. "Y'all into X?" he asked the women.

Both sidled up to him, clearly giving their answer. Billy looked left out, and as he was the key to the operation, Trufante told them it was his friend. With Sadie hanging all over Billy, Dannie and Trufante followed them out of the square. Trufante could feel the pressure of some of the not-so-committed partiers pushing behind them as the rain increased. He knew most would quickly flee, but there were always a few that remembered Lieutenant Dan from *Forrest Gump*, thinking the hurricane-force winds would cleanse their souls as well.

Trufante had a different answer for his soul, and when they reached Billy's rickshaw, he climbed in back with one girl on each side. Billy hopped onto the bike, and started pedaling.

The streets were quiet now. Anyone planning on evacuating was already headed to the mainland; those who had decided to ride out the storm were hunkering down in their homes. Many of the houses they passed were boarded up; several had lights on, though most were dark. If Trufante were a thief, this would be a banner night.

Cruising North Roosevelt, they passed several banks with digital signs. Between the storm warnings, the displays showed it was almost four a.m. Trufante sat back, realizing he was tired. The rush from the coke that Billy had shared was long gone, and he felt the early stages of a hangover. Hopefully the X would get him through. If it didn't, it'd be close enough to dawn that he could make his way back to the marina and see what Mac was up to.

He started to feel melancholy. It was times like these, the early hours of the morning, that he really missed Pamela. He knew at almost fifty that he was getting too old for this, but it was in his blood. After decades of all-night parties, he wondered if that part of his life was almost over, and he started to think about how to get Pamela back.

The thoughts ended when Billy stopped in front of an old Conch house. They were in a neighborhood of single-story homes, looking like they dated back to the forties, when they were used by the armed forces stationed here. If not for the colorful paint and unique fences and rails, it would have looked like a thousand communities across the country, but the eccentricity of Key West saved it.

"Hang out for a minute. I'll go set it up." Billy climbed down from the bike and walked up the path to the house. The door opened, and he entered, leaving Trufante alone with the women. Dannie's head was resting against his shoulder and Sadie was leaning against the cab. He moved just enough to see if Dannie was awake, and when she only grunted, he knew the party was over.

One of his saving graces, through all the screw-ups and bad decisions, was his hard-wired code of chivalry. Most of his acquaintances, including Billy, would ditch the women, but

Trufante wasn't like that. He remembered the name of the hotel they were staying at, and slowly, he lifted Dannie's head from his shoulder and placed it against the other side of the cab. Stretching one long leg, he eased himself over her, extricating himself from the cab, and climbed onto the bike. Tru didn't have a second thought as he started pedaling down the street. His code didn't extend to Billy Bones.

SEVENTEEN

MAC WAS UP BEFORE THE SUN. SURPRISINGLY, HE HAD slept a few hours, and as the coffee brewed, he scanned his phone, piecing together the forecast models and reports from Ruth. The National Hurricane Center was the authority, but slow in acknowledging that the European models, with more data points, were more accurate than their own forecasting. Instead, Mac went back to Mike's Weather App, where everything was combined. The models now formed a consensus that the eye would pass well to the north and east of Key West. That he was safe here was little consolation when he thought about his and Mel's island home.

There was still danger here, though—primarily tornados spun from the outer bands, as well as the storm surge. The devastating winds were usually close to the eye wall, but surge, expected to be six to nine feet, was the deadlier component. They appeared lucky that Ruth, if she didn't stall out, would make landfall at low tide this afternoon. Even though the tidal range was less than three feet this far south, that could make the difference between the trawler floating high in its slip or sitting on Caroline Street. Deciding it wasn't worth the risk, while he waited for Trufante and Ned, he started readying the boat to depart.

For the last few hours it had been raining on and off as the outer bands of the storm approached. Huddled in the wheel-house, he drank his coffee, watching the minutes tick down until six. Ned would be here, but Trufante was currently AWOL. Finally, Mac saw Ned approach.

"Appreciate this, Mac," he said as he climbed over the tran-som. "Where're you figuring on running?"

"Storm's going north. We can make Fort Jefferson in about three hours. The harbor is well protected there; we should be okay."

"Make sense. Where's Tru?"

"MIA," Mac said. The possibility that Trufante wouldn't show up was very real. Mac had made it clear in his text that if Trufante wasn't here on time, the boat was going without him. That was before Pamela emerged from the cabin with her hair askew, rubbing the sleep out of her eyes.

"Tru show?" she asked.

"Who you got here?" Ned asked.

"Pamela, Ned." Mac made the introduction brief. Despite their bonding session last night, she still scared him. And now, with Trufante missing, he wondered how she would react.

"We have to find him," she said.

"No. We have to get out of here," Mac said. Reaching for the ignition, he was about to start the engine when she stopped him.

"No, Mac Travis, we have to find him."

Mac had seen the look on her face before, and released the key. The stubborn mix of desperation and commitment was one of the few traits Pamela and Mel shared. And that meant his plans were about to change.

In response, he looked down at his phone and studied the

radar image of the swirling storm. Wood's island was already engulfed in yellow, with red approaching, but as the tentacles rotated counterclockwise around the eye, they seemed to break up after passing what would be due west of the island.

"What do you think, Ned?" Mac asked, handing him the phone.

"Until you offered the boat ride, I wasn't going anywhere. The shield around Key West appears to still be intact."

Mac thought Ned was right, but there was too much at risk here. He wasn't in a position to sacrifice his uninsured boat to Ruth. It was a point of contention between him and Mel that stemmed back to Wood's distaste for anything to do with the government or bureaucracies. On a day-to-day or even year-to-year basis, money wasn't a problem. Mel owned the island free and clear, and they had no debt or bills. It was pretty easy to make ends meet. But having to replace the boat, especially after the new electronics and engine, would force them into a situation he didn't want to think about. Financing was not an option when the gross income on your tax return didn't have many places to the left of the decimal point.

Looking back, he saw the center console in the next slip. Towing it in the current conditions to the Dry Tortugas would burn too much fuel. Reluctantly, he decided it would have to ride out the storm here.

He made some calculations in his head. Moving at fifteen knots, as last reported, even if Ruth veered south and west, it would take five or six hours to reach the Tortugas. Rain wasn't a problem, but the spinning storm was already kicking up the seas. He figured he had an hour window before they were stuck here for the duration—not a spot he wanted to be in.

Pamela had been staring at him as he computed the odds of losing the boat. "One hour."

"Agreed," she said. "One hour and *Ghost Runner* is doing what she does best."

"You named the boat?" Ned asked.

Mac shrugged him off. "He's got to be close to Duval," he said, turning and ducking into the cabin. A minute later, he came out with two bright-yellow rain slickers and handed one to Pamela. "We stay together," he said, figuring that, at a fast walk, they could cover the street and get back in forty minutes.

NOTHING FELT RIGHT: the inferior suite, the carpet, the air. Bugarra cut a path across the floor as the Weather Channel played in the background. If he looked, he could have seen the depressions made by his feet from the last twenty minutes of pacing around the suite.

He didn't fail often, but he had to admit his inability to obtain Gross's research from Travis was just that—failure. Without knowing what Mac held, Bugarra had to wonder if it was Ruth that had brought him to Key West or something else. The wind-driven rain striking the patio doors brought him back to reality, but still a part of his mind wouldn't let it go. Was Travis shrewd enough to use the cover of the storm to investigate Gross's find? The answer slightly calmed Bugarra. Travis was an able salvor, but he had never been bitten by the treasure bug. Looking at his phone, Bugarra dialed one of his men to see if there was any movement at the marina. The two men in the Yellowfin who had screwed up the attack on the island had followed Travis down and had been watching his boat all night.

Deciding against riding out Ruth in the hotel room, Bugarra had prepared his boat, figuring Travis might head out. Reaching for his rain jacket, he abandoned his route across the carpet and left the suite. Standing under the overhang covering the walkway, he pulled out his phone and pressed the contact for one of his men.

"There are three aboard. Looks like they're getting ready to head out," the man said.

"Three? Describe them."

"Travis, an old man, and some hot-looking tall chick."

"No sign of his mate?"

"No, just the three. They look like they're arguing." He paused. "Wait, now they're leaving the boat."

"One of you stay put. The other follow them."

Bugarra couldn't figure out what they were up to. Though he'd known who Travis was for years, dating back to his days working for Wood, Bugarra had never gotten a sense of the man. He had a reputation for being capable; "a good hand" was what Bugarra remembered Wood calling Travis, which was high praise from the old engineer. There'd been rumors about some of Travis's subsequent adventures that, if they had any degree of truth, showed he was more than just capable. What was missing from the man, and why Bugarra was having a hard time figuring him out, were the two traits abundant in salvors: greed and paranoia.

Travis was a different animal, but Trufante was not. He was made of greed and paranoia. Maybe not as much as Slipstream, who was sitting in Raiford Prison serving his time for killing Gross, but the Cajun was a known quantity—and Bugarra understood that.

He took the stairs down, exited through the lobby, and started walking. There was little traffic, and no cabs, so he continued on foot, turning left onto White Street. Even on the quiet side of the island, he could tell that Key West was in a different kind of mood. The point of no return had been passed sometime last night, when it became safer to stay than leave. Known for being lawless, the city was strikingly quiet, almost as if the usual state of affairs was more show than go. Emergency services had been suspended and the Coast Guard had enacted Port Condition Zulu, closing the harbors. Most other cities would be experiencing a crime spree, but Key West danced to the beat of a different drum.

Walking was not Bugarra's preferred mode of transportation. The abundant pink cabs usually cruising the island were nonexistent, but he did see a scooter rental place with several randomly parked in front, as if they had been abandoned. Checking one, he saw the key was in the ignition and hopped on. He felt like a gorilla riding a tricycle, but it got him across the island. The predawn glow showed the marina was as quiet as the streets. Protected from the winds, the boats bobbed on the light chop. He spotted Travis's boat and found his men.

IT HAD BEEN the quickest ride to Key West in history, Kurt thought, as he drove Justine's car across the Stock Island Bridge. With a short diversion off the turnpike, they could have switched to the larger park service pickup he usually drove, but decided the car was something they owned and would be safer in Key West. Allie was excited. Not really aware of the danger, she sat in the back texting friends and posting on Facebook.

Kurt had never been through a hurricane, but he'd been around enough wildfires to know how dangerous nature could be. Justine was anxious. A lifelong South Florida resident, she'd experienced one major and several minor storms. It wasn't surviving Ruth that worried her. Their destination was just outside of the furthest model. It was the aftermath that concerned her.

They had barely reached Key West, and waves and spray were already crashing over the seawall, as Kurt turned left onto

South Roosevelt. The entrance to the airport came up on the right, and he turned in and drove past the deserted terminal to the FBO area. After parking, he locked the car, and they headed toward the trailer to the right marked Seaplane Adventures.

The office was locked, and Kurt had started to make a plan B if they had missed their ride, when he saw two men talking on the tarmac. They walked out to the planes and waited while the men readied one of the planes to ride out the storm.

"Hey, you Hunter?" one of the men asked.

"Yeah." Kurt introduced Justine and Allie.

"Gary. Hop aboard. I'll be right there." Gary continued to work on the other plane, cranking down a ratchet on one of the tie-downs.

Kurt led the way to the twelve-seater and waited while Justine and Allie climbed aboard with their bags. He followed, spacing out their baggage to balance the load before moving to the right-hand seat in the cockpit. A few minutes later, Gary climbed aboard and shut the door.

"Gonna be a little bumpy," he said, as he strapped himself in and started running through the preflight checklist. "Put on the headphones," he called back to Justine and Allie. Kurt donned the pair by his seat and waited.

His stomach dropped as a gust caught the small plane on takeoff, and he was about to reach for the barf bag when the plane leveled out, its tail wagging back and forth as the engine fought for altitude. The feeling quickly left, and he could see Gary relax as their altitude increased. Twenty minutes later, the weather changed for the better and the ride smoothed out.

Gary's voice came over the headset. "Since the weather's good, I'll give y'all the ten-cent tour." He started an almost continuous monologue as the plane flew first over the Marquesas Keys, then passed the Quicksands. The view removed all worries of the hurricane they had left behind. Two wrecks were visible as they passed, one from Mel Fisher's *Atocha* fleet, the other a bombed-out hull used by the Navy for practice. It soon became quiet as the brick fort became visible and the plane landed in smooth seas. Gary taxied into a small beach by the fort.

"You'd never know what we just left," Justine said as she climbed down onto the float.

"That was awesome," Allie said behind her.

EIGHTEEN

Trufante woke with a start. No stranger to waking up and not knowing where he was, he looked around in an effort to get his bearings. A dim light crept through the semi-closed shades. It appeared to be a small hotel suite, and he was surprised to find himself alone on the couch. A queen-sized bed in the corner revealed two lumps.

The night came back to him slowly. For the way he felt, it would go down as a disappointing effort. He got out of bed, wanting to leave before the women across the room woke. Just as he stood, the strands of violet hair occupying one pillow moved. He sat up slowly. It wasn't like he'd done anything wrong—or anything at all, for that matter—and he didn't feel any further responsibility toward the women.

"What are we going to do about Ruth?" she asked, lifting her head.

Trufante remembered she went by Dannie. The *we* was not sitting well with him, and now he knew why Mac hated the word. "I gotta go find Mac."

"Who's that?"

"Never mind. Get some sleep. This place looks pretty well

built." In fact, he had no idea, but it was by the cemetery, which he knew was the high point of the island. Standing, he looked on the coffee table, then around the room for his phone. It wasn't visible anywhere, and he checked his pockets.

"You lose something?"

"My phone. Can I borrow yours?"

"Sure," she said, getting out of bed. She picked up her phone from the nightstand, punched her code into the screen, and brought it to him before heading to the bathroom.

Dannie emerged from the bathroom. The streaky makeup was gone and her hair was brushed. "Coffee?"

He nodded, dialing, and waited for the call to connect. "Hey," he said into the phone, and gave Mac the address, already knowing he was in trouble. He turned to Dannie. "Be safe now. See y'all on the other side."

SKETCHY CIRCUMSTANCES WERE the norm for Trufante, but it looked like Mac had finally found him. With his phone still in hand, he entered the address Trufante had given into the map app. Anyone else, under any other circumstance, he would have told to get here now, but with Pamela freaked out and the clock ticking, Mac decided to find the Cajun and provide an escort.

Ned had gone back to the boat. Pamela had refused, and together she and Mac jogged across the island. Cursing his sea legs, he struggled to keep up with her. Finally, they found Trufante walking down the sidewalk with his grin leading the way. Seeing Pamela it quickly disappeared.

"We need to get moving," Mac said. From his last glance at the radar, Key West was clearly not going to take the brunt of the storm, but the next few hours were not going to be pretty either. For now, in the calm between the tips of the squall bands whipping around the eye, it was almost pleasant standing on the street, but he knew it wasn't going to last.

"Storm's going to hit early this afternoon. That gives us just enough time to reach the harbor at Fort Jefferson." The plan was still the plan. If Key West was only experiencing mild effects of the storm, at seventy miles away, the Dry Tortugas would be virtually untouched.

Mac was thankful for the tailwind and, with a sense of urgency, the three of them ran back to the marina. The slightly downhill slope from the cemetery to the water also helped. Reaching the marina, they boarded the boat, and, without wasting time to catch his breath, Mac started the engine. With Ned and Trufante handling the lines and fenders, they were underway in just minutes, and Mac, anxious that their window was closing, pushed down on the throttles. His worries were not unfounded, as the wake from the trawler was smaller than the waves being pushed by the wind out of the harbor. Taking one last look at the center console, he turned into the water being pushed toward them by Ruth.

Once clear of the point, he selected a half-dozen waypoints that would keep them well clear of the shallows and entered them as a route in the chartplotter. Engaging the autopilot, he stayed at the helm for several minutes to make sure the equipment was working properly before handing over the helm to Trufante. After pointing out the route on the screen, he stepped back to the cockpit and motioned for Pamela and pulled her into the cabin. The tension between them was unbearable and Mac needed to fix it—at least for the duration of the trip.

"I need you to be good with him," he said. He saw her face start to screw up and cut her short. "This is gonna be a rough ride. I need my mate. Whatever feud you two have going waits until we hit dry land."

She nodded like she understood and turned back to the cockpit. "I want to let you-all know that the cloud over this boat is gone now. We will have safe passage aboard *Ghost Runner*," Pamela declared.

"You named your boat?" Trufante asked. "The console too?"

"*Reef Runner*," Pamela said, quietly.

For the second time in as many hours, Mac had to admit he was shocked at her vision. "*Reef Runner*," he said, almost embarrassed to hear the words out loud. He wondered why Ned and Trufante thought it so out of character that he had named the boats. It was just something Mac had never thought of. But now it felt right. "There's beer in the fridge," he said, as he eased Trufante away from the wheel and took back the helm.

"Naming your boats and offering beers. Highly suspect," Trufante said, as he disappeared into the cabin.

Despite its forty-two-foot length and twelve-foot beam, the boat felt crowded. Still not entirely trusting the new electronics, Mac checked the chartplotter. Aside from being swept slightly off course when large waves pushed the bow sideways, the instruments reacted correctly, and he watched as the boat turned to starboard, heading toward the waypoint he had placed at the entry to the Northwest Channel. He continued to watch as *Ghost Runner* maintained a straight course through the channel, then made a turn to port after reaching the next mark. In deeper water now, the seas were still big, but the ride leveled out. Mac looked over at Trufante, who was standing next to him with a full beer—probably his second, at least.

"You're going to have to talk to her," Mac said.

"Yeah," Trufante muttered, and drank.

Mac looked at the sky. The horizon was clear. Behind them, a dark cloud was moving toward Key West. Not many people would have thought that going to sea in a storm was a good idea, but Mac felt more comfortable aboard the boat than he would have on land. With a thirty-foot reading on the depth finder, he pushed the throttle down. The engine reacted and settled into a comfortable twenty knots.

Sitting in the chair at the helm, Mac glanced back at his passengers. They had settled in as well, and although the seas were running about five feet, the steel hull of the trawler sliced through them easily. Trufante had gone back into the cabin, obviously drinking another beer while avoiding Pamela, who sat on the port bench talking to Ned. Satisfied with the autopilot, Mac looked up, scanning the water around them. A ray of sunlight made its way through the swirling clouds behind them, and he saw the distinct reflection of glass. He stared at the location, then the compass. After calculating the reciprocal course, he grabbed the binoculars from the electronics box. Putting them to his eyes, he braced his elbows on the back of the seat and scanned the water. He had been right. Maybe a mile behind them was another boat.

NINETEEN

With a renewed sense of purpose, Bugarra scanned the water ahead with his binoculars. He first thought he had lost them. Then, on his way to Travis's boat to interrogate the old man who was still aboard, he saw the three figures running toward the marina, and scrambled back to his boat.

The twenty-eight-foot Yellowfin had twin two-fifties and a small cabin forward of the console. With its narrow beam, it was built for speed, not comfort. In these conditions and following Travis's trawler, the opposite would have satisfied Bugarra.

"Just enough speed to keep him in sight," he said to the man at the helm, wishing the boat was equipped with radar so he could track Travis without the risk of being seen. "Either of you see radar on his boat?" He tried to remember if he had seen a bar or dome on top of the wheelhouse.

"I think there was a dome with a pair of VHF antennas and the outriggers," the helmsman said.

Bugarra had seen the twin displays mounted in the dashboard, and now his man confirmed how well equipped Mac was. Two VHF antennas would mean he had a single-sideband radio as well. The other problem was fuel. Travis had a destination in mind. Without knowing where he was heading, Bugarra did not have the ability to run at the Yellowfin's optimum efficiency. He moved next to the helmsman and pressed several buttons on the engine gauges. The top one showed his consumption, and, as he thought, they were in a bad spot. A little faster would be better for the twin engines. Having to hold back kept the boat not quite up on plane and sucking thirty gallons an hour. Travis was probably running right in his sweet spot and using less than half that. Although the gauges showed the tanks almost full, Bugarra knew not to trust them. The loading of the boat and its attitude in the water could throw off the gauges by as much as a quarter tank.

Studying the chartplotter showed only one likely destination: the Dry Tortugas. On their present course, there was nowhere within either boat's round-trip range that had a safe harbor. There were anchorages in the Marquesas Keys, but Fort Jefferson made more sense. If he were heading there, Travis's intention was probably a safe harbor to wait out the storm—unless he knew something else. And with that thought, Bugarra's paranoia increased.

He crossed in front of the console and sat in the chair on the portside. Just as he sat, the helmsman eased back on the throttle as the boat ahead appeared to slow, and Bugarra went back to the helm.

"What's he doing?"

"Just came down off plane. I'm not sure, but you said to stay back."

Bugarra picked up the binoculars and scanned the water ahead. The trawler had slowed to almost a stop. "Shadow him from here," Bugarra said. He handed the binoculars to the other man, who climbed onto the gunwale to get a better look. There could be a hundred reasons why Travis had slowed.

Switching the VHF on, Bugarra turned to channel sixteen

in case the other boat was in trouble. The airwaves were quiet, and he lowered the volume. If Mac wasn't in trouble, there must be something significant to the location. The chartplotter showed them past the Marquesas Keys near an area called the Quicksands.

Famous as the final resting place of the *Atocha*, the shallow area's shifting sands were a cemetery holding dozens of lost wrecks. But he wondered why Travis had stopped. Shallow areas like this were better explored during flat-calm conditions, not in six-foot seas that could expose the bottom.

"They're moving again," the helmsman said.

"Follow them until we're sure of the heading. Then we can circle back and see why they stopped." Bugarra moved the cursor over the area where Travis's boat had slowed and set a waypoint there. His impatience was growing with each wave they slammed into. The men he had chosen for the mission were two of his best. After blowing the assault on the island, they would want retribution. Bugarra did some quick math and realized that with the speed difference between the boats and no backup available, this was as good a time as any to take what he wanted from Travis.

MAC WAS TUNED in to the vibrations of the boat. It didn't take a name to make a bond between boat and man, and he'd had one with *Ghost Runner* long before last night. Every noise meant something, and running through these conditions, missing something could be fatal. Condition Zulu meant that not even the Coast Guard was going to rescue an errant boater today.

"Mac!"

The sound of his name penetrated the tunnel vision he had

extended toward the crew. On the small boat, the only way to get space was in his head. He turned to Ned when he heard his name called again.

"This is one of the spots in Gross's research. Stayed up all damned night sifting through it."

Mac instinctively cut back on the power, then realized that searching now would be futile. "Seas are up, and with low tide, low pressure, and a storm surge, I can't trust any of this," Mac said, waving his hand at the electronics. Newton's discovery that every action had a reaction was true with storm surges. The wall of water pushed ashore when a hurricane made landfall had to come from somewhere. What he was seeing here was just that. He also knew the low water here might be adding to the surge slamming against his house right now. That explained the turbulent seas as the receding water acted like low tide against the wind.

"Just saying," Ned said.

Mac had to admit that he was intrigued. "We don't have a lot of equipment, but we can take a look on the way back."

Because of the shallows and shoals, a direct route to Fort Jefferson was impossible, and Mac entered a route in the chart-plotter around them. He listened to the sound of the engine, and his knees absorbed the steady pounding of the waves under the boat as it started to accelerate. He heard it in the sound of the engine and felt the seas, but he couldn't regain the flow state he had been in earlier.

As they travelled away from Ruth, the wind and waves subsided. It was still what the old-timers called *nautical*, but the worst was behind them, and Mac was satisfied with how the trawler cut through the four-foot waves. Earlier he had to drive each wave, increasing and backing off power to adjust to the larger ones. Now, Mac started to relax, and re-engaged the autopilot. He stared out at the water ahead of them and felt his eyes grow heavy. Fighting to stay focused, he jerked upright in the chair just as something passed by his head and ricocheted off the steel frame of the wheelhouse.

This wasn't the first time he'd been shot at. "Get down and hold on," he called out as he pressed down on the throttle and cut the wheel hard to starboard. The boat didn't respond, and he had a moment of panic until he realized that the autopilot was still engaged. Hitting the standby button returned control of the vessel to him, and he made the ninety-degree turn. With Ned's interruption, Mac had forgotten about the reflection he had seen before.

Looking back, he could see the shape of the boat running toward them. He immediately realized that there was no chance of outrunning them. If they were to escape, it would be through evasion. Turning the boat back to port, he steered toward the shallow water.

Trufante emerged from the cabin with a four-beer look on his face. For many people, this might impair them, but the Cajun looked ready.

"Shotgun and power head are in the rack." Mac tried to think of anything else that might be effective, but came up short. He wasn't even sure if there was any ammo left for the shotgun.

"What's going on, Mac?" Pamela asked.

"You and Ned go down into the cabin and stay low."

"Just because—"

Mac was not about to have this discussion. Another bullet struck by his head. "Now." He continued to steer toward the shallow water while Ned and Pamela crept into the cabin. Trufante was back with the shotgun and a half-box of shells. He started to slide them in, and Mac heard the reassuring click as Trufante chambered one. It might sound good, but Mac knew it would be of little use at this range. Glancing back, he saw the boat veering down on them.

"Don't waste 'em, but throw a little lead their way." Working on instinct now, he grabbed the microphone for the VHF radio and put out a mayday call. As soon as he issued it, he realized that, with all the agencies shut down by Ruth, it was futile, and was about to set the microphone back in the holder when he heard a response.

The chase had drawn them within Fort Jefferson's range, and Mac quickly explained their position and circumstance. Help was promised, and Mac dared a look back. Figuring he had about five minutes before the boat caught up, glanced down at the chartplotter, looking for refuge. With help coming from Fort Jefferson, he could halve their response time by heading directly toward it, but that wouldn't be enough. He needed to buy another ten or fifteen minutes.

Rebecca Shoal was coming up to port. It was the last obstacle between their current position and help. Somehow, he would have to make it work. Steering toward the tower on the horizon, he tried to make a plan.

TWENTY

Mac had been able to run a comfortable line with the bow slightly tilted away from the beam sea. Now, trying to reach the shoal before the boat behind them did, he had no choice but to turn to port and face the waves head-on. Slamming into the face of the storm-driven waves, he fumbled with the touchscreen plotter, finally getting close enough to see that the shoal was six miles off. The soundings he already knew in these conditions were meaningless, and he stood on his tiptoes, struggling to see the water color ahead.

Behind him the boat was still closing, and he pushed the throttle to its limit. He could see the boat clearly and hoped his heavy steel-hulled workboat might have an advantage over the lighter fiberglass of the other boat. His insistence on adding extra horsepower paid off as the big diesel pushed the boat through the waves.

Bearing the full brunt of the waves, the trawler cut through the crests, which threw up huge sheets of spray that covered the cockpit. With his passengers all forward, Mac gritted his teeth and plowed ahead. Risking a glance behind him, he saw that his tactic, though uncomfortable, had worked. The other boat was still behind them, but didn't seem to be gaining ground. As the waves tossed the lighter boat around with each strike, its course turned into a zigzag of corrections, increasing the distance they were covering.

There was also something to be learned by watching how the captain handled the boat. A patient man would have cut his speed and worked with the seas rather than against them. Whoever was after them was impatient, and that could be used against him as well.

Mac stared at the sixty-six-foot tower growing on the horizon. He started to calculate speed and distance both for the *Ghost Runner* and for whoever was coming to their aid out of Fort Jefferson. It would be close if the boat in pursuit was unable to gain an advantage. Gripping the wheel tightly as it fought for an easier course, he continued to plow toward the light.

He'd been to the Dry Tortugas several times, mostly to fish the pristine reefs lying within site of the brick fort. It was still U.S. soil, so he had not been required to check in with the authorities there, and struggled to remember who had jurisdiction. He did recall several soft-sided RIB boats with twin outboards. The boats would be perfect in these conditions. He only hoped they were fast enough to reach him in time.

A plan was brewing in his head, and he looked over at Trufante. Using his long legs like shock absorbers, he stood next to Mac, lightly gripping the seat for support with one hand and gripping the shotgun with the other. His thousand-dollar grin was full on, and he looked like he was enjoying the ride. The only discomfort Mac could see was that he needed the one hand to secure himself, meaning that he couldn't hold the ever-present bottle of beer.

"Get the power washer ready," Mac yelled over the engine noise.

Trufante gave him a questioning look, but released his hold on the seat and, grabbing for anything that would steady him, made his way to the stern. He wobbled back and forth with each wave, finally reaching the hose. It had been a useful addition to the boat. The strong stream of water was useful for cleaning traps and jetting out sunken objects, but Mac had no illusions it could stop bullets. What he was hoping for was that it was enough to throw the captain off balance, forcing him into a mistake.

They were within a mile of the shoal now, and Mac scanned the opposite side of the tower for any sign that their help was approaching. The horizon was empty except for the tower and the lines of white-capped waves moving toward them. That didn't mean that the boat wasn't close. If he was right and they were coming in one of the soft-sided craft, the waves would easily disguise it until the last minute.

Gradually, so that the other boat might not notice, he started to slow. As they approached the shoal, he zoomed in on the chart showing on his left-hand screen. The soundings were decreasing, and just ahead he could see waves breaking over rocks where there should be three feet of water. The storm surge was wreaking havoc on the soundings, but now he knew by how much. Either unaware or not caring that he had slowed, the other boat was within a hundred yards of them when several rounds struck the trawler.

Trufante looked back at Mac, but he knew it was too soon to show his hand. Sliding his body against the wheelhouse, he used the structure as a shield and continued on. When they were twenty yards away from the rocks, he dropped speed to just above an idle and spun the wheel hard to port.

"Ready!" he yelled back to Trufante.

The other boat was late in reacting and flew past them. More shots were fired, this time going wide. Mac had seen the impatience of the helmsman earlier, and he was counting on it now.

Continuing his course, he circled the light, waiting for the other captain to commit. "Here he comes."

It was up to Trufante now. His Cadillac grille shone brightly as he rose and aimed the wand at the oncoming boat. Mac flipped the switch to activate the pump and reached for the shotgun that Trufante had stashed by his side. Firing several rounds in the direction of the boat to distract them, he counted the seconds in his head and waited until the boat was within range of the power washer. With the seas moving each vessel independently, it was a long shot that any of the buckshot would hit the boat, but the distraction seemed to work. A second too late, the driver saw the rocks, and, just as the boat slowed, Mac called to Trufante.

The stream of water slashed across the bow of the Yellowfin. Before Trufante could adjust the aim of the water, Mac sent several more rounds toward the boat. He ducked and watched as the Cajun stood tall and raised the stream until it hit the driver squarely in the face.

Instantly, the boat spun out of control as the driver was blinded and thrown off-balance. Mac turned back to the wheel and increased power. He continued his circle, moving the trawler to the opposite side of the tower to use its steel frame as cover in case the other boat was able to recover.

Mac heard Trufante let out what sounded like a Cajun war cry from the cockpit and turned to see the other boat had capsized, floating perilously close to the rocks. He saw three men in the water swimming for the tower.

KURT, Justine, and Allie stood on the beach looking out past the float plane that had just delivered them. Far to the north, they could see the faintest sign of the squalls marking the outer band of Ruth. It was an odd feeling, standing on a white-sand beach surrounded by gin-clear water when their homes were inside the black mass.

A man in a park service uniform came toward them. "You must be Hunter?"

"Right. I'm Kurt. This is my wife, Justine, and daughter Allie."

"I'm Richard Farnsworth, the park director. Grab your stuff. I'll show you to your rooms."

They followed Farnsworth around the beach, where they reached a walkway that crossed what looked like a moat. The water was clear enough that Kurt was able to see schools of small snapper cruising around the shallow water.

"It's really six feet deep," Farnsworth said.

"Looks like a lot less than that," Allie said. "Is it a real moat?"

"It was built to hinder a land invasion, yes."

They entered the main gates of the fort and found themselves looking out on a large, grassy area.

"Our housing is in that newer building on the other side. Come on; I'll give you a quick tour on the way."

The fort was unlike anything Kurt had ever seen. He recalled from the narration on the flight that it covered sixteen acres, most of the island. Farnsworth rattled off dates and statistics as Kurt studied the architecture.

"That building was used to heat the cannon balls before they were shot." Farnsworth indicated a freestanding structure with an odd-shaped roof.

"Why?" Allie asked.

"Fire is a deadly threat to every ship at sea. By heating the shot, they were able to both damage and set fire to approaching ships."

"Were there any battles here?"

"No, the fort was actually never finished. Rifled cannon made it obsolete, and it was turned into a prison."

Kurt saw a woman running toward them.

"Special agent, we need you ASAP."

Kurt looked around for a second before realizing the woman was talking to him. There seemed to be urgency in her voice, and he handed his bag to Justine. "I'll catch up to you guys in a bit."

"Cool. Can we see Dr. Mudd's cell?" Allie asked Farnsworth.

Kurt remembered from Gary's briefing that the doctor who had set John Wilkes Booth's broken leg after he shot Lincoln was the most famous prisoner housed here. The description faded as he was hustled back out the entrance and to a dock on the right of the ferry pier. A man waited there.

"We've got a distress call out by Rebecca Shoal," the man said, tossing Kurt a horseshoe-shaped inflatable PFD. "You're the special agent in charge. Sounded like there might be some foul play."

"What about the Coast Guard?" Kurt asked as he slid the collar over his head and attached the straps around his chest.

"They bugged out because of Ruth."

"Is it safe?" Kurt adjusted the straps on the PFD.

"Totally. Seas are running four to six feet." The man hopped onto a twenty-odd-foot soft-sided RHIB boat.

Kurt followed and moved to the helm while the man started the engines. Seconds later, they sped off across the clear water. It took a few minutes for Kurt to get acclimated to the boat. The twin two-fifties each putting out over forty-four hundred RPM were pushing the boat over forty knots. The soft sides of the boat absorbed the brunt of the waves, but with their speed, the larger waves launched the lightweight boat into the air. Kurt held one of the grab-rails as the craft slammed back against the water. Still, it was exhilarating. In these conditions, his center console would be lucky to push ten knots.

"The shoal is about twenty miles out." The man pointed to a mark on the chartplotter.

Kurt estimated that was less than a half-hour. "How long ago did you receive the distress call?"

"Logged it at eleven twenty."

Kurt looked at his watch. That was ten minutes ago. Add the half-hour trip, and he wondered if they would reach them in time. "Any idea what we're dealing with?"

"Just a mayday. They were probably at the limit of the VHF range. Couldn't get much info."

He felt the engine noise rise a notch and looked down at the gauges. They were moving at fifty knots now. With nothing to do but hold on and hope that they got there in time, Kurt alternated staring into the clear water and watching their progress on the screen. Ten minutes later, the tower marking Rebecca Shoal came into view, and he felt his hand instinctively move to his waist. Having no idea what they were facing, he wanted to check his weapon, but it was packed in his bag back at the fort.

"Are we armed?" he asked the man, who also wore no sidearm.

"Got a rifle in the hold there," the man said, nodding in the direction of the console door.

Releasing his grip, Kurt reached around and unlatched it. The door swung open, and he eased around to the opening. He found the barrel of the rifle and, sliding his hand down, released it from its restraint. Moving back behind the protection of the enclosure, he checked the magazine.

"Haven't ever had to use it," the man said.

"I'm from Biscayne. With Miami close, we get some interesting action."

Both men were silent, observing the scene in front of them. Two boats were in view now, and both looked in danger of grounding. The sound of gunshots echoed across the water, and Kurt gripped the stock of the rifle. They were too far away to see what was happening aboard the vessels, but he could see how they were moving. Suddenly, what looked like a stream of water shot from the lead boat. The other boat foundered, its captain probably blinded by the water. It moved toward the shoal and, in what looked like slow motion, capsized.

TWENTY-ONE

MAC SAW HELP SPEEDING TO THEIR AID JUST AS THE BOAT that had been chasing them capsized. He idled until he was downwind of the shoal and let the trawler drift. Picking up the binoculars, he scanned the water, looking for survivors. After they had clearly tried to kill him, he was more interested in their identities than saving them. Trufante stood next to him, shielding his eyes from the sun.

"Bugarra," he said softly.

Mac moved the binoculars in the direction Trufante was looking and confirmed the sighting. The other two men in the water with Bugarra looked familiar, but he couldn't place them. "What about the others?"

"I think those dudes were the ones on the island."

Mac's blood started to boil, and he breathed deeply, trying to control his emotions. He knew in his current state he was not rational. Pamela and Ned emerged from the cabin.

"I heard Bugarra's name," Ned said.

Mac offered him the binoculars and pointed at the larger man in the water.

"Once I saw what was on that flash drive, I figured it

wouldn't take long for him to surface. He always thought it was easier to steal things than earn them."

Ned had known the treasure hunter since the old days when Wood was still around and Bugarra was a struggling diver. One lucky find, piggybacking on someone else's work, had elevated Bugarra to superstar status. It hadn't even been from a wreck, but just the coins he'd pulled from the sands near Sebastian Inlet that were both very rare and easily documented. Secrecy was a highly coveted commodity in the world of treasure hunting. Unless you dotted every *i* and crossed every *t*, there was always a chance that a discovery could be discredited. Bugarra played the game by a different set of rules. A media hog, he often claimed success before he had it, in an attempt to attract more dollars for his company.

"Bad business when he's around," Ned said, handing the binoculars back to Mac.

The rescue boat was close enough now that Mac could see the National Park Service logo stenciled on its side. It was less than a quarter mile away and had dropped off plane. Raising the binoculars, he recognized one of the men aboard.

"We have to save them," Pamela said, distracting him.

"Park service'll take care of it now."

"We ought to skedaddle before they start asking questions," Trufante said.

Mac knew that since he had spotted Kurt, there was a good possibility that Kurt had recognized him or his boat. "We'll stick around and see if they need help."

Trufante suddenly disappeared into the cabin. Mac wondered for a second what he was hiding, but was distracted by Kurt's voice on the hailer. Mac decided to respond face to face. Bugarra would hear anything said over the loudspeaker, and the VHF was an open channel for anyone listening. Seeking discretion, he waved at the boat and idled toward it.

"Kurt," Mac called out, then called for Trufante to set the fenders. There was no sign of the Cajun, not unusual when there was law enforcement around.

"We got it," Kurt called back, and flipped several large red balls over the gunwales.

Mac maneuvered the *Ghost Runner* next to the park service boat and grabbed a line. The seas were still too rough to sit side by side without the fenders. "You guys take care of those men, and we can pull the boat out of here."

The man at the wheel nodded. Mac tossed the line back to Kurt. Before they were out of earshot, he called to him, "We're heading to Fort Jefferson—we can catch up there if you need a statement."

Without waiting for an answer, Mac idled away. He was all business now, and called to Trufante that the coast was clear of whatever it was that he was avoiding. The coward peered out of the cabin and came back on deck. He and Mac focused on the capsized boat. Trufante's grin was back when he realized what Mac had in mind. They both knew they were looking at a six-figure boat. As a salvor, Mac would benefit from the recovery of the vessel, and Trufante knew he'd get his share. Taking the boat out from under Bugarra would just be icing on the cake.

The Yellowfin was drifting away from the shoal, and they were a good hundred yards away from the men in the water. The park service boat was moving toward them. "Let's get a line on her," Mac said, turning his attention away from the rescue to the drifting boat.

"What'cha got in mind?" Trufante asked.

"Let's just get ahold of her for now. Once the park service picks up Bugarra and his men, we're gonna flip it."

"Parbuckle would be the correct term," Ned said.

"Right." Mac idled toward the boat. Trufante reached into

the portside hold and removed a coiled line. "Gonna need three before we're done."

Trufante pulled out two more lines and laid them on the deck. "Bow or stern?" he asked, as he stripped off his shirt.

"Bow first. We'll get the stern once they're out of sight." Mac was upwind of the disabled boat now and set his engines into neutral. The trawler slowly drifted back to the capsized vessel. Trufante was on the dive platform with the end of a line in his hand. Ned had the coil ready to pay out line as he needed it. When the boats were fifty feet apart, Trufante jumped into the water and, dragging the line behind him, swam toward the bow of the capsized boat. Treading water, he took several deep breaths and dropped below the surface. Mac started to idle forward, and a second later, he saw the thumbs-up signal.

Slowly, Mac idled into deeper water until the slack was out of the line and waited while Trufante used the rope to pull himself back to the trawler. After hauling himself onto the dive platform, he sat with his feet in the water, catching his breath.

With the boat in their possession, all eyes turned to the park service boat just in time to see Bugarra being helped aboard. He shrugged off the helping hands and turned to face the *Ghost Runner*. They'd drifted several hundred yards apart, but even from that distance, Mac could see the hate in the man's eyes. A few minutes later, the other two men were aboard and the park service boat accelerated. Mac acknowledged Kurt's wave, and they watched the boat come up on plane and head toward Fort Jefferson.

"Okay, let's get 'er done. Pamela, you better stay clear. One of those lines snaps, it could take out an eye."

"Not on your life, Mac Travis," Pamela replied. "I want to watch."

Mac shrugged. He wasn't running tours here, and if she wanted to be on deck, so be it. "At least go forward so we can keep the cockpit clear," he said, waiting for her to climb around the cabin and situate herself on the foredeck.

"Ready?" Mac called to Trufante. "Use the portside cleat."

Ned brought in the slack line as they backed down on the boat. Line management was critical in this maneuver, and Mac was glad the old man was here.

"Go," he yelled to Trufante. With the line in hand, Trufante repeated the procedure. A few minutes later, he was back aboard, and Mac started to move *Ghost Runner* away from the capsized boat while Ned payed out the line. When both lines were taut, he repeated the same procedure with the third line, this time to the cleat at midship. "Hold on!" he called out, and accelerated.

The deck vibrated as the engine fought with the load behind the boat. Mac continued to apply pressure, looking behind him as he pressed down on the throttles. It wasn't a complicated procedure, but the seas were making it difficult, and he had to slow several times to adjust the lines to allow the boat dragging behind to sit on top of a wave instead of in the trough. When he felt it was right, he applied power and, with one eye on the tachometer and the other on the boat behind them, pushed the engine into the red.

Suddenly, he felt the speed increase and the RPMs drop. He'd found the sweet spot, and behind him, the rotational pressure on the hull flipped the boat over. Once it started to turn, he immediately called for Trufante to release the stern and midship lines before it rolled again.

Trufante let out a loud hoot when the boat, now righted, turned bow forward and accepted the tow. Mac slowed and, wary of entangling a line in the propeller, dropped to neutral. "Ned, bring the free lines in. Tru, haul the boat closer." It was a long tow to Fort Jefferson, and rather than dragging a thousand gallons of water behind him, he wanted to make sure the bilge pumps were working.

With the vessels alongside each other, Mac and Trufante climbed onto Bugarra's boat. There was no apparent damage other than some chipped fiberglass where one of Mac's rounds must have hit. The Yellowfin was well built, and despite having been upside down and exposed to the water, the downward pressure on the hatches had kept water from entering the battery compartment. Water spewed from either side as the bilge pumps did their work, and when they sputtered, Mac shut off the battery switch. He had already decided to tow the boat back to the fort. It was fifty-fifty whether the Yellowfin would start, and having it come into port under her own power might taint his salvage rights. He and Trufante climbed back aboard *Ghost Runner*, and Mac breathed deeply. The run to Fort Jefferson had accomplished several things in addition to the payday being towed behind him. Bugarra had been exposed, and there was a good chance he would face charges for shooting at them. Kurt Hunter appearing at the scene had been an unexpected bonus. Mac had spent several days in Miami in the last few weeks helping him with Gross's murder. Now, he hoped the special agent could repay the favor.

Ned and Trufante had made a bridle from the lines, and Bugarra's boat, now with two cleats sharing the load easily, followed the trawler. Mac thought about the logistics of towing it the twenty miles to Fort Jefferson, then covering the same ground again to get it to Marathon. He pulled the phone from his pocket and opened the radar app, but it wouldn't load. There was no signal, so he put the phone back in his pocket. Even with new technology, he still depended on the accumulated knowledge and experience of his twenty-five years on the water, and studied the waves and sky.

There was nothing alarming above, with only puffy

cumulus clouds scattered through the sky. The seas were more difficult to read. It was easy to see the wind waves coming from the north, but there was a distinct groundswell caused by the storm coming from the east. Towing the boat fifty miles to Key West in these conditions was not a good idea.

Decision made, he set course for Fort Jefferson and sat back in the captain's chair. The seas were easy on the boat and passengers, and the mood was light. To help things along, Trufante had handed beers to everyone. Mac took the one offered him and, after checking the tow, finally relaxed. With his feet on the wheel, using them to make subtle adjustments, he sipped the beer and steered toward Fort Jefferson.

As they approached the fort, Trufante was the only one who appeared anxious, and Mac remembered how he had disappeared when the park service boat showed up. Under other circumstances, Mac would have dismissed it as Trufante's instinctive reaction to law enforcement, but Trufante knew Kurt, and had stayed down after they had recognized him. That led Mac to think it was Bugarra that Trufante was worried about, and the knowledge put Mac on edge.

TWENTY-TWO

As they approached Fort Jefferson, the seas calmed. Glancing over his shoulder every few seconds to check on the tow, Mac did what every salvor does after making a recovery—calculate the worth.

Trufante had probably done the math, which should have lifted his mood, but something was troubling the Cajun. He sat alone on the port seat with a beer in his hand. It was the same position Mac could have found him in almost any other day they were out, but that thousand-dollar Cadillac grin was missing. Whether Mac liked it or not, his fortune was often tied to Trufante's, and that made him a concern.

Mac placed the boat on autopilot and asked Ned to take the wheel. The old man nodded and moved to the captain's seat, where he scanned the seas ahead as the hydraulic motor tied into the autopilot steered the course Mac had laid out.

"Old Wood'd be rolling in his grave if he saw all this mess. You got cable too?" Ned asked.

Mac ignored him. Like Wood, he had grudgingly accepted the early technology, loran and paper depth plotters were often hard to use and inaccurate, but now he was sure his mentor would approve.

Mac left Ned and turned to Trufante. "Need another one?" Tru shook his head as Mac moved toward the bench. The trawler was all function with minimal form. Except for the cabin, which was well appointed, the decks were bare of cushions or seats. The bench running along the port gunwale was used to move crab and lobster pots from the winch near midship to the slide on the stern. Across the cockpit, the other bench had a rack behind it to hold dive tanks and offered room to gear up. Both men were acting out of character. Mac rarely offered Trufante alcohol, and Trufante more rarely refused.

"That boat was a nice surprise. Should be a good paycheck." Mac was about to sit, but felt uncomfortable enough standing. Heart-to-heart talks were not in his wheelhouse.

Trufante nodded.

"You know that Pamela came to me because she was worried about you," Mac said, so only Trufante could hear. The Cajun sat motionless. Mac looked at his beer and saw there was barely a quarter left. Ignoring Trufante's refusal, he went to the cabin and grabbed two bottles. If Trufante didn't want one, Mac would drink them both. That didn't turn out to be necessary, as the Cajun reached for the bottle and nodded his thanks.

"And y'all sat up all night naming boats," he finally said.

Mac sensed the jealousy in his voice. "It was you she was looking for."

"Well, you found me."

Mac retreated a step as if he'd been hit. In all their years together, he'd never seen Trufante act this way. There had been other women before, but none had the effect that Pamela did on him—not even close.

"Suit yourself," Mac finally said, and moved back to the helm. He looked forward and saw the red-brick fortress rising from the water, thinking, for the first time in his life, that land might be preferable to a boat.

He and Trufante had been here before, anchoring in the protected waters at night on fishing trips, so Mac watched Ned and Pamela as they stared at the fort. The sixteen million bricks shipped from Pensacola formed an impressive structure, until they got closer and could see what the ravages of time and a salt-water environment had done to it. The fort had never been completed, and the harsh climate, along with bad engineering, had taken its toll, causing huge chunks of the structure to deteriorate and fall into the sea.

Mac evaluated the key, not from a tourist's point of view, but as a captain and salvor. Far enough away from the storm and with Bugarra in custody, he was concerned for his prize. "We're gonna anchor out." Even with Kurt involved, he was still worried about how Bugarra would spin the story. Shots had been fired from both vessels, and there was a lack of reliable witnesses. Bugarra, after years of bribing state officials, had influence, and Mac guessed that as soon as Bugarra could get to a phone, one of his teams of attorneys would be enlisted.

"*Ghost Runner* to park service headquarters Fort Jefferson," Mac said into the VHF microphone. The name still sounded foreign, but good. His first choice had been to call Kurt directly, but there was no cell service here.

"Copy, *Ghost Runner*. Switch to channel nineteen."

Mac entered the channel into the radio's keypad and called again. He asked to speak to Agent Hunter and was asked to stand by. While he waited, he idled into the harbor on the north side of the fort, dropped anchor, and, with Ned's help, pulled Bugarra's boat alongside, where they dropped fenders to separate the hulls, and tied it off.

"You want to see what you can do with the engines?" he asked Trufante. It was more an order than a question. Trufante lifted his head, drained his beer, and slid over the gunwale, dropping easily to the deck of the other boat. Once aboard, he worked slowly but methodically. As much trouble as he could be to have around, the Cajun could easily take apart an engine and put it back together. As Mac watched, he saw Trufante's attitude change as he started checking the batteries and electrical connections. If the boat could be started, Trufante would be able to do it.

Mac turned back to the VHF when he heard his boat called. Kurt Hunter's voice came over the speaker.

"I'll need you to come ashore and give a statement," Kurt said.

Mac recognized the businesslike tone and figured that Kurt wasn't alone. He requested a tender be brought out to pick him up and went to talk to the others. With Trufante occupied, Mac needed to talk Pamela and Ned into staying aboard. There was no telling what either would say. Ned would be helpful in recounting the story, but Pamela was a wild card. Someone needed to keep an eye on her, and she seemed to be intently listening to Ned's history of the fort.

Several minutes later, Kurt waved from a small, soft-sided boat and sped toward them. After promising Pamela she could see the fort before they left, Mac waited for Kurt to come alongside, timed the wake, and hopped down to the waiting boat.

"Appreciate you helping me out here," Mac said, as Kurt spun the boat, facing the bow to the small beach, where a seaplane was secured. Kurt accelerated, passing the empty ferry, turning to the docks, and coming alongside several other Park Service boats.

"Bugarra is a piece of work. He's spinning this to make it look like you sunk his boat."

"I did, but it was to avoid being killed."

"Let's leave that first part out," Kurt said, leading the way to the fort's entrance. Once inside, he turned to the left and entered a small door marked "Park Service Only."

Mac ducked to enter the door and stood hunched over in the humid office. The low-ceilinged room's veneer was failing, exposing the brick beneath it. A small air conditioner struggled to cool the space, trying to extract the moisture from the porous brick walls. It was treading water at best.

"Have a seat," Kurt said.

Mac again noticed the businesslike tone and waited while a man who appeared to be Kurt's boss walked in, sat behind a desk, and pulled out a notepad.

"I'm Richard Farnsworth, the park director. Hunter here says he knows you. That would recuse him from the investigation, but I'll allow him to stay as a witness."

Between the legal tone and with Kurt sidelined, Mac's advantage had disappeared. He started to wonder if Bugarra had gotten to the director.

"I already have Mr. Bugarra's statement. Let's start when you left Key West." Farnsworth held up his phone and pressed several buttons before setting it on the table. "I'll be recording this as well. Do I have your consent?"

Mac nodded.

"You can start whenever you're ready," Farnsworth said.

Mac started to recount their morning, being sure to emphasize that he had a boatload of misfits anchored here that he had saved from the storm. "That was my only purpose in being on the water today." The last thing he wanted was to sound like they were out for a joyride.

"You understand that the Coast Guard declared Condition Zulu and closed the port last night?"

"I was only trying to save my boat and friends. I had no intention of needing a rescue until I saw the other boat following us."

"Why don't you describe what happened, then," Farnsworth said, inching closer to the table.

"Just past the Marquesas, the sun came out and I saw a reflection on glass behind me. I found it strange that two boats would be out on a day like this and following the same course."

"And what did you do?"

"Nothing, until he shot at us," Mac said. There was damage on both vessels from the rounds they had exchanged. He had to establish that Bugarra shot first and Mac was only defending himself, his passengers, and his boat. "This falls under the Castle Law," Mac stated. The Florida law allowing home-owners to protect their home if their life was endangered had been extended to boats in 2011. It turned out that living with a lawyer and having Trufante as your mate provided a substantial legal education.

"He went as far as to accuse you of piracy. The men with him corroborated his story."

"That's absurd. He shot first." Mac was scrambling now. What he'd thought was going to be a slam dunk to get Bugarra off his back was now looking like it could land him in jail—ironic, since he was inside Fort Jefferson, which was used as a prison for several decades after the Civil War.

"We'll need to talk to your crew. What are your immediate plans?"

This was going downhill. They might be able to get a coherent story from Ned, but there was no telling what Pamela and Trufante would say, and then there was the question of what the Cajun was hiding. "We planned on waiting out Ruth here."

"We have no detention facilities, but we will ask you to remain on site until the Coast Guard is back in Key West and can take over the case."

Mac had never had a good experience when the Coast

Guard was involved. He was about to ask about the salvaged boat when Farnsworth answered that for him as well. "The boat reverts to Mr. Bugarra until the dispute is settled."

Trufante was working on the engines, and, barring something unforeseen, Mac was confident he would have the boat running shortly. The electronics might be shot, but the cowlings would have protected the engines from the short exposure to the saltwater. Mac needed to get back to the boat and stop him.

"Doesn't seem to be any cell service out here. I'd like to call my lawyer."

"You can use the phone here," Farnsworth said. "Service has been erratic with Ruth, but you're welcome to try."

"This would be a confidential call," Mac said, wanting the agent out of the room. Alone a minute later, he dialed Mel's number, only to have a tone blast in his ear and a recorded voice tell him that all circuits were busy. He rose and left the room. Kurt and Farnsworth were waiting outside. "No service," Mac said.

"I'd like to get those interviews done today," the director said.

Mac needed to delay this until he could reach Mel. He wasn't sure the park service had jurisdiction here, and Farnsworth had as much as confirmed that they would hand the case over to the Coast Guard. "I'd like to check my boat for damage. Some of those shots were close to the waterline," Mac said.

"Agent Hunter can run you back out," Farnsworth said, and turned to Kurt. "Take their statements and collect any evidence you can while you're out there. Mr. Bugarra's boat, too."

Mac had just lost whatever leverage he had. Somehow he had to hope that the truth would prevail. That hope would be backed by whatever he could do to sabotage Bugarra's boat.

TWENTY-THREE

MAC WAS QUIET ON THE WAY BACK TO THE ANCHORED
boats. Bugarra had reacted quickly and reached deep into his
pool of resources. What an hour ago had looked like a profitable
day with the added bonus of Bugarra going to jail was now
turned on its head.

"I've seen Bugarra in action before," Kurt said. "If there's
anything I can do to help ..."

"A satellite phone would be good for starters," Mac said.
"Looks like Ruth took out the lines to the mainland."

Reaching the *Ghost Runner*, Kurt turned into the side of the
trawler and cut the engine. The soft-sided boat slid against the
steel hull.

Trufante reached down and tossed a line to Mac, who
secured the bow. Kurt was already at the stern. With the Park
Service boat secure, they boarded the trawler, where Mac
explained to Ned and Pamela how Bugarra had outmaneuvered
them.

"Maybe Mel can help," Ned said.

"Already tried," Mac said. "There's no cell service out here,
and Ruth must have taken the landlines down." They all

instinctively looked to the northeast. Like windblown smoke against the blue sky, the faintest tendrils of the farthest bands of the outer ring of the storm were barely visible.

"We've got a radio tower back at the station," Kurt said. "This is the first time I've been here, but it looks like a cell tower. There's gotta be some way to reach her through that if she's not in the path of the storm."

"She was headed to New Orleans to do some research," Mac said.

All eyes moved from the horizon to him. Ned gave Mac a quizzical look that only old men can give. Everyone knew they were on a treasure hunt and he was withholding information, but Mac chose to ignore them and moved on. "Kurt's going to collect some evidence and interview you guys before towing Bugarra's boat back to the dock."

Mac winked at Trufante, hoping he understood, and waited for Kurt to return to the park service boat for his evidence kit before yanking Trufante inside the cabin.

"What's up?" Trufante asked.

Mac saw the look in his eyes and realized Trufante had misunderstood. Tru's first reaction was generally wanting to know what he had done wrong. He had joked about it, often apologizing before asking what he'd done.

"Did you get the boat running?" Mac asked.

"Easy. The water hadn't breached the cowlings. Had to prime the engines, but they started right up."

"Well, go un-start them." Mac waited until he saw that Trufante understood. "And do it so they'll need parts or something. Don't just start yanking wires."

"Got it." Trufante turned to leave.

"It's got to look like a result of the capsize."

"I got this."

"Perfect." Mac wondered if that was the first time he had

ever said that to Trufante. Usually his responsibility for the Cajun was to keep him on the right side of the law and out of jail. This time was different. With Bugarra already manipulating the perception of what had happened, it was Mac's law that was going to be the right side.

The two men walked back into the cockpit, squinting against the sunlight.

"Just gonna go check her out," Trufante mumbled as he crossed the gunwales and hopped down to the Yellowfin.

Mac turned his attention away, knowing he would have to trust Trufante. "Maybe you want to take statements from the others?" Mac suggested to Kurt, who was watching Trufante as he removed the cowlings from the twin engines. Mac could only hope he'd play along, knowing that Kurt, like him, had his own sense of right and wrong.

"Good idea." Kurt took a picture of a dent in the wheelhouse.

Mac wondered if the ding was actually from Bugarra's weapon. This wasn't the first time he had come under fire. "Not much for evidence." Kurt pulled a notepad and pen from his pocket. "I'll get the statements and process the Yellowfin at the dock."

"Don't think we hit it with anything but the pressure washer," Mac said.

"Gotta be sure, or Justine'll have my head."

Ned stepped forward first and recounted the incident. He emphasized that it was Bugarra who was after them and had fired multiple shots before Mac returned fire. Once Ned was finished, Kurt turned his attention to Pamela. Ned nodded toward the cabin, and Mac followed him in.

"What's Mel looking for in New Orleans?" Ned asked.

Mac looked out on deck and saw Kurt talking to Pamela. She was not known for being succinct or truthful; Mac guessed she would supply a wealth of misinformation and probably keep Kurt busy until Trufante finished his work.

"She wanted out of Atlanta," Mac replied. "Looks like Ruth's going to blow up the peninsula and wreak some havoc in Georgia too. Thought with Lafitte being mentioned several times, if there was any place that would have anything useful, it would be New Orleans."

"She's looking for a needle in a haystack," Ned said.

"That's what she's best at." They both knew her reputation for working the hardest cases that many thought unwinnable. It had taken years, but she had finally set her ego aside and admitted she was tired of the ACLU's agenda of manipulating legislation by prosecuting handpicked cases. Once she was able to see the big picture instead of her tunnel vision of each case, she saw that the group really cared little for the downtrodden and those they claimed to help. Their agenda had become clear to her, and she left. But her skill-set remained finely tuned from dealing with Big Sugar. If there was something there, she would find it.

"I've been reading some of the documents on my phone while y'all have been busy," Ned said. "It may be that this does have something to do with Lafitte. But separating the rumors from the facts is going to be a task. There's some photocopies and pictures of journal entries, but on this thing"—he waved the phone in the air—"they're damned near unreadable. Be good if we could get a look at the originals. I still can't wrap my head around the connection between that scoundrel and Henriques."

"As soon as we can get a call through and I explain what happened, I'll let you have her ear."

"Good enough. I sense there is something big here. We've all been conditioned to the Spanish way of documenting everything. Looking at Gross's files under the lens of a pirate changes a lot."

Mac wanted to continue the conversation, but when he looked up, he saw that Kurt was finished with Pamela. Mac decided to ask Ned more about Henriques later. Just as Pamela finished, Trufante appeared over the gunwales and nodded at Mac.

Kurt must have seen it too. "Does it run?"

"I got it started," Trufante said.

Trufante was almost as good at evading the truth as Mel was at finding it. "You want to run it back to the dock, I'll see what I can do about getting you a phone line," Kurt said.

This time, Mac decided to take everyone to shore. There was no boat to guard, and he knew that with Pamela and Trufante on the island, if he needed a diversion, all he needed to do was add water. Pamela seemed genuinely interested in the fort's history, or maybe the ghosts of the lives lost there, and was talking to Ned about visiting Dr. Mudd's cell. Trufante decided to stay aboard and guard the beer. He shook his head and went into the cabin.

Once ashore, they split up, with Ned starting a guided tour for Pamela. Kurt and Mac left them at the moat and walked through the sally port—the main entrance to the fort, as Ned had informed them. Kurt bypassed the office where the meeting with Farnsworth had occurred and walked toward a building whose white siding and architecture looked more modern. Mac guessed these were the living quarters for the park service employees stationed here.

"Hang out for a second," Kurt said. "I've got to check in with Justine and Allie and have a look at the communications."

Drawn by the turquoise water he could see through the embrasure, Mac walked over to a run-down section of the old fort and looked out at the waters surrounding the key. It didn't take long for his imagination to be drawn back to the nineteenth century. He overheard Ned lecturing Pamela from the adjacent gun placement.

On first appraisal, Garden Key, where the fort was eventually built, had been deemed both insignificant and inadequate—add to that the lack of fresh water, and the Navy had decided to leave it a barren rock. Later on, because of its location that decision was reversed in the interest of protecting trade with the Gulf Coast. In the 1840s, the fort was started, but never used as intended, nor was it completed.

Mac heard Ned explain the complicated cisterns located below the fort used to collect fresh water. Sand-filled columns built into the structure were intended to act as filters for rainwater, but had failed, leaving the cisterns under the parade ground and two steam-powered desalinators as the only sources of freshwater.

"Are these windows lined up for the stars?" Pamela asked.

Mac heard Ned grumble, and the lesson ended.

The pair moved on, and Mac looked back toward the building. Kurt was coming toward him with Justine and a girl carrying snorkeling gear. Mac nodded at Justine, unsure what the social protocol was. She solved his quandary by hugging him tightly.

"Mac, my daughter, Allie. Allie, this is Mac," Kurt said.

"Hey," she said to Mac and turned back to her dad. "Can we go snorkeling now?"

"Sure. One of the rangers said that the old steel pilings were pretty cool," Kurt said. "I've got to help Mac out for a few minutes. You guys go have fun."

After Allie and Justine walked away, Kurt led Mac into the building. "Justine figured out there's a landline and also a cellular connection here. As long as Mel's not in the Keys or South Florida, you should be able to reach her." He opened a door, and they entered a small room that had a table holding what looked more like a ham-radio outfit rather than a surveillance setup run by the CIA he had expected. That wasn't his concern, though, and he thanked Kurt when he pointed toward a phone on a desk. "I used it a few minutes ago to check in with Allie's mom," Kurt said.

Mac picked up the receiver. It had been so long since he had held a landline-type phone in his hand that it felt odd. He punched in Mel's number from memory and waited for the call to connect.

Kurt had given him some space and was across the room filling out a form that looked like an incident report. With his back to the door, Mac couldn't see the hallway, but did see when a shadow cast across the doorway and cleared his throat, hoping that Kurt would hear.

Kurt looked up, and they made eye contact. Mac put two fingers to his eyes and pointed to the hallway. Kurt was halfway out the door when Mel answered. Mac paused for a second, not sure if he should reveal himself.

"Hello," he heard Mel's voice through the receiver.

In the hallway, a door slammed and he heard voices. One was Kurt's, but he couldn't make out the other.

"Hello?" she said again.

"Hey," he whispered into the phone.

"Are you okay?" Mel asked.

He listened for a second and heard more voices outside the room.

"Yeah, but I gotta go."

TWENTY-FOUR

THE MAN INTRODUCED TO BUGARRA AS SPECIAL AGENT Hunter seemed familiar, but he'd met a lot of people and shaken a lot of hands in the past few weeks, let alone the dozen interviews for the cable networks trying to capitalize on Gross's murder.

He'd carefully woven his current story of how Travis had pirated his boat and left him stranded. Farnsworth, the director, seemed to believe the story, and with a little encouragement was solidly in his corner. The other man, Agent Hunter, appeared skeptical, but it wasn't his call to make. The director had allowed Bugarra use of their satellite phone system to contact his attorneys. For the first time since he'd found out Travis had Gross's research, he had leverage on the man. Now, he sat in the small room in the park service living quarters where he'd been temporarily assigned, waiting for his chance to pry the location of Gross's last find from Travis—however he had to.

Looking out the window, Bugarra stared at the water through the openings in the fort. Aside from the phone call the director had let him make from their communications room, he was isolated from the world. It didn't really matter that there was no cell service on the island; the entire state of Florida was on lockdown. The state would stand still until tomorrow morning, making it the perfect time to make his move.

His eyes instinctively moved to the parade ground. On a normal day here, he suspected that, with the ferry and seaplanes running tourists in and out, there were probably over a hundred people on the island. Today it was vacant, except for the park service employees, his men, and Travis's group. This made the two women walking across the parade ground holding snorkeling gear and a beach bag seem out of place.

On closer inspection, one was older, maybe mid-thirties, and the other a teenager. He watched as they walked toward the fort's entrance, and leaned forward when he saw them stop by Travis and Hunter. He couldn't hear the conversation, but he could tell from their body language that they were more than friendly, especially Hunter and the women. A minute later, they separated. The women continued toward the entrance; Hunter and Travis walked toward the living quarters.

Wondering if this was his chance, Bugarra got up and left his room. Knocking on the closed door of the next room, he waited until one of his men answered, then instructed them to follow the women. Continuing down the hallway, Bugarra carefully stopped near a corner, and listened.

The sound of a door being opened caught his attention, and he tried to place himself in the building. From what he recalled, the hallway off to the right led to the communications room. If Hunter was taking Travis there, Bugarra would lose his advantage.

He waited several seconds until he was sure that was where the men had gone, then, with his back to the wall, he slid around the corner. At the partially opened door, he could hear the two men talking. It sounded like Travis was about to make a call.

That call, Bugarra suspected, would go to Melanie Woodson, something he could not afford.

He'd dealt with Wood, her father, over the years. There'd been some good deals in the beginning. Bugarra's company, Treasure Hunters, had just started to flourish, but the bills quickly mounted. Learning how expensive search and salvage could be when you only had centuries-old information, he'd burned through most of his reserves before unleashing his current business model. Back in the day, he thought the money was in actually finding the treasure, not in recruiting backers. When he made the switch, Wood couldn't stomach it, and they had fallen out several times. Like her father, Melanie Woodson had the reputation of being a crusader. She was just the type of person who could bring down his empire.

Travis knew Bugarra was on the island and would be naturally suspicious. He decided to use that to his advantage, and took several steps toward the door, making sure his footfalls were heard. Hunter was wearing a sidearm now, and Bugarra would have to be careful—step loud enough to make Travis suspicious, but quiet enough that neither man would do anything rash.

He didn't have enough time to see if his ploy worked. Travis said something barely audible, then he must have heard Bugarra, and disconnected the call. Taking another step past the door, Bugarra started walking faster toward a glass exit door at the end of the hallway. Though constructed to look like a residence, the building was a commercial structure, with exit signs and crash bars on the doors.

Just before pushing through the door, he paused to look back and saw Hunter coming toward him—alone. Spinning, as if he had forgotten something, Bugarra crashed into the special agent.

"I'm so sorry," he said, loud enough, he hoped, for Travis to hear his voice. He had to play his hand and let Travis know he was here.

"Something I can help you with?"

"Just taking a walk and forgot something. Your boss said that my boat would be returned this afternoon. Thought I'd go have a look."

Just before Hunter stepped aside, Bugarra saw Travis in the doorway. Turning away quickly to avoid eye contact, he started to push the crash bar to open the door. Travis would have seen him, and that was okay—what he couldn't afford was confrontation. The agent was clearly on Travis's side, and his own men were following the women. It suddenly dawned on Bugarra that the women were the key.

Moving quickly now, he exited the building. Hunter, obviously not sure if he had reason to follow, held back a few seconds. Looking back over his shoulder, Bugarra saw the two men talking. He picked up his pace to a fast walk in the direction of the fort's entrance.

MAC WATCHED as Bugarra walked quickly toward the sally port. There was something about his look that Mac didn't like, and when Kurt came up beside him, Mac guessed that he had seen it, too.

With just a look between them, Mac and Kurt followed, increasing their pace when they saw Bugarra walk up to one of the men who was looking at the water. They saw Bugarra point at something near the fort's crumbling walls: the tips of two yellow snorkels sticking out of the water, and start running toward the dock.

"That your girls out there?" Mac asked Kurt.

Before Kurt could answer, Bugarra and the man moved

toward the ferry and walked across the gangplank connecting it to the dock. A minute later, the two men emerged with snorkeling gear. At the side of the boat, they removed their shirts and put on the gear.

"We have to get out there," Kurt said.

The two men slid off the side of the ferry. Mac took off at a run, with Kurt right behind. He would have preferred his own gear, especially his long freediving fins, but his boat was too far away. They needed to be in the water now. Together they ran through the small picnic area and crossed the dunes to the beach.

The sun reflecting off the water temporarily blinded Mac as he searched for the pair of yellow snorkels. After scanning the fort's walls, where he had seen the women earlier, he moved his gaze to the open water, remembering that Kurt had recommended snorkeling near the steel pilings. Mac spotted Justine and Allie halfway between the fort and the old dock, swimming directly toward Bugarra and his man.

"Come on," Kurt said, pulling off his deck shoes and shirt.

Mac followed suit. Kurt headed straight for the water, a shorter distance, but Mac chose to run across the beach, realizing that crossing the sand was faster than swimming. When he reached the end of the beach, he stopped to locate the snorkels again. They were just past the point and turning toward the old steel piles. The only problem was that Bugarra was waiting aboard the Yellowfin.

Kurt was swimming toward his family, stroking quickly through the light chop. Mac gauged Kurt's speed and knew right away he'd never make it in time. It would be up to him to save the women. Looking around one more time to get his bearings just before he dove in, he saw Pamela and Ned coming toward him.

"Get the director," Mac called. "Bugarra's after Kurt's wife and daughter."

He didn't wait for a response; he dove in head first and pulled hard with his arms. He saw the snorkels at the first piling and knew he wasn't going to get there in time. Treading water for a second, he watched Bugarra in the Yellowfin idling toward the group. The two men in the water noticed it as well and made their move on Justine and Allie.

Before Kurt could reach them, the women were subdued and hauled aboard the boat. Kurt swam up beside him in time to see Justine putting up a good fight until one of the men slammed a fist into her chin. She crumpled onto the deck, and Mac felt Kurt's anger. He sensed Kurt was about to scream and start after the boat, and put a comforting hand on his shoulder to stop him. It wouldn't benefit anyone to have Bugarra see them in the water. They turned and swam back toward shore.

Mac followed. Though Mac was a stronger swimmer, Kurt, fueled by fury, reached the beach first.

"Wait. We need a plan," Mac called after him. Before he could see what Kurt was doing, he heard a familiar sound and turned to see his trawler heading directly toward them. "Over here," he yelled to Kurt, and jumped back in the water. He didn't wait to see if Kurt would follow—Mac knew he would.

The bow wake hit them, causing them to duck under the waves and time their ascent to not hit the hull. Trufante had slowed to an idle, but momentum was pushing the boat toward them. Signaling to Kurt to stay where he was, Mac surfaced and saw Trufante above the gunwale at the wheel. The trawler was circling them like they were trap buoys. Trufante was playing it right. Mac again motioned to Kurt to stay put and wait for Trufante to pick them up. The steel hull slid alongside him, and Mac heard the click of the transmission when Trufante dropped it into neutral. Safe from the deadly propeller, Mac stroked to the dive platform and climbed aboard, Kurt right behind him.

Trufante didn't wait until they were situated. He understood the urgency of the situation and spun the boat in the direction of the fading wake of the kidnappers' twin engines. Mac moved toward the helm and turned on the radar. They had little chance of catching the faster boat, but dialing in the boat's profile while it was still in sight made tracking easier once it disappeared over the horizon.

"Thanks, man," Mac said to Trufante, slicking his hair back and wiping the seawater from his face. "We got 'em. Just have to hang on until the engine blows." That funny look was back on Trufante's face, and this time Mac was done guessing. "Spit it out."

"I only had time to crimp the fuel line to the starboard engine. If I could have yanked wires, it would have been easy, but ..."

"Just keep an eye on them." Mac couldn't fault the Cajun for doing—or not doing—as asked.

Trufante nodded, and Mac went back to the starboard bench, where Kurt was sitting with an arm over the gunwale, staring ahead at the boat that held his wife and daughter.

"We'll get 'em. I have the radar signature dialed in, and Trufante did a little work on the engines." But it was hard to reassure the agent as Bugarra's boat disappeared over the horizon. "Ned and Pamela are back at the fort. They're going to find Farnsworth and get help."

Kurt seemed to snap out of it now that there was something he could do. Pushing past Mac, he reached the helm and grabbed the VHF microphone. Mac watched as Kurt switched to channel nineteen and hailed the fort. Mac and Kurt huddled around Trufante, straining to hear over the speaker what the director would do.

The answer came quickly: "Stand down."

With two words, the wind had been spilled from their sails.

TWENTY-FIVE

Trufante didn't waver. He kept a firm grip on the throttle. No one said a word; they were all stunned by the director's response. Mac broke the spell. "Shut it down," he said. It took a while for Trufante to process the command, which was contrary to what he expected Mac to do. Normally averse to orders, especially from an office man, Tru expected his boss to do the opposite.

"Our goal is not to catch them," he said. Kurt and Trufante turned to face Mac, shock on their faces. "Our goal is to save Allie and Justine." Mac looked at Kurt. He could tell Kurt was nervous, but was being patient. Though he might not agree, his direct supervisor had ordered him to stand down, and unless a better option presented itself, he would comply.

"We've got them locked on the radar. The range is good for a hundred miles. It shouldn't be any problem to track where he's headed. Besides, Bugarra didn't take them to kill them, or we would have picked up their bodies outside the harbor. He intends to use them to leverage us." Mac saw that everyone agreed. Trufante bumped the throttle forward to just over an idle, keeping his course the same as the boat moving ahead on the radar screen.

Mac leaned over him and tapped the red icon. A small cursor appeared over the boat, and he selected "track" from a pop-up menu. A circle appeared around Bugarra's boat. "That way we can keep an eye on him." He turned to Kurt. "I expect once he reaches Key West he'll send over his demands."

"Should we call the FBI? This is a kidnapping."

"Any other day, maybe, but every office in the state is shut down now. Ruth's had its way with the Keys, but the rest of the state is not going to be free of it until tomorrow. It's up to us for now."

"I should call in to headquarters and see if he relayed a message."

"He knows how to find us. We have a single-sideband radio that should cover Key West to the Dry Tortugas," Mac said,

"If it's all the same, I'd rather be closer than further away," Kurt said.

Trufante had been listening to the exchange, and looked at Mac. He nodded, and the Cajun pressed down the throttles. It took a long moment for the boat to get up on plane, but soon enough, they were traveling at twenty-five knots. Trufante checked his course against the icon on the screen representing Bugarra's boat and adjusted slightly to match it. Mac zoomed out the screen. About thirty miles ahead of Bugarra's boat was Key West. Mac had guessed that was where Bugarra was going; now he knew for sure. If it wasn't Key West itself, Bugarra was clearly heading for the chain of islands.

Mac adjusted the volume and squelch on the SSB and VHF radios. Even though there was still no signal, he had Kurt turn up the volume on his cell phone.

"Dial her back to eighteen hundred," Mac told Trufante. He complied, easing the throttles down while watching the tachometer. When the diesel settled into the range he wanted, there was an audible drop in the volume. It was just barely enough power to keep the steel hull on plane and was more fuel efficient. Checking the fuel levels, Mac saw the tanks had a solid half in the port side and about a third in the starboard. He switched over to the port tank; he would allow the tank to go down to a quarter before resetting the switch. The difference in weight between the tanks was hard to detect from the decks, but Mac saw how Trufante was having to goose the starboard trim tab to lift the hull slightly. Once the weight of the fuel in the tanks was equal, the boat would ride better.

Mac didn't need a calculator to tell him they had enough fuel to reach Key West. With the Marquesas appearing on the horizon, they were already halfway back. Again, he checked the radar screen. Bugarra's boat appeared to have slowed, but he was a captain as well and knew that his boat was faster than the trawler. As they moved through the storm-churned water, Mac had to keep reminding himself that this was not a race. They had to be smart. Even if they could overtake the faster boat, it might panic Bugarra into doing something that nobody aboard the trawler wanted.

Mac saw the troubled look on Kurt's face and tried to figure out what to do when they reached Key West. The other consideration was if there still was a Key West. It would take another day or so for the seas to calm, but the sky was clear and sunny. There was no telling where the eye had passed, and whatever damage it had done was already in the books for the Keys. He wished anyone still in the eye's path the best of luck and focused on what he had to do. For them, it was time to recover.

"Bugarra's going to want whatever information we have from Gross's files in exchange for your family," Mac said, after pulling Kurt back into the cabin, where it was quieter. "We've got to get ahold of Ned. He sounded like he was onto something, and he's our best hope of figuring out what Bugarra wants. The sooner we can do that, the better the chance for getting Justine and Allie back."

"I can radio the fort," Kurt said. "I'm also going to email Martinez for a leave of absence as soon as we get reception. If we're going to get them back, I can't be bogged down with the park service regulations.

"Sounds good." Mac had a thought: "Maybe one of the seaplanes can get Ned back to Key West. The storm's about gone; they should be okay to fly."

Kurt pulled something out of his pocket. "I have the pilot's card here."

"Let's see if he'll do it, then."

Kurt texted the number. "It won't go through."

Mac pulled out his own phone and pressed the home button. "No service."

"Maybe it'll go through once we're closer."

"We can't depend on cell phone networks. There's no telling what kind of war zone we're walking into. If you can get either of them on the VHF, we ought to try."

Kurt moved back to the helm. He picked up the microphone from its clip and changed the frequency back to channel nineteen, then started hailing the fort. Nothing. He tried the SSB next and was able to reach one of the rangers, who promised to find Ned and the seaplane pilot.

"Okay, the sooner we're all together, the better chance we have." Usually Mac liked to work alone, but Kurt and Ned were valuable allies. Looking over at Trufante at the helm, Mac wasn't so sure about the Cajun, but decided it was better to have a loose cannon in your backyard pointing at your neighbor than the other way around.

Moving back to the helm, Mac stood behind the captain's chair and checked the radar screen. "Looks like your bit of sabotage did the trick." The icon was moving slower, although the gap still remained. Mac figured they could get about ten knots an hour more out of *Ghost Runner*, but deemed it not worth it. Better to conserve fuel and watch the other boat. For now, they had plenty of fuel, but there was no telling when the next time he could top off the tanks would be. Pumps needed power, and even if Key West had dodged the brunt of Ruth, there were likely outages. Sooner or later, Bugarra would stop and make the call Mac knew was coming.

Thirty minutes later, the world came back to life. Within a few minutes, everyone's phone was pinging and the radio crackling. "If we've got cell service now, let's hold off on that radio call," Mac said, preferring the privacy of the cell network over the open airwaves of the VHF.

As if on cue, Mac heard the new name of his boat hailed over the speaker: "*Ghost Runner*, this is the National Park Service, Fort Jefferson." It was Farnsworth. Turning the radio off, Mac decided the name that Pamela had christened her with was definitely appropriate.

Mac watched as Trufante dropped speed slightly and programmed a course around the small keys dotting the water between their current position and Key West. Trufante looked at Mac for assurance and, when he nodded, set the autopilot.

The communal feeling they'd felt on the run back from the Dry Tortugas ended with that first phone ping. Mac and Kurt were both looking down, their faces buried in their devices.

As Mac checked his, he looked up at Kurt, who shook his head, indicating there was no message from Bugarra. Mac asked him to try Justine's, but she had left hers in the fort when she and Allie went snorkeling.

"I'm going to send that email to my boss," Kurt said.

Mac nodded and checked the notifications on his screen. He saw a dozen texts from Mel, opened the last, and saw *Call me when you get service.* He also saw several voicemails. Two were from her. Checking the timestamp, he saw they were from several hours ago. She was likely trying to reach him after he had disconnected so abruptly in the communications room.

Now, over fifty miles from Farnsworth's inquest and Fort Jefferson, Mac felt like he had regained some power. Bugarra had his boat back and had fled as well. Neither was going to jail, and Mac knew from the way the cards had been dealt by the administrator that was as good a resolution as he was going to get.

His next voicemail was from an unknown number with a 305 area code.

"Shut her down," he called to Trufante. When the engines died, he held up the phone. The group gathered around, and he pressed connect. Bugarra's voice came through the speaker. There was engine noise in the background, but the words were distinct.

"I'm sure you know I have your two women. They will be safe as long as you comply with my demands. I know you are in possession of the research from Gross's hard drive. That will be returned to me in due course. But before I release these two, I want what Gross was looking for. Please acknowledge receipt of this message. I will expect an update every twelve hours starting at six o'clock tonight."

TWENTY-SIX

·

SITTING ON THE DECK BY THE TRANSOM, JUSTINE AND Allie huddled together as the boat sped away from Fort Jefferson. Justine grasped Allie's hand and gave a reassuring squeeze, thinking the self-assured sixteen-year-old had held it together pretty well. Justine was as proud of Allie as if she was her own daughter.

Justine had been too surprised to react when the two thugs attacked them in the water. Their snorkels had been visible behind them for a while, but she had thought nothing of it. Now, she realized her mistake—there had been no tourists at the fort. After being pulled from the water, it took her several minutes to realize it was Bugarra at the helm. Rage overcame her at the thought of endangering a young girl because of a treasure that might not be there. Her fists clenched, showing the hard muscles in her forearms, toned and built by hours paddling her stand-up board.

It was sunny and warm, yet she felt Allie shivering, and pulled her close. She doubted it was from the elements; it was a hot, humid day, and the water they had been snorkeling in had been bathtub warm. Justine knew that, despite her stone face, Allie was scared—Justine was, too.

The twin engines behind them were surprisingly quiet and, sitting below the gunwales blocked it further allowing them to be able to talk.

"Your dad and Mac will come get us. You know that, right?" she said. Although she had no doubt the men were in pursuit right now, she was not the kind to wait passively. Trained to observe detail, she had studied and memorized everything about the boat and the men who had taken them. She had already seen Bugarra in action, both at the Shipwreck Ball, where she and Kurt had saved Gross's daughter from Slipstream and the state archeologist Jim DeWitt, and just hours ago, when Bugarra had tried to kill Mac and his crew. She knew he was involved in the business at the Savoy with Maria Gross, but the investigation quickly had ended with Slipstream's confession. Justine had no illusions—if Kurt and Mac couldn't produce something of the treasure, she and Allie would be dead.

"I know they will," Allie said, squeezing Justine's hand. "But we have to be ready."

Justine smiled and teared up at the same time. "Look around. Watch everything they do and listen to everything they say. We'll get our chance."

She estimated it had been an hour since they had been pulled from the water, and tried to remember the trip down. From her present position, all she could see was blue water. Slowly, so as not to attract attention, she lifted herself up just enough to see that ... there was nothing else to see. The limited view of the horizon didn't tell her much, but she figured they were doing around forty knots and Key West was seventy miles away. The math wasn't hard. The Marquesas Keys would be coming up soon.

She returned her focus to the boat and glanced around at

the two thugs who had yanked them from the water. They were laughing and talking, probably trying to figure out how to spend the paycheck Bugarra was sure to have offered them for their services. With no threats in sight, they were relaxed and not paying attention to Justine or Allie.

Justine's first thought was to take them now, while they had their guards down. But, weaponless and in the confines of the boat, there was little chance for success. Patience was a virtue, but not one of hers, though she knew it was their only way out. She and Allie clung to each other, watching and waiting. Justine had evaluated every item in sight for its value as a weapon and decided there was nothing they could do until they reached their destination.

The whine of the engines and movement of the boat had almost lulled her to sleep when she felt the attitude of the boat change. A few minutes later, it slowed, then stopped. She could tell there was land nearby—first, from the shade of a large cloud overhead, and then from a sound she knew well from staying on Adams Key: the rustling of the breeze through the mangroves.

The men were more alert now, and she moved slowly, rising from the deck and stretching. A wide cove in the shape of a half-moon extended in front of them. Mangrove-lined shores stretched from the water's edge a quarter mile in each direction. She surmised they were in the Marquesas Keys. An escape plan flashed through her mind. With their snorkeling gear by their sides, they could probably be in the water and moving toward the shore before the men could react, but once they reached the thin strip of land, her plan dissolved. The population of the small islands was comprised of stinging insects and snakes. There was no way to sustain themselves or communicate with the outside world, if they were to avoid being recaptured.

Sitting back down, she looked at Allie and whispered, "We're in the Marquesas."

Bugarra must have heard her. He turned toward them and spoke for the first time since they had been taken. "You'll be fine. Your boyfriend and Travis will do what I want."

"And what is that?" Aside from it being the key to their survival, Justine was just plain curious.

"Don't be naïve, girl," he said. "You know very well what Gross was up to when those two idiots killed him. The *Sumpter* was just the beginning. If they had just waited, they could have let him take them right to the mother lode."

"And what might that be?" Justine asked. She'd seen his ego on full display at the gala.

"We'd need Gross's research to tell us that, wouldn't we?"

"All very interesting, but what do you expect Mac and Kurt to do?"

"Gross was onto something big."

"I think you're expecting the impossible," she said, trying to figure out if it was even possible that Kurt and Mac could satisfy Bugarra's demands.

"Don't underestimate Gross. He was the best."

"Is that remorse I hear?"

"It wasn't me that killed him, and I didn't sanction it."

He said it easy, like he had killed before, which confirmed Justine's feeling that she and Allie were disposable.

———

MAC LOOKED AT HIS WATCH. They were within sight of Key West, near Man Key, just to the west. There was still no information coming from the Keys about what Ruth had left in her wake, and that bothered him. The last thing he wanted was to pull into the port and find anarchy, but he needed to stay close. The radar signature from Bugarra's boat told him they were nearby.

"Any word on getting Ned flown in?" Mac asked Kurt.

"The pilot said he needed to make sure the runway was clear of debris before he made the trip. He was thinking it would be tomorrow."

"That's too late," Mac said. Bugarra had been clear about being updated often, and Ned was crucial if they were going to solve the puzzle. Mac knew they needed to work on two fronts. One to satisfy Bugarra—provide him with what he wanted, and they would get Justine and Allie back. The second was to get the two back without providing the treacherous salvor any useful information. The word *useful* stuck in his mind.

"The only way to get Ned here tonight is to go get him here ourselves," Kurt said.

Mac knew he was right. Avoiding Key West because of what *might* be going on there was a cowardly approach to this business. "All right."

The determined look on Kurt's face was enough to tell Mac he had made the right decision. He'd been there before himself, when Mel had been abducted, and knew exactly what was running through Kurt's mind. "Whatever it takes," Mac said.

With somewhat of a plan, Mac watched the water ahead knowing nothing else could be done until they reached Key West. When they finally approached the marina, Mac started looking for signs of what to expect ashore. He'd been here twenty-five years, through Wilma and more tropical storms than he could recall. So far, the water remained clear, a good sign. If the island had been leveled, the first thing he would see was brown water from the erosion of the shoreline. Then the organic debris: trees, stumps, branches, and leaves. If devastation had occurred, there would be parts of buildings in the water. He saw none of that. Key West had done what it did best—survive.

The marina was much like he had left it. Several boats whose owners were either out of town or confident that their insurance would cover any damages were askew, but they were all still in the water. The boats whose owners had taken precautions were mostly intact. Mostly what he saw as he backed into the slip was leaves and garbage. Ruth had been here, but it looked like the damage had been minimal.

"We need to get to the airport," Kurt reminded Mac as he secured the lines.

Mac looked around the marina, but the Yellowfin was not there. He knew there were as many slips in Key West as barstools on Duval Street, so he wasn't overly concerned.

Once they reached dry land, Mac's guess that Key West had been spared was proven accurate. There were branches and litter everywhere. Several trees were down, some unfortunately landing on structures, but for the most part, the city was unscathed. Hard to believe just slightly more than twelve hours had passed since the *Ghost Runner* had left the marina that morning.

"Look at that, your old *Reef Runner* made it through," Trufante said.

Mac glanced over at the center console. There were some fresh dings where it had slammed into the dock, and he was relieved to see it whole but just now he needed land transportation, not another boat.

"We need to get to the airport," Mac repeated Kurt's words, as he secured the stern lines.

"I'll stay and watch the boats. You never know what kind of unsavory elements are out after a storm," Trufante said.

Mac dismissed his offer, thinking he was probably trying to avoid walking across the island. A pink cab cruised by on the street and he remembered the young driver he had exchanged numbers with. He was kind of relieved he had an excuse to call her and make sure she was all right. It wasn't his style, but he felt an odd connection with the girl. Texans had strong roots, and it might have been their common link to Galveston that did it, or any number of other instincts that bound people together. His brain was going down a road that would benefit no one, and he pulled himself back to the present and pressed the phone icon. The phone rang several times, and he was composing a voicemail in his head when she picked up.

"Hey."

"This is Mac Travis—remember the guy from the cab?"

"No offense, but a lot of guys ride in my cab." She paused. "But I remember you."

"Did you get through the storm okay?" Mac asked, noticing the others were eyeing him. Trufante made a joke about him making small talk with the girl—something very out of character.

"All good. Power went back on about an hour ago, and we've got plenty of food and water."

"Looks like the island dodged a bullet. How about your cab?"

"Nothing fell on it, if that's what you mean. I haven't been out yet."

Mac asked her to pick them up, telling her to use the main streets, as they would be cleared first. She agreed and said she'd be there in fifteen minutes.

She arrived several minutes early with a report that the roads were generally passable. Mac watched for signs of damage as they went. Palm Avenue was clear, as was the causeway. Sonar turned onto First, which turned into Bertha, then turned left onto South Roosevelt.

The windward side of the island showed more damage, but it was still minimal. The beaches were littered with debris, some having been swept over the road by the storm surge.

When they reached the airport, she turned left. Mac could see several pieces of heavy equipment working to clear the main runway. He directed Sonar to drive past the terminal to the FBO area, where they stopped. The runway was covered with leaves and littered with palm fronds and branches, and it had a light coating of sand.

"Call the pilot," Mac jumped out of the cab, ran through the open gate in the chain link fence, and waved to a driver working a bulldozer to clear the runway, and saw him head toward the FBO area.

TWENTY-SEVEN

THE SMALL PLANE APPEARED TO COME AT THEM RIGHT OUT of the setting sun. It banked slightly as it flew overhead, and Mac could see the pilot looking out the window. The airport was still officially closed, meaning no one was manning the control tower. That wasn't an issue, though. Only a fraction of the airports in the country actually had a manned tower, and Mac knew pilots landed all the time by using a hailing channel to state their intentions. Anyone else in the area would hear, and the pilots worked out any conflicts themselves.

Under the circumstances, it was a good practice to fly over the runway before attempting to land. As the first plane in after Ruth, any debris would be the pilot's problem. He wiggled the wings of the floatplane as he passed, indicating that all was good, and continued flying until Mac again lost sight of the small plane. As it turned, a glint of metal reflected the setting sun, and Mac was able to follow the approach. This time the pilot came straight in and landed easily. He taxied to the FBO area and cut the engines.

A few minutes later, a shaky Ned and an excited Pamela

exited the plane. The pilot followed and waved to Kurt. Ned came toward them.

"You okay, old man?" Mac said. "I need to put you to work."

The hazy, airsick look in Ned's eyes vanished, replaced by cold determination. "That won't be a problem. Though it might be a while before I can unclench my hands."

They walked out to the curb and he asked Sonar to take them to Ned's house.

"I've got Justine's car parked over there," Kurt said, pointing at the small lot behind them. "I'll meet you at Ned's."

Mac glanced at his watch. "We have to call Bugarra about fifteen minutes ago."

Kurt nodded and jogged toward the car.

As they cruised through the side streets, Mac saw that the residents were out, checking the damage to their properties. The relief on many of their faces was clear.

The mood in the car was the opposite. They needed to get to Ned's and make a plan.

A few minutes later, Sonar pulled up to the curb in front of Ned's house. Trufante, Pamela, and Ned got out of the back. Mac waited behind until the group followed Ned inside.

"What do we owe you?" Mac asked.

"This one's on me. Thanks for caring."

Mac peeled a couple of hundreds off the soggy pile of bills in his pocket. "I have a feeling we'll be needing you again before this is over."

She started to refuse, but he pushed them across the seat. After Sonar finally took them, he exited the cab and walked up the driveway. Kurt had arrived and was waiting anxiously by the door.

"Let's go talk to Ned and call Bugarra. We'll get them back." Mac checked his watch before entering Ned's office. They were already a half-hour late, and he knew Bugarra was not going to take that well.

"We need some information now," he told Ned, who was already on the computer, pecking furiously at the keyboard.

Now he stood behind Ned, frustrated as he watched him click back and forth between windows."Dual screens would really help," Mac said. It had taken a lot of convincing for Mac to go that route on his boat, but once he had them, he'd never go back.

"It's got to be something with Lafitte and Henriques. That's where everything points." Ned pointed to the screen, which showed the files in one of the many folders on the drive.

"Conversos? I never heard of that. Open it up." Instead of the boat names that he'd expected, Mac saw only people's names. "What do you make of it?"

"You need to learn your history of the Caribbean. Wood was too impatient to do the research, but I guess that's why he had me," Ned said. "Turns out the apple didn't fall far from the tree."

Mac wanted to protest, but let him continue.

"The history of the Jews in these waters goes all the way back to Columbus's era, when edicts banned them from Spain and then Portugal. Many sailed as 'Conversos,' Jews who had converted to Catholicism. They were skilled traders, among other things, and needed in the New World. For years, the local governments went along with the ruse, but the Inquisition was like a dog with a bone. When they ran out of Jews to persecute on the Iberian Peninsula, they came here."

"We have to call him, even if it's just for a history lesson," Kurt said.

The three men looked at each other, and Mac pulled out his phone. He pressed Bugarra's number and waited. The call was answered almost immediately.

"We have some leads, but are going to need until tomorrow to track them down," Mac said, revealing nothing of what they'd learned. If at all possible, he wanted to hold his cards close.

"By six o'clock tomorrow night, I want to see results."

Mac disconnected. He turned to Kurt, who was standing close enough to have heard the conversation, and told him they had twenty-four hours.

"I think we should split up and try and find them," Kurt said, looking stressed.

"Probably a good idea, but that's more your line of work than mine."

Kurt started toward the door.

"Just keep in touch. We'll keep working this end," Mac said. He was both relieved and concerned at breaking up the group, but knew Kurt's skill set was better geared toward finding Justine and Allie. Mac just hoped Kurt was patient enough to call for backup if he found them.

BUGARRA SET the phone down on the coffee table and looked around his suite. He was used to expansive water views, so it felt like the walls of the room he had chosen because of the storm were closing in on him. The woman and the girl were in the next room being watched by one of his men. The other was on guard outside the door of the suite. They would be fine for now. What was bothering Bugarra was Travis. He knew Travis was withholding information, and he needed to find out what it was.

He decided to leave his men to watch the women. In retrospect, it had been a rash act to take them, but Bugarra knew Travis had the information he wanted, and at the time taking them seemed the only way to get it. He'd left bodies in his wake before, but they were usually competitors or their henchmen, not someone's wife and daughter. In a rare show of concern, Bugarra hoped Travis came through so he could release them.

He'd been in a dangerous business for too long not to know how to mitigate risk, and the best way this time was to keep an eye on Travis. Bugarra was familiar enough with his reputation. Travis would try and get the women back *and keep* the treasure.

Bugarra ordered the men to make sure that Hunter's family was comfortable and had food and water, then left the suite.

Hitting the streets, thinking he was probably going to have to walk, he saw a cab cruising by and whistled. The pink-haired woman driver did a quick U-turn to pick him up.

"Can you take me to the marina?" Bugarra asked. The woman nodded, and he saw her glance at him in the mirror. He let it go, thinking that anyone out tonight might be up to no good. "And if you have a few free hours, I'll be needing a cab for a while."

There were few cars on the streets, making for a fast ride across the island. Bugarra saw a few lights on, probably from people who had stayed. Most of the houses were dark. Normally the streets were alive and busy once the tropical sun set; tonight was quite the opposite. They arrived at the marina a few minutes later, and he asked the woman to wait. She nodded again and looked down at her phone.

He didn't think anything of it, as that was what most people did when they had more than thirty seconds with nothing to do. Leaving the cab, he walked past the closed Half Shell Oyster Bar. The docks were dark, and he guessed the management had turned the main breakers off as a precaution. Tonight had a different feel about it, like fatigue had overtaken the city. Debris from the storm surge covered the dock and sidewalks. The boats, usually lit by the pedestal lights at each slip, as well as their own spreaders, looked like shadows against the water. From the dim lights in the three or four illuminated cabins he passed, he suspected the shore power was off as well.

The blackout forced him to survey most of the marina on foot, but he soon found Travis's boat. Staying in the shadows of an adjacent trawler, he watched the dark boat, finally deciding that it was empty. He backtracked to the cab and found the girl still there, staring into space now. She jumped when he opened the door and he checked his phone before asking her to take him to an address on Whitehead Street. He'd thought he had startled her, but her nervous eyes kept making contact with his in the rearview mirror. With the two women hostage, his best defense mechanism was his paranoia, and he wondered what she knew as she drove past Duval and turned onto Whitehead.

One phone call had gotten him the old man's address.

TWENTY-EIGHT

It took all Kurt's willpower to stop himself from blindly running after Justine and Allie. Instead, he channeled his fury into something productive. He needed information before he could act. Finding where Bugarra was staying would have been possible if the island's law enforcement was working, but with all departments—including the police, fire, and EMS—still shut down, he had no alternatives. His contacts with the FBI would also be useless, as the closest office that might answer their phone was probably several states away. His cell was working again, and he checked the locations of Justine and Allie's phones. Neither registered, and he assumed that Bugarra had turned them off, before remembering the phones were probably in their rooms at Fort Jefferson.

Working for the National Park Service, Kurt had spent most of his time in wilderness areas. He'd been working in the Plumas National Forest in Northern California when he found the pot grow that had changed his life. Even at work, he liked to interact with the land and water, and often had a fishing pole in his hand or, at least, aboard the boat. An errant cast from his fly rod had led him to an irrigation pipe sucking water backward through an eddy in one of the national forest streams. Following the pipe had led him to the grow, and that had, at least temporarily, ruined his life. After losing custody of Allie when the cartel retaliated, he had been relocated to Biscayne National Park.

Though he had been involved in several high-profile cases since arriving in Florida, his five-figure attorney, Daniel J. Viscount, had convinced his ex that his lifestyle was not a danger to Allie, and, with a big assist from Justine, Kurt had won his custody hearing. For the last year, he and Justine had been spending most weekends with his daughter. He now regretted bringing Allie along this time, though there had been no way of knowing it was going to turn out like this. Looking at his phone, he knew he should call Jane and tell her, but decided against it. Ruth was as good an excuse as any. He could easily delay the call until morning.

He'd only been to Key West once, and Duval Street acted like a magnet on him, so it was the first place he went. Looking at the bars, now empty after the storm-fueled parties were over, he realized this was the last place Bugarra would take the women. He continued until he reached Front Street where he pulled over and opened the maps app on his phone.

Working both the remote wilderness and expansive waters, he was used to, and comfortable with, charts and maps. Now, he studied Key West. The first thing he noticed was that the marinas were all on the north side of the island. Realizing the only lead he had was knowing Bugarra's boat, he figured that finding it would be the logical way to start looking for Justine and Allie. Parking the car, he followed Duval to where it dead-ended and started walking along the historic boardwalk, back-tracking to the cruise ship pier, then moving east.

It looked like electricity had been restored to most of the island, but as the sunlight faded, he could see the docks were still dark. Unable to identify the boats from the boardwalk, he was forced into the time-consuming task of following every pier, and was about to give up when he reached the Key West Marina, where Mac's boat was docked.

He saw a single taxi idling by the entrance to the pier. The driver's face was partially lit by a phone, and, seeing someone familiar, he approached the cab.

"Sonar?" He tapped on the window.

She jumped and looked up. Kurt took a step back to avoid looking intimidating, but in the process, that scared her worse. On any other night, the streetlights would have easily illuminated him, but tonight they were dark. In the long minute it took for her to recognize him, Kurt spotted someone approaching. Sonar froze, and Kurt took another step back into the darkness. He could see sudden tension in her face, and, as the man came closer to the cab, there was enough light for Kurt to see it was Bugarra. Kurt sank into the recessed entrance of a storefront and watched as Bugarra got into the cab. His hunch had been right.

The car took off, and Kurt stepped out of the shadows. He started to follow it. There was little chance he could keep up on foot, but with no other clues, even knowing the general direction would help.

Running along the boardwalk, he tried to keep the taillights in sight. The storm surge had come up over the walkway, and he slipped on the long strands of seaweed. As he ran, he was forced to alternate glances at the ground ahead and the taillights of the cab. Several times he lost his footing and thought he had lost the cab. When he reached the higher ground of Front Street, the footing improved, and he was able to make up some distance, but as the taillights disappeared around the corner of White-head Street, he stood with his hands on his hips, spent, gasping for air, and wondering where this left him.

His only hope was that Sonar would let Mac know what happened after she dropped the kidnapper off. Kurt pulled his phone out to alert Mac.

MAC WAS WALKING out the door when his cell rang. He answered the call, but put Kurt on hold so he could text Sonar and get her location. She texted back that she was at the house, and Mac ran toward the front window; he saw Bugarra was sitting in the backseat of the cab. Switching back to Kurt, he explained the situation.

"I'm down the block now. I see them," Kurt said.

"We're going out the back. There's a detached garage. We'll meet you there." Mac disconnected and nodded to Trufante and Pamela, who had agreed to stay behind to make it look like someone was home and create a diversion. They finally had a clue, and Mac didn't want Bugarra following him.

"Go," he whispered to Ned.

Staying to the shadows, using the house as cover for as long as possible, they regrouped in the dark back corner. The garage was only ten feet away, but exposed to the street. Mac could see the back of the cab. Bugarra's head was clearly visible in the backseat and he appeared to be looking at the front of the house. Mac tapped Ned on the shoulder and, a second later, followed him to the garage.

Opening the garage door would attract too much attention, so they wheeled Ned's bikes to the swing door and waited for Kurt. He appeared a minute later, and Mac directed him toward the third bike. The beach cruisers weren't fast, but were efficient for getting around the flat island. When the three men were ready, Mac turned his back to the door to cover the light from the screen of his phone and texted Trufante.

A second later, a loud crash came from inside the house, followed by a woman's scream. They hoped the diversion would give them enough time to get the bikes into the neighbor's yard. What sounded like a fight between a man and a woman started. That hadn't been part of the plan, and Mac wondered if leaving Trufante and Pamela together had been a good idea. There was no time to think about that, though, and he was first to leave the garage.

In single file, they walked the bikes across the grass, tripping several times on the exposed roots of a large banyan tree. The heavy beach cruisers were not made to navigate rough terrain, and Mac could hear Ned struggling behind him. He laid his bike down after clearing the root system and turned to help Ned. A minute later, the three stood in Ned's neighbor's driveway, looking at the back of the cab. There were no signs that they had been seen, and Mac decided to cross one more lot before hitting the street. The three rode around the block, stopping about a hundred feet short of the corner a block ahead of the cab. Mac texted Trufante. One at a time, the lights in the house were extinguished.

A second later, he heard the garage door open and the car engine start. With most of the residents gone and the streets empty, Mac couldn't remember a time when the island was so quiet. The silhouette of a head in the back of the cab could be seen turning toward the sound as Trufante backed the car out of the driveway. Fortunately, Bugarra had positioned himself to watch the front of the house, and the driveway was a blind spot. He would see the car, but hopefully not be able to identify the occupants. Trufante backed into the street going the opposite direction that Bugarra was facing and took off.

Mac's breath quickened. Bugarra could do one of two things: He could stay in the cab and follow the car, or he could break into the house to steal the data. Mac suspected he'd pick the former. Being a salvor himself, he understood the paranoia Bugarra was feeling right now, and his sense would be to follow the pair he thought was Mac and Ned. He guessed that Bugarra was thinking: If they had found something, they would lead him to it, and they likely had Gross's research with them anyway. Losing them would ruin any chance to take it from them.

Mac watched as Trufante turned onto Front Street. He lost sight of him, but knew where he was going. His suspicions about Bugarra were confirmed when the cab started, backed into a neighbor's driveway, pulled out, then disappeared around the same corner.

Mac, Ned, and Kurt started pedaling down the street. Despite the lack of normal nightlife, they were counting on the Key West phenomenon that it was still faster to reach anywhere on the island by bicycle. Mac was surprised that Ned was appearing to effortlessly keep pace with him and Kurt, until he realized that the old man lived here, and most residents put more miles on their bikes than on their cars.

Mac wove his way through the side streets, trying to gain an advantage and stay on a direct route to the marina. There were only a few cars out, and he feared he would be too late, but when the marina was in sight, they kicked it into high gear and coasted to a stop behind Turtle Kraals just before they saw the headlights approach.

TWENTY-NINE

Mac and Ned got off their bikes and started to head toward the dock.

"I'm staying," Kurt said. "I can't leave the island knowing Allie and Justine are here. You guys draw him out. If he follows, we'll know if they're with him. If he doesn't, you can circle back."

"Makes sense, Mac," Ned said.

Mac was quiet for a few seconds. Kurt was right, but they had to act now or lose their advantage. "Me and the old boy'll take the boat now and see if he follows. I'll have Tru meet us around the bight, and we'll switch. Let him and Pamela take the boat ride."

Kurt faded into the shadows while Mac and Ned ran to the *Ghost Runner*. Once aboard, Mac sent Ned to the helm while Mac readied the trawler. The engine started at the same time as he tossed the lines, and Ned pulled forward out of the slip. "I got it," Mac said.

"I've been driving boats since before they had motors. Tend to your business. I'll take her around the bight."

Mac grunted and moved to the side of the wheelhouse.

From here, he could watch Bugarra. The cab hadn't moved, but he saw the interior light go on. Assuming that a door had opened, he asked Ned to slow down. They were baiting a trap, not escaping one. Unable to see in the darkness, Mac killed all the lights and studied the pier. He thought he saw a shadow, there for a second, then gone. A figure appeared a few feet from the dock. Mac's eyes locked on the man as he moved down the dock and stopped at one of the boats.

His phone had Trufante's number already on the display, and he pressed the connect icon and waited. When Trufante answered, Mac explained what he wanted Trufante and Pamela to do. "He's coming," Mac said to Ned. "Give her a little push. Not so much he loses us, but we need to make the swap before he gets to the Cruise Ship Pier."

Ned shot Mac a look that said he understood and didn't appreciate the coaching. "We'll get 'er done." He passed the breakwater and pushed down on the throttles. "You got a fuel issue if you want to go much further."

Mac moved to the helm and read the gauges. Both read about a quarter tank, but he knew this was a high estimate. Their current speed was not fast enough to get the boat up on plane, and with the transom down and the fuel sensor located in the rear of the tanks, the reading was misleading. Instead of relying on the gauges, he looked at the hour readout on the tachometers. Some quick math told him they had only about fifty miles of range remaining. Normally, with marinas dotting the waterways, this wasn't a problem, but after Ruth, there was no telling what was available. They weren't going far enough to worry about it now, and he dug five hundred-dollar bills out of his stash in the cabin to give to Trufante. Some of the cash would inevitably go to filling the refrigerator with beer, but if most of it got into the tanks, Mac would be happy.

Looking up, he saw an iron railing to port, which told him

they were passing Mallory Square. If a cruise ship were in port, it would be visible from here, but none appeared. Any ship that was capable of diverting around the storm or running from it had left days ago.

Mac looked back and saw the green and red lights from Bugarra's bow. He had taken the bait.

"He's behind us and moving fast."

The trawler shot forward as Ned applied more pressure. Mac turned back to his phone to call Trufante, but saw Ned's old VW parked by itself near the pier. Two tall figures stood by the railing. One pointed at the boat, and he swore he could see Trufante's grille. Picking up the phone, he called Trufante and directed them to the end of the pier.

"Right there," Mac said, pointing to Trufante and Pamela.

"I can see," Ned said, squinting.

Mac fought the instinct to take the wheel, but resisted. They would be better served if he worked the lines. As Ned approached the pier, Mac looked back and saw Bugarra round the point of the bight. The plan was working. It looked like Bugarra was going to maintain the gap and see where they were headed, rather than come after them.

Ned slid the boat within a few feet of the pier while Mac coiled a third of the line in his right hand. With the remainder in his left hand, he tossed it across the water to Trufante. The lanky Cajun easily caught it, and together they pulled the boat until it was only a foot from the dock. Mac motioned for Pamela to come aboard, then helped Ned onto the higher dock. Mac followed and, after giving Trufante a few instructions and the money, the boat moved off. It had taken less than ten seconds to switch crews and only a small detour in course.

Mac and Ned moved back into the shadows and watched as Bugarra continued to match the trawler's speed. When his boat passed by them a few minutes later, it was clear that there was only one man aboard. Mac called Kurt to let him know that Bugarra was alone, and Mac and Ned turned to the street.

"You said something about the Conversos?" Mac asked. He had gotten Bugarra off the rock, which would give Kurt a better chance of locating Justine and Allie, but finding the treasure was still the best way out of this.

"Let's go visit the synagogue. Hopefully the rabbi stayed behind."

They reached Ned's car and, with Mac driving, headed toward United Street. Mac wasn't sure where this was going to lead, but he had no other clues.

The predawn streets were clear of traffic, but this was the time Key West was normally asleep. Avoiding several branches and palm fronds, Mac wove through the streets. They reached B'Nai Zion a few minutes later and left the car out front.

Ned led the way to the side door and knocked. For a few minutes they thought that the rabbi had evacuated, but after striking the door harder, they heard noise inside. The door cracked open, and the rabbi smiled when he saw Ned.

"An old friend appears," he said, opening the door.

"I figured you'd ride it out," Ned said, entering the small apartment.

"This time of night I don't think you're just checking on an old man?" the rabbi said.

"We're in a bit of a bind," Ned said.

Mac looked on, sure that the rabbi would help if he could. He knew genuine caring when he saw it, and the rabbi had it. He had opened the door and greeted them with no questions asked. After declining coffee, Ned explained what they wanted and the urgency of their situation.

"Most of the old books and journals relating to the Conversos are in back. Come on."

There was a space where academics dwelled that adventurers were loath to enter. As they walked through the apartment and into the synagogue, Mac knew he was out of his element. Ned became more and more animated as the rabbi led the way to an old library.

"The Jewish community of Key West goes back centuries. Although there was little in the way of records before the city was incorporated in 1832, the Jewish presence here was well known. Most were the ancestors of the Conversos, Iberians running from the Inquisition. They found a safe haven here, and, finally able to openly return to their faith, established themselves." The rabbi went to a shelf and pulled down several old journals.

"Gross's work was mostly centered around the period before the Civil War," Ned said. "Quite a few mentions of Lafitte and Henriques."

"I've heard before that there was something between those two."

Mac started pacing the old tile floor, wondering how the men could have anything in common when they were separated by two centuries. He knew there was no other option, but for a man inclined to action, library research was painful. Mac looked over Ned's shoulder as the rabbi opened one of the journals. He blew off a layer of dust and started paging through it.

"Here we are. Nicholas Van Doren."

Like every other salvor on the east coast, Mac knew his pirate history, but this name was not familiar. Despite his impatience, he listened to the rabbi.

"Van Doren and his family were captured by Gasparilla in the early 1800s. There is no record of what became of his parents, but one can assume." He paused. "Gasparilla must have seen something he liked about the boy and took him under his wing. When the Navy took out the old pirate, Nick escaped with ten men, a handful of small boats, and several chests containing Gasparilla's treasure."

"How does that tie in with Lafitte?" Mac asked.

"We'll get there. It's important to know who you're dealing with."

Ned was leaning over the rabbi's shoulder looking at the journal. "This is the journal Gross had pictures of."

The excitement running through the three men became palpable.

"Nick never wanted to be a pirate, and spent years trying to prove he was otherwise. It seems he was about to head across Panama to the Pacific and start fresh, when his boat was blown up off the Yucatan."

"And that boat held the treasure?" Mac asked.

"That's another story entirely, but he recovered much of it. What we're looking for here is much bigger."

There were stories about buried treasure and lost mines in that area, going back to Columbus. Mac knew most were myths, and the ones that were real would never be found.

The rabbi must have seen his interest waning. "After losing his ship, Van Doren needed help and turned to Jean Lafitte."

"Why him?" Mac was skeptical.

"To start with, Van Doren had met the old pirate several times previously while he was with Gasparilla. Back in the day, the two pirates ruled the gulf. From what Van Doren says, it was apparent to both that they shared a common ancestry. It's come to light lately that Lafitte was a Sephardic Jew. Amsterdam had become a safe haven for Jews, and knowing that's where Van Doren was from, it's a pretty good chance he and Lafitte shared the same heritage. The Middle Eastern features of the sect was a trait that would have made them look like brothers.

"How does that bring them back together in Mexico?" Mac asked.

"Rumor had it that after the Navy had run Lafitte out of Galveston, he had taken refuge in Campeche."

"So, Van Doren was close by, sought him out, and Lafitte offered his help?" Mac asked.

"For a price, yes. Until Lafitte double-crossed Van Doren," the rabbi said.

"How does this tie into Gross's research?"

Ned interrupted. "Gross could have been focusing his efforts on the federal waters of the gulf in general to escape the oversight and greed of the state of Florida. I know what's being spread around, about him selling out, but that's mostly coming from Bugarra. Gross was a dreamer. He wanted a galleon, not just gold to sell."

The pieces were starting to fall into place. Mac looked again at the rabbi, anxious for him to continue the story.

"It appears that Van Doren had regrouped and, with the help of another Sephardi he had found shipwrecked on the Mexican coast, discovered Henriques' treasure while salvaging what was lost when his own ship was destroyed. Which is where things get interesting."

"Who's Henriques?" Mac asked.

"Another pirate Jew," the rabbi said. "Moses Henriques captured the entire sixteen-ship Spanish plate fleet in 1628. He took the treasure to Brazil, where he established an island colony, but the Inquisition found him, and he fled to Campeche.

"It was purely by coincidence, almost two hundred years later, that Campeche declared its independence from Mexico and offered privateers commissions to anyone who would sail against their enemies. Lafitte, having been removed from Galveston by the Navy, was now based out of the rebel state. As he had done in New Orleans and Galveston, he cornered the market and soon had a fleet of ships patrolling the gulf waters.

"But Lafitte was a true pirate. He found out about the treasure and tried to double-cross Van Doren. Van Doren took the bait, but was able to hide the treasure before Lafitte found him."

"This is an interesting story, but it's getting us no closer to finding it," Mac said.

"The journal mentions Garden Key. Do you know what that is now?"

Mac shook his head.

"Fort Jefferson."

THIRTY

JUSTINE GLANCED AT ALLIE, THEN STUDIED THE ROOM, looking for anything that might aid in an escape. The TV was on, and the man left to watch them had a smile on his face as he watched the early reports of the destruction Hurricane Ruth had wrought. His reaction to the misfortune of others only infuriated her more. With his pistol sitting on the table in front of him, there was no way she could subdue him and escape. The only way out was subterfuge.

She was a scientist, and critical thinking was her wheelhouse. Her work as a forensics tech for Miami-Dade often made her think outside the box, and that's what she had to do now. She'd had offers of higher-paying research positions in the private sector, but Justine liked the excitement and intrigue of using science to solve cases, plus the added complexity of people in the puzzle. At first it had been all about the science of forensics, until she learned there was an art to interpreting the evidence as well. Now, she sat staring at the news, trying to figure out how to use her background to escape.

The first tendrils of light were just visible around the borders of the blackout curtains. Her stomach grumbled and she realized that unless you counted a few bottles of water and a candy bar, she and Allie hadn't eaten since being abducted yesterday. She remembered Bugarra instructing the men to keep them comfortable.

"Hey, we're hungry," she said to the man.

He turned toward them and grunted. Justine could see he was tired and probably hungry too. The two men were taking turns watching them, and she had studied them both. From their looks and the way they responded to Bugarra, she assumed they were ex-military. She had garnered from their conversations that they were from Miami and not all that happy that they had been forced to leave their families to weather the storm alone.

"Yeah, I'll get my buddy to bring some food."

Justine had hoped that he would go next door, giving her and Allie a chance to hop the second-floor balcony and escape, but instead, he texted his partner. Watching him type, she heard the conversation pinging back and forth.

"If he can find something open, we'll get some food."

She cleared her throat. "We need some girl stuff too—you know, that time." Allie gave her a questioning look, but Justine ignored it. "Some rubbing alcohol, too—helps with the cramps." Chances were strong he didn't know if that was true or not, and she hoped he wouldn't question it.

She saw his look change and knew she had gained her first advantage, though she wasn't sure if it was sympathy for her or the guilty pleasure of his partner having to make an embarrassing purchase. He put his head down and texted the additional requests. As badly as she wanted to tell Allie what she had planned, Justine just squeezed Allie's hand, trying to tell her that they were going to be all right.

WITH NED LINGERING BEHIND, Mac excused himself, thanking the rabbi for the information. Once outside, he called Trufante. The cat-and-mouse game with Bugarra was about to run its course, and if they were going to head back to the Dry Tortugas, he needed the trawler. Pamela answered, and he asked her to have Trufante bring the boat around to the Edward Knight Pier on the east side of the island. Anywhere on the Atlantic side of Key West would have been battered and possibly even seriously damaged by the storm, but Mac expected the concrete and steel structure on the east side would be intact.

"I'll need you to stay here and coordinate everything," Mac told Ned when he came out.

"If you're going after it, I'm going with you."

Mac decided that argument could wait until later. "I'm meeting the boat in a few minutes," he said, and turned to the rabbi. "Can we get some copies of the journal?"

"Of course, as long as I get the full story when you get back," the rabbi said. Taking the journal, he stepped out of the room. The rabbi was back a few minutes later and handed two copies of the journal to Mac. They thanked him and promised updates.

"Let's go," Mac said, hopping in the passenger seat. Ned started the old VW and headed toward White Street, where he made a right and drove toward the pier. It was immediately apparent that the Atlantic shore had taken the brunt of Ruth. The island had fared well with the wind, but the debris line brought in by the storm surge was well past the road. They crossed Atlantic Boulevard.

"Here's good," Mac said. "It'll be faster on foot. This might take a while—you sure you don't want to go back and start reading? Once we hit the water and we're out of cell range, it'll be hard to look up anything."

"Damned well can't lug my whole library around. You leave me, Travis, and there'll be hell to pay."

Mac took the win and left the car. As he ran down the pier, dodging piles of seaweed, buoys, line, and all manner of refuse, he hoped they'd found the answer. As he reached the end of the narrow walkway, the pier opened up to a wider area. Mac went to the rail and scanned the water. He saw his boat coming and waved.

THIRTY-ONE

Kurt peddled the beach cruiser into Ned's driveway. At the same time the VW, after almost sideswiping him, pulled in. He had been spinning in circles trying to canvas the island on the bike and opted to come back for the car.

"Any luck with those girls of yours?" Ned asked as he climbed out of the VW.

Kurt shook his head. The sun was climbing into the sky now, and he knew time was running out. On the way into the house, Ned updated Kurt on what he and Mac had found. Just as he finished, his phone rang. Mac.

"I'm back at Ned's," Kurt said when Mac asked for his status.

"Find Sonar. She may have a lead. I'll send you her number."

Kurt heard the sound of engines in the background. "Ned says you're heading back to the fort?"

"Small problem in the way." Mac explained that Bugarra was still following the boat.

Kurt thought for a moment. The best-case scenario was to lure Bugarra back onto land and hope he would lead them to

Allie and Justine. Allowing Mac to go find the treasure without Bugarra on his tail was an added bonus.

"Send me Bugarra's number. I have an idea."

They disconnected, and Kurt waited while the two messages with Bugarra and Sonya's contact info came in. He pressed Bugarra's number. Whether it was the unknown number or Bugarra couldn't hear his phone ring over the boat's engines, the call went to voicemail. Kurt left a message that he had some information, then texted him the same.

"You have anything with more firepower than this?" Kurt motioned to his sidearm.

"Course. Come on in and check out the armory."

Ned led Kurt into the office, where he opened a closet, revealing a large gun safe. He hit several keys on the keypad and turned the handle. Kurt was surprised at what he saw when the door opened. On the right were a half-dozen rifles and shotguns, and on the left several shelves containing handguns with boxes of ammunition stacked below.

"Don't have much use for them anymore, but in the old days, this place was like the wild west. Have a look and take what you need."

Kurt went to the safe. He saw a Barrett M82 and carefully removed it from the holder. "This oughta do it."

"A little on the heavy side. How about the Remington?" Ned asked.

"I'll take the weight for the firepower. You have any fifty-cal rounds?"

"Don't have any armor piercing, but these steel-core ones ought to work."

Kurt took the box and rifle. Now he just needed to lure Bugarra to a spot where he could disable the boat. "Thanks."

"No problem. I've been relegated to desk duty. Don't think

for a minute I wouldn't rather be out there with you guys, but somebody's got to do it."

Kurt didn't doubt that for a second, and hoped he would be as put together as Ned at that age. "Where do you think would be a good ambush spot? Mac said Bugarra was off the pier on the east side."

Ned crossed to the desk, where he pulled out an old map of the island. Kurt had seen bits and pieces of the map on the screen of his phone, but there was nothing like a paper map to get the feel for a place. "Right here would be good," Ned said, pointing. "Mac's gonna be needing some fuel, too."

"Robbie's marina? That's Stock Island."

"Problem is, everything on that side of Key West is shallow water. The boat will be too far offshore, and you won't get the accuracy you need to take out both motors."

Kurt picked up his phone and texted Mac with the location. By the time Kurt had written down the directions and loaded the weapons in the car, Mac had confirmed an ETA of ten minutes. Kurt hoped that would be enough time. He thanked Ned and backed out of the driveway.

People were out and about now, and traffic was picking up. He had heard of the unusual phenomenon of disaster tourism, and it certainly looked like anyone who had stayed behind was driving around checking to see what damage the island had sustained. Fortunately, the traffic was mostly cars. There were few of the scooters and bicycles that made Key West a nightmare to drive in. Even without them, it took close to ten minutes to reach the Stock Island Bridge, and Kurt started worrying that he was too late. Once he was across, though, traffic thinned out, and he reached Robbie's a few minutes later.

Another set of problems confronted him when he turned into the yard and saw several boats knocked off their supports and lying on the ground, blocking the driveway. With no choice, he left the car, grabbed the rifle, and ran to the end of the yard. Just as he reached it, he saw Mac's trawler slow and pull in.

With only seconds to spare, he found an old lobster trap to use as a support and slowed his breathing as he sighted the weapon. Through the scope, he saw Bugarra's Yellowfin turn the corner. Loading a round into the chamber, he watched as the boat approached. It seemed to pass in slow motion, and finally the engines appeared. Inhaling, he aimed and slowly released his breath at the same time as he squeezed the trigger. The backlash surprised him, but he was able to chamber another round and fire again before the boat was past.

THIRTY-TWO

MAC FLINCHED WHEN HE HEARD THE SHOTS. HIS FIRST reaction was that Bugarra was shooting at them, but when he turned and saw black smoke coming from the transom of the Yellowfin, he smiled. With many of the slips empty, it was a simple matter to turn the trawler around in the narrow channel, and a few minutes later, he sped past the crippled Yellowfin, ducking as Bugarra unloaded the magazine of his pistol in their direction. the shots went wide and Mac assumed they were a warning; Bugarra needed him alive—for now. As they passed the point, Mac saw Kurt raising a rifle in a victory pose.

Mac hoped that Bugarra would lead Kurt to his family. With only the copies of Van Doren's journal to guide him, the last thing Mac wanted was the pressure of having to find the treasure in order to save Justine and Allie. Looking back at Pamela, he remembered her and Mel being taken by a ring of slavers, and how that had shaken him. What Kurt was facing with his two loved ones held captive was equally unimaginable.

Fuel was his biggest concern now. The tanks were showing close to empty, and there would be no chance to recover the treasure without it. Robbie's marina had a fuel dock, but with

Bugarra behind them, that was not an option. Instead, Mac headed back to the Key West Bight, hoping the gas dock would be open. Passing the wheel to Trufante, he sat on the port bench behind the helm and took out his phone. Next to refueling, information was his next concern. He knew where to go, but not where to look.

After checking his messages, he texted Kurt to tell him they were heading to Fort Jefferson, and wished him luck, knowing they were going to be out of range in less than an hour and working independently.

His next call was to Mel. He brought her up to date. Mac could hear the concern in her voice when he told her that Justine and Allie were being held by Bugarra. She offered to fly back and work the legal end, but Mac had another idea. He told her the rabbi's story and asked her to find out whatever she could about Lafitte and Campeche. New Orleans hadn't revealed any useful information, and she had thought about following Lafitte's path. While he told her his plan to head to Fort Jefferson, she found a flight that would arrive in Cancun later that evening.

His next call was to Ned.

"You going to keep interrupting me, or can I get some work done?"

"Settle down, old man. Just wanted to see if you had anything. We're heading around to fuel up, and then we're off to Fort Jefferson. Probably be out of range in an hour."

"On my way," Ned said, and disconnected.

Mac was torn. Ned could be as much of an asset as a liability. Mac was past fifty himself, and the thought of how he was going to age was never far from his mind. His eyesight had been the beginning, but he had noticed other, more subtle changes, especially when physical work was involved. Putting himself in Ned's shoes, Mac knew he couldn't leave the old man out. Mac would rather die trying, and he knew the same was true of Ned. Looking down at his phone as he drove, he hit the recent calls button and told Ned to meet them at the marina.

With everyone up to date, he looked at the shore as they rounded the southernmost point of Key West. He hadn't seen what Ruth had done to this part of the coast from the water yet. Boats were strewn along the shore. Several floated freely, listing badly and drifting with the current. For centuries, the Keys had been a wrecker's haven. The dangerous reef and frequent storms were a hazard to the ships trying to ride the Gulf Stream north, or avoid it by staying closer to shore on their southward runs. The wreckers had been there in the past to save lives, as well as enrich themselves. Now the twenty-first-century versions would be out in full force. Looking over at Trufante, he saw the grin, evidence that he's seen the money, too. In another time, he regretted that it might actually have excited him.

The closer they got to the marinas on the western side of the island, the worse the damage appeared. He looked over at Trufante, who was also looking around, probably counting dollars as they passed the wrecked boats. From the smile on his mate's face, Mac expected that he would be shorthanded when this was over.

They reached the marina, only to find the fuel dock deserted. There was no sign of life at the office, either. After directing Trufante to pull into a nearby dock, Mac took one line over the gunwale with him and tied it off to a nearby cleat.

As he suspected, the fuel pumps were locked. That shouldn't be a problem, as he had bolt cutters aboard, but with the power out, they wouldn't pump. He took a quick look around, but there was no breaker box in sight. Even if he did find it, there was no guarantee that it would be live. The clock built into his head was ticking. They had to get to Fort Jefferson soon. There was no time to waste trying to find fuel legally, so he went for the alternative. Looking around the marina, he spotted an unlimited supply of fuel. The problem was that the built-in fuel tanks were set low in the water—below the water line, making siphoning from them into the trawler's tanks impossible without a pump. He looked around and saw a dozen boats in the marina's small yard, blocked up and on the hard. They would be easy prey for anyone with empty fuel tanks and a garden hose.

It wasn't hard to rationalize his decision. Lives were clearly in jeopardy, and doing nothing wasn't an option. Promising himself that he would reimburse the owners later, he returned to the *Ghost Runner* and told Trufante his plan.

"Hot damn, a Cajun credit card," he said, holding up the hose.

Siphoning was slow work. It would take too long to fill the tanks from a single boat. Using the two eighty-gallon bladders he had aboard, they could pull fuel from two vessels at once. He would only be able to partially fill them; empty, the bladders were simply heavy; full, they would weigh over six hundred pounds—each.

Mac ran to the office, where he saw a pile of wheelbarrows used by the boaters to load gear and ice. Placed that way to weather the storm, he grabbed two off the top of the stack, returned to the trawler and loaded a bladder in each. He and Trufante picked their victims, and several minutes later, they were both siphoning fuel.

Mac checked the bladder in his wheelbarrow, which was close to half-full; it would be ungainly , but he figured he and Tru could move three hundred pounds each. Stopping the flow, he capped off the rubber tank. Since the bladder was already in the wheelbarrow, he folded the sides in, trying to balance the weight. Even then, it moved awkwardly across the dock, directed more by the weight of the sloshing fuel than by Mac's efforts to correct it. He found that slower was better and made it to the trawler. Trufante was already waiting with his wheelbarrow, and with Pamela's help, they were able to wrestle one bladder onto the deck. Wiping sweat from his eyes, Mac wasted no time in loading the other tank. Within a few minutes, both were lying on the cockpit deck, releasing their fuel into the *Ghost Runner's* tanks. While they emptied, he made some quick calculations. To reach the Dry Tortugas and get back with any kind of margin for error, they would have to repeat the procedure several times.

While the third round was dumping into the trawler's tanks, Mac looked around for Ned and saw him hurrying down the dock. He came aboard, and Mac looked around to see if they were ready. "Let's go," Mac said, helping Trufante release the last of the fuel in the hose back to the donor vessel.

He checked his phone on the way out of the marina, taking the wheel from Trufante just as they passed the last marker. He'd often found it was easier to think when he was doing something. He pulled up the same route he had used only yesterday, and, still with no idea what to do when he got there, started toward Fort Jefferson.

A WAVE of satisfaction swept over Kurt when he saw the twin motors smoking. After a frustrating night, he had finally accomplished something. Now, he just needed Bugarra to lead him to Justine and Allie. Mac's boat had swung around and was about to pass on its way out of the channel. He raised the gun over his head, both in victory and to wish them luck. If he failed, they would have to come through with the treasure to save Allie and Justine. There was little doubt in his mind after the past few minutes that Bugarra would up his game.

The trawler disappeared around the corner, and Kurt turned his attention to Bugarra. The Yellowfin was disabled and drifting toward one of the docks. With the tide helping, Kurt waited until the boat touched the dock and Bugarra stepped off before running back to the car.

Kurt saw Bugarra a minute later standing in the shade of a large metal building. He was talking on the phone, and Kurt eased closer, hoping to hear. By the time he reached a suitable spot to listen, Bugarra had disconnected. He stood there for several minutes watching the road until, finally, a pink cab appeared. Kurt recognized the driver and smiled. Mac had sent Sonar's number over earlier, and Kurt opened the message app on his phone to find it.

Calling was out of the question. Her wrong reaction, or Bugarra overhearing anything, would put her in jeopardy. Kurt quickly composed a text asking her to let him know where she had dropped Bugarra off.

Once the cab was out of sight, he ran to the car and drove back to Key West. Traffic was picking up as residents returned home, and it took three lights to get through the intersection at Roosevelt. As he waited, the adrenaline rush from shooting out the motors started to drain from his body, and Kurt's anxiety level started to rise. He had already lost them at the light, and if Sonar didn't return his text, it would all have been for nothing.

Finally, he was able to make his way through the intersection. With a map of Key West open on his phone, he followed Roosevelt until it turned into Truman at First, where he turned left and headed toward the interior of the island, figuring the more centrally located he was when Sonar gave him the drop-off location, the faster he could get there. He had just accelerated when the phone vibrated on his lap. With vehicles riding his bumper, he pulled over to read the text.

Sonar had sent an address. He thanked her, then clicked the

link. The directions from his location quickly appeared, and he tried to control his breathing during the short drive to the Casa Marina Hotel. Pulling up under the porte-cochere, he stashed the rifle under the back seat, grabbed his Glock, and headed to the entrance. Dodging two large potted plants that had blown over, he reached for the door handle. He entered the lobby, trying to compose himself, but still felt his heart pound as he approached the front desk, pulling out his credentials. Martinez hadn't responded to his request for leave, which meant he was still officially working, but either way, he knew he could get fired for what he was about to do.

Placing his badge and ID on the counter, he got the attention of the clerk, and asked for Bugarra's room. A look of indecision crossed the young woman's tired face, and Kurt realized he needed to back off. "It's pertaining to a case. Just a few questions for him."

"I can ring him for you, sir," she said.

Kurt knew she was doing her best to protect a valued guest. Asking for a manager might end with the same result, or worse, they would call Kurt's office. Looking at the counter, he noticed the large keypad on the phone; he would be able to see the number she punched in.

"Okay, that would be great."

He watched as she pressed the three-digit room number, and just before it connected, he stopped her. "Maybe, on second thought, I'll email him," he said. The girl nodded, obviously relieved, and Kurt quickly left the lobby and returned to the car. After moving it around the building to a parking space near the back corner and out of sight, he looked for a service entrance, but found only an emergency exit that was locked from the inside. To his left was a fence; after checking for witnesses, he used the hood of a car as a foothold, pulled himself over, and landed inside the hotel grounds. The room number was 202, so

Kurt headed for the second floor. He choose not to use the elevator, instead taking the stairs two at a time. He had just turned down the hall when a door opened.

Kurt found himself standing face to face with Vince Bugarra.

THIRTY-THREE

JUSTINE COULD FEEL THE BLOOD POUNDING IN HER EARS AS she waited and worked out her plan. Finally, the second man returned with a bag of food from a convenience store. Her heart dropped when she saw that he had disregarded her request for the personal items, but, after taking a ribbing from his partner, he pulled a small bag from the larger one, handing it to her. Now she just needed to make the plan work.

She thanked the men and after giving Allie a reassuring nod, took the bag to the bathroom. Once inside, she locked the door and breathed deeply. Now that she could take action, she felt better. Taking out the rubbing alcohol and tampons, she quickly filled one of the hotel glasses with alcohol, then pushed the tampons out of their applicators into the alcohol. They quickly soaked up the fluid, and she decided to go big, and added some more alcohol and another tampon.

An ignition source was her problem, but she'd had hours to work out the details. Earlier, she had seen a complimentary grooming kit in the bathroom; she now opened it and took out the nail clippers. The cord to the hairdryer proved surprisingly tough to cut, and she started to worry if the men outside were getting suspicious as she hacked away at the rubber coating. Finally, she saw the copper wires and stripped them of the remaining insulation.

She set the wires down, removed the alcohol-soaked tampons from the cup, and set them on a towel. After taking a deep breath, she was ready, and picked up the cord. With the insulation removed, she found it easy to separate the two wires. Holding them apart with one hand, she inserted the plug in the outlet and, being careful not to touch the ends together, took one wire in each hand. Leaning over the towel, she held one wire on a tampon, then touched it with the other.

The spark blinded her temporarily. The room went dark when the circuit breaker tripped, and the next few seconds seemed like an eternity. Finally, she saw a small blue dot that started to brighten and ignite. Surprised by the intensity of the flame, she smiled.

With no idea how long it would take for the alcohol to burn off, she reached for the door and cracked it open. Holding the tampons by the strings, she pushed through the door.

"Allie, let's go," she said.

The room was very dark. With the light from the burning tampons, Justine was able to see that only one man remained. The other must have gone to get maintenance to reset the breaker. Allie reacted quickly, and Justine handed her one of the tampons, then tossed the other at the man.

The man was taken by surprise and flinched as the tampon hit him in the face.

"Get the gun," Justine said.

Allie hesitated, and the man started to move. Justine slid around behind him and, once in his blind spot, held the burning tampon to his neck. He screamed in pain. She had hoped he would drop to the floor and submit, but he fought back, sweeping his arms wildly, causing her to drop the burning tampon.

"Allie. Now!"

Allie snapped out of her daze and lunged for the pistol. Justine had been on the fence about Kurt teaching his daughter to shoot, but now Justine appreciated it, as Allie came into a shooter's stance, pointing the barrel at the man. He raised his hands, and the escapees bolted through the door. Leading Allie down the corridor, Justine looked around for the other man and decided on heading the opposite direction from which they had entered.

It was a typical hotel layout, the walkway to the left mirroring the one to the right with a stairway at each end. Deciding to go right, they reached the bottom of the stairs. She saw a potential problem when the two exit paths, after weaving around several landscaped areas, merged, before going through a breezeway to the lobby. It was a classic pinch point. She could see the chain-link fence with razor wire just outside the landscaped perimeter. In the land of many homeless, these types of security measures were common to keep the indigent population from setting up camp. Climbing the fence would both slow them down and prevent anyone from seeing them. Instead, she decided to go through the lobby. The sooner they were seen by anyone outside Bugarra and his men, the better.

Turning back to the walkway, she started to lead Allie toward the lobby when a figure emerged through the breezeway. Startled, she pulled Allie back behind a large sago palm and waited. Justine saw that the girl's pupils were dilated and she was breathing quickly.

"Breath, girl. You're doing great," Justine said, squeezing Allie's shoulder.

From Justine's vantage point, the man's gait looked familiar, but she couldn't see any of his features. Thinking it was just the adrenaline racing through her system playing tricks on her, she was about to move back onto the path when she realized who it was.

The second thug was alone and looked angry. He was moving quickly, as if he knew something was wrong. But he was focused on getting upstairs, and not on what was in front of him. Justine and Allie froze, staying low and using the landscaping for cover. He walked right by them. Justine waited until he had climbed the first set of stairs; as soon as his back was facing them, she pulled Allie out of the bushes and ran toward the lobby.

Before they reached the double glass door and freedom, she heard a man call out from above. Recognizing the voice, she looked up and saw Kurt on the second-floor breezeway. Her fear turned to joy when she saw him, but the moment was short-lived as she stepped into the open to call out to him. Just before she opened her mouth, she saw Bugarra appear from a doorway behind Kurt.

Kurt had a pistol in his right hand, but Bugarra had a gun as well. His arm started to rise. Somehow, she had to let Kurt know not only that Bugarra was behind him, but that she and Allie had escaped. She felt Allie squeeze her arm when Bugarra raised his weapon.

Allie jumped out from the cover of the breezeway and raised the pistol. Kurt saw her and froze. Justine reacted without thinking. An instinct deep within her wanted to protect Allie, and she reached for her, but Allie resisted, fighting to keep the weapon pointed at Bugarra.

"No, there's another way," Justine said.

Just as she said it, she reached for the gun, and it fired.

Bugarra's aim snapped back to them. Justine looked up at the breezeway and saw only one man standing. Allie saw, too.

"Dad, oh my God! Dad, are you okay?" Allie called, running out from the cover of a column, where Justine had pushed her.

Justine knew it didn't matter if they were seen. She had to know as well. "Kurt?"

"I'm okay," he called down.

He didn't sound okay, and Justine and Allie both knew it. "Let me help him," Justine called to Bugarra.

"Both of you, upstairs, now," he replied. "Drop that gun and take it slow. Let me see your hands the whole time."

Bugarra ordered his henchman to retrieve the gun and escort them upstairs. Justine had to hold Allie back. She didn't want her to race to her dad and risk Bugarra's fury. With the thug's gun at their backs, they started to climb to the second floor. Justine reached the landing first and saw Kurt on the ground clutching his leg. A pool of blood spread under his thigh, and her first instinct was to run toward him, but with Bugarra's gun trained on her, she knew she'd better ask first.

"Let me take care of him."

"Get a blanket and haul him in the room," Bugarra ordered the other man, who had just emerged from the room they had been held in. He had a towel around his neck and scowled at Justine as he passed.

Justine and Allie both ran to Kurt. He was still conscious, but there was a faraway look in his eyes. Working forensics, Justine had seen a lot of dead bodies. Kurt, probably in shock, looked like he was close. Stopping the bleeding was the first priority. Once they were inside, she could have a better look at the wound. Removing her belt, she made a tourniquet around Kurt's thigh and cinched it tight. The man appeared with the blanket, and Justine wasted no time laying it next to Kurt. Together, she and the man rolled Kurt onto it and, being as gentle as they could, pulled him into the room.

"In the bathroom. I don't want them charging me for blood-stains," Bugarra said, as he closed the door.

MAC DECIDED to stay at the helm and run the boat himself, rather than let the autopilot do the work. He needed to think, and the routine tasks of checking course, fuel, and the gauges occupied his conscious mind, allowing his subconscious to work. He'd been around Ned and Wood long enough to know that there was something to the Van Doren story. Firsthand accounts were usually the best one could hope for, and the journal appeared to be just that. It rang true to Mac.

Ned's history of the fort had only added to the layers of confusion Mac felt as he steered toward the Marquesas. Van Doren's journal was dated 1822. The fort, built in the middle decades of the 1800s, could very easily have been built on top of the cache, or it could be on one of the other six keys in the archipelago. If Van Doren were on the run from Lafitte, as the journal said, the Tortugas were an unlikely spot to stop. Mac wasn't sure when the original name, given by Ponce de Leon for the abundance of turtles in the area, was amended to include *Dry*, but it had been done for a reason.

As he veered away from the treacherous waters of the Quicksands, it suddenly came to him. If Van Doren were a shrewd captain—and from his writing, it appeared that he was to some extent educated—the Tortugas might have been the perfect spot. The reason the fort had been built there—despite the inhospitable conditions was its strategic importance. In those days, with the U.S. trying to eliminate piracy from its waters, Van Doren would have stayed north, hoping Lafitte would shy away from the Navy that had recently removed him from Galveston. Taking the northern route would have likely brought Van Doren within sight of the islands.

Mac was starting to believe there was something to the story, but the question remained—Where could the treasure be hidden? He had the feeling that Mel was on a wild goose chase, but at least he knew she was safe. His thoughts turned briefly to Kurt and his family, and Mac noticed he had eased off on the throttle and increased speed.

"How much further?" Pamela asked.

Mac looked down at the chartplotter. "We're about halfway. Maybe an hour and a half."

"We need to go faster. Something's happened. I can feel it."

He had known her long enough not to dispute her claim, and he instinctively reached into his pocket for his phone. He wondered about his knee-jerk reaction to something going wrong was to check his phone. Not too long ago, he never turned it on. Now it was attached to him. He tried to rationalize it as a necessary tool as he opened the main screen and saw there was no service. Not a surprise. He knew the signal from the cell towers only reached about six miles offshore. What surprised him was the uncomfortable feeling he had not been connected. In the past, he'd welcomed being off the grid, and he wondered where he had gone wrong.

Now was not the time to fix that, and he stashed the phone and checked their position. The Quicksands were behind them now, and Rebecca Shoal, where they had parbuckled the Yellowfin, lay ahead. As they passed the light, Mac wondered how much simpler this might be if they hadn't tried to salvage the boat.

There was something magnetic about making landfall after a passage, and Pamela and Trufante both came up behind him as the fort came into view. Standing proudly above the horizon, the other islands were just dark marks on the water, and Mac wondered how the same scene looked to Van Doren before the fort existed.

It's important to know who you're dealing with. The rabbi's words echoed in his head. It was a reminder of something he already knew: In order to find something, the thought process of the person who hid the thing was often more important than the clues. Using this premise, Mac turned to the west. He wanted to come up on the Tortugas the same way Van Doren had.

He felt Pamela grab his shoulder for support as he made the turn. Trufante was steadier on a boat than on land, and his sea legs easily adjusted to the course change.

"Where are we going?" Pamela asked.

"I want to see this the way Van Doren did. We'll head to the west, turn, and come back." Mac studied the chartplotter, trying to find the route that a nineteenth-century sloop would have used. Zooming in on the area around the fort, he saw just how complicated the passage was, even with his electronics. Almost two hundred years ago, unless you knew how to find the channel, it would be deadly.

THIRTY-FOUR

JUSTINE HAD STOPPED THE BLEEDING. FOR THE TIME BEING, Kurt was not critical, but he badly needed a doctor. There was no exit wound; the bullet was embedded in his thigh. Fortunately, the bullet seemed to have missed the femoral artery. Using torn pieces of the hotel towels, she continued to work on the wound; she had cleaned it with the remaining rubbing alcohol, used the rest of the tampons to absorb the blood, and bound it with a towel. Though Allie had been brave during the escape attempt, now, with the shot having coming from a gun in her hand, tears streaked down her face as she sat against the tub with Kurt's head in her lap.

"You didn't do it. It was my fault," Justine said.

"That doesn't make it any better," Allie said.

Justine knew there was nothing she could do now except continue to search for an opportunity to escape and provide whatever medical help she could to Kurt. She did curse the bad timing that had brought Kurt to their rescue at exactly the same moment she and Allie had tried to escape. Justine both loved him more for coming to rescue them, and was mad that now they were all Bugarra's captives.

"He's going to be okay," Justine said to Allie. She saw the muscles in Kurt's arm flex as he squeezed Allie's hand.

"What are we going to do?" Allie took a section of towel and started to clean her face.

Justine knew how resilient she was. "Remember that place in your head you were when we walked out that door?"

Allie nodded.

"You need to go back there. This isn't the time to wallow in self-pity."

"I know that, but who else is going to find us?"

"Mac Travis is out there."

"I thought Dad said that he had gone after the treasure?"

Kurt had quietly given Justine an update while she cleaned and bandaged his wound.

"What time is it?" he asked.

Justine turned the watch on his left hand over. It was almost five.

"Mac is supposed to update Bugarra at six."

She looked through the partially opened door at Bugarra, who sat on the edge of the bed, typing on his phone. He had turned out to be as careful as he was flamboyant, which led her to believe that his public persona was fabricated; inside was a different, darker man. She guessed it had taken the pressure of a hurricane bearing down on them for Bugarra to drop the facade. Now that his true nature was exposed, he was even more dangerous.

Working for Miami-Dade was like continuing education for Justine. Every day she was faced with new problems, from the evidence and the people. She had heard the detectives talking about how people snapped, then became remorseful. She hoped that was what Bugarra was going through. If he was, she intended to turn it to her advantage. They had almost escaped, but she knew it wasn't likely to happen again with Kurt injured. She needed to think of another way out.

"We're going to need supplies," she called out, slowly releasing the tourniquet. Kurt started bleeding again, and she placed another large towel under his leg. He looked up at her, and, seeing the pained look on his face, almost had to look away. Once the towel was saturated with blood, she retightened the tourniquet, stood, and held up the towel.

"We've got to get him some help or he's going to bleed out. He might even be paralyzed." The last was an overstatement. One of the first things she had done after basic first aid had been to check for feeling in his toes. Drops of blood fell from the towel onto the tile floor as Justine watched Bugarra process the information. He was in deep, probably much deeper than he had wanted to be, but desperate people were hard to predict.

"There's a line between kidnapping and murder." She had nothing to lose. It was all she could do to hold her tongue while he processed everything Though Bugarra was a big guy, she suspected he was the bully type who avoided physical confrontations. She'd assessed the situation and decided that while she might be quicker, he was a big man, and the pistol still lay within his easy reach. There was little chance she could reach him before he grabbed it.

"Do you want him to bleed out on the floor?" Justine said.

That, at least, got a reaction. Bugarra walked into the bathroom. Justine backed away just enough for him to see the blood-soaked towels.

He turned away. "Get him ready to move."

Knowing they would be leaving gave Justine hope, and she smiled at Allie, trying to reassure the girl that she was happy with the development. Once they were out of the hotel room, there would be a much better chance for Justine to engineer an escape.

THEY HAD MADE it to Fort Jefferson. Now Mac faced the challenge of swaying the park service director to his side in case help was needed in the search. Mac also hoped that Farnsworth knew that Bugarra had kidnapped Justine and Allie and was seventy miles away. Mac had sensed disdain, or even dislike, when he had been interviewed earlier, and was sure that Farnsworth had been bribed by Bugarra. He could only hope the distance and urgency of the situation would affect the director. Mac wondered if he was the right person to approach the career bureaucrat. If Mel was here, she would have been the natural choice. Trufante and Pamela were out, so Mac turned to Ned. "Think you can talk to the director? I didn't exactly hit it off with him."

"One of these days, you'll learn a little finesse," Ned replied. "It's an improvement, though—ten years ago, you would have stormed the fort with a flare gun."

Mac held his tongue, knowing Ned was right. It had taken a few decades for Mac to think before he acted. "His name's Farnsworth."

"Well, are you going to take me over to the dock, or make me swim?"

Mac idled the boat to an empty slip at the park service dock. "Maybe I should go with you."

"Maybe you should trust an old man. Stand by on channel seventy-two," Ned said, climbing over the gunwale, and stepping gingerly onto the wooden dock.

Ned's pride was evident as he struggled to get his land legs. He wavered slightly, and Mac almost went after him, but held back. It took until Ned reached the edge of the dock before Mac thought the old man could pass a sobriety test, but once he hit dry land, he walked straight and proud. As Ned walked away, Mac went into the cabin to get a bottle of water and saw the folder containing the copies of Van Doren's journal. When he brought it out onto the deck, Pamela and Trufante began eyeing the papers. If he was going to find the treasure, he needed to get into Van Doren's head, and to do that, he needed to be alone. Turning his gaze to the fort, Mac wondered if there was any trouble Trufante could get in on an island in the middle of nowhere. The fact that there was no alcohol for sale persuaded him to cut the Cajun some slack. "Go ashore if you like. Just stay close."

Trufante wasted no time in hopping onto the dock, and looking back at Pamela. She didn't seem quite as excited as he did, but followed. Mac watched them walk away, and as they approached the moat, Ned entered the sally port. Taking one last look around, Mac checked the VHF, then sat in the captain's chair with his feet resting on the wheel.

Van Doren's writing was archaic, but he appeared to have been a literate man. Mac had seen plenty of old documents that were almost impossible to read. At least Van Doren's was legible. Mac thumbed through the pages, then started at the beginning, soon becoming fascinated with the story:

I knew Lafitte was too shrewd to give us a fast boat. The worm-eaten hull of the ship he had offered was a guarantee that we would not or could not flee. What he had underestimated was the determination of myself and our crew. Rhames and the others left from Gasparilla's men despised Lafitte, partly for the heritage that bound he and I together, and now he had attempted to double-cross me, someone he had once called brother.

It seemed, at least for the present time, that even the weather was in our favor, and the ship ran in front of the wind. What she lacked in maintenance, she had in sail, and with every scrap we could find pushing us forward, we were making good time. What we didn't have were guns. Promising the protection of the two schooners that now trailed behind us, Lafitte had stripped the ship of anything we could use that didn't interfere with the recovery of the treasure in our holds.

I stood next to Mason, who was by the binnacle studying the charts showing the water that lay ahead. We were heading back into familiar territory now, and we both looked for anything that could aid our escape.

When I had first seen her, I noticed that the ship rode low in the water. In an effort to improve the trim and gain more speed, we decided to dump the ballast and bring the treasure into the bilge. Having used the cover of ballast stones before to hide the silver we had recovered from the wreck of the Ten Sail in the Cayman Islands, we hoped to lighten the load.

I left Mason and grabbed Rhames and several of the freedmen. We went below and, forming a chain, started bringing up the ballast stones and replacing them with the treasure. Saving a layer of rock to conceal what lay below, we soon felt much lighter, and I could see from the old water line that we had risen a good foot.

Back on deck, I saw the effort had gained us a knot or two of speed. That was well and good, but we were without a destination. Our plans had been to sail to Panama and cross the Isthmus, hoping to lose the label of pirate that had been plaguing us since the U.S. Navy sank the Floridablanca, and Gasparilla with her. But heading into the unknown waters of Central America in this ship was not a good idea.

Our safe haven for the last year had been Great Inagua. It was in exactly the opposite direction of where we wanted to go, but I knew our old ship the Cayman would likely be there. We were also in good favor with Potts, the governor, whom we had helped ascend to his current post from his position as the clerk for the corrupt governor of the Caymans. I also knew Lafitte would *be wary about leaving the gulf waters and entering the eastern Caribbean.*

Plotting our course on the chart, I saw that the Tortugas lay in our path—another boon, as we knew those shoal-ridden waters. I could only hope the captains of the ships behind us didn't.

Mac could not have been more drawn in if it was a best-selling adventure novel.

When he finished reading, Mac put the papers down and stared out at the water. Somewhere within the range of his vision, Van Doren had hidden his treasure.

Before Mac could continue reading, Ned's voice came over the VHF. Mac picked up the microphone to answer, only to hear Farnsworth order Mac to stand down and surrender himself.

Mac turned off the radio without answering, started the engines, and tossed the dock lines. Backing out of the slip, he saw several uniformed park service employees hustling out of the sally port. Mac had learned from Kurt that the NPS had no jurisdiction outside the park boundaries, so he wasted no time and spun the wheel, heading toward open water.

The pages of Van Doren's journal rustled in the wind, and just before they scattered across the waves, Mac grabbed them and stuck them in the compartment below the wheel. He looked back, seeing the park service men running toward the dock, and a minute later smoke rose from one of their boats as the engines started. The soft-sided twin engine was coming after him. There was no point in estimating the speed of the boat. As soon as it came up on plane, he knew it would catch him.

The only question—how quickly?

THIRTY-FIVE

IGNORING THE JARRING OF THE CHOPPY SEAS, MAC PUSHED the throttle to its stop in an effort to reach the park boundary. He looked back often to check on the park service vessel in pursuit, and couldn't help but sympathize with what Van Doren must have felt with Lafitte's men chasing him through these same waters. The instruments had changed, the boats had changed, these were different times, but the waters and shoals were the same as in the nineteenth century. The pages might reveal the secret, but as the boat slammed into the waves, there was no way to decipher it.

Mac saw the park service's RIB boat struggling with the head seas and spun the wheel slightly to starboard, changing his course to go directly into the waves. Taking a slight angle was preferable both for speed and comfort, but he saw the inflatable slow as the soft bow had to fight through each wave, while his steel hull sliced easily through them.

Slowly, he started to pull away from them. Checking his position in real time on the chartplotter gave Mac an advantage that Van Doren didn't have. He was in the southeast channel now, moving quickly toward the boundary line. Boundaries ashore were often based on landmarks, such as rivers or mountains. There was nothing to tell him he was safe here except the dotted line on his screen. With what he had seen of Farnsworth and his crew, Mac worried that they would not respect the boundary.

Mac knew the park service could call the Coast Guard or the Florida Fish and Wildlife Commission for either permission or help. He was banking on both agencies still either being shut down or in emergency response mode. Looking down, he saw the red line was underneath the icon of the boat on the screen, but he was in no position to relax. Checking the gauges, he kept the engine red-lined and crossed into federal waters.

He had to make a decision. Running only saved himself. It had been a gut reaction and probably the right one at the time. There was nothing he could do for Kurt and his family from inside a cell. Now, he was free, if at large, and needed to figure out how to help his friends.

Something was nagging at him from the earlier pages in Van Doren's journal. There were several entries from before the chase, describing how they had recovered the sunken treasure. After training as a commercial diver and spending a half-dozen years working on oil rigs in the Gulf of Mexico, Mac had an interest in the origins and history of diving. What Van Doren had described using appeared to be some of the most innovative techniques of the time.

Diving bells had been around in one form or another since Aristotle. Advances were made over the years, but none were widely publicized, as they gave an advantage in warfare, as well as salvage, to the country that used them. Van Doren, working independently, had used some of those innovations. He started to wonder if his original assumption was wrong. Maybe Van Doren had stashed the cache underwater, where only he could recover it?

The red line on the screen was clearly behind the boat now, and with GPS tracking on, Mac would have a record of the crossing. That didn't stop him from wanting a little more water between him and the park service boat, and he continued for another mile before dropping speed and looking behind him. The inflatable seemed to be hovering around the line, as if daring him to come back and cross it. He switched the radio back on and set it to channel nineteen, one of the stations assigned to law enforcement. He heard no communication between the park service and any other agency. Relaxing his grip on the wheel, he changed course to the south, putting the seas on the front quarter of the trawler, instead of directly ahead. The boat immediately responded and settled into the easier line.

Mac was going nowhere, and he knew it. He was on the perfect platform to recover the treasure—if he could only find it. In addition to fishing, the *Ghost Runner* was set up to dive and salvage. It lacked only mailboxes, the large pipes that treasure hunters used to blow sand off the bottom. Mac had gotten around that by using a high-pressure raw-water pump and several fire hoses. It wasn't as easy as dropping the huge pipes and running the props, but it was equally as effective. The only problem was that he needed a crew.

Trufante, for all his problems, knew the equipment and procedures. Being only a few miles away put his resume on the top of the pile. Getting him aboard without going to jail himself was a problem, and Mac swung his gaze to where the park service boat had been. With seas running four feet, from this distance they blocked his sight angle. Switching the right-hand screen from the depth finder to radar, he zoomed in and quickly located the boat. It was still sitting where he had last seen it at the park line.

Knowing they were in a standoff if the park service boat had radar and was tracking him, he took a chance, recalling Kurt complaining several times about how the feds were reluctant to spend their budget on equipment. He changed course to the northwest and, still staying outside of the red line, started to work his way behind Loggerhead Key. He kept one eye on the radar and, seeing the icon of the park service boat remain static, set a course that would put him just behind the narrow island, both out of sight and beyond the park boundary.

He would have to wait a few hours for darkness before he could enter park waters and find Trufante, but that would give him the time he needed to finish reading the journal. Mac had Van Doren's voice in his head, and he was sure if he continued to read about the escape, he could find the treasure.

JUSTINE CHECKED Kurt's vital signs and bandage. He was feverish and in pain, but lucid, and Justine updated him in a muted whisper while Allie used her body to strategically shield them from Bugarra. It was important, if they had any chance of escape, that they keep up the illusion that though Kurt needed medical attention, he was in worse shape than he really was. Justine had been trained as a first responder, and she was careful to layer everything she said to Bugarra in medical jargon. So far, he had bought it.

Looking over Allie's shoulder, Justine could see that he was on the phone, though she couldn't hear the conversation. He disconnected, stood up, and came toward them.

"Get him ready," Bugarra said. "We have to go."

"He needs a doctor."

"It looks like he's doing just fine. Take some extra towels if you want, but we're out of here now."

Justine scowled at him, grabbed the towel strips she had

torn, and asked Allie to bring the two remaining clean towels. Bugarra made a move to lift Kurt, but Justine intercepted him and, with Allie's assistance, helped him up. The first few steps were a struggle until Kurt discovered how much weight he could put on his injured leg. Justine was pleased when she saw how well he could walk, but silently encouraged his limp.

Even though the lobby was empty, shattering Justine's hope that they would be seen, Bugarra glanced back impatiently several times until they were finally outside. With every step, Justine was looking for a way out, but nothing had presented itself.

"Give me his keys," Bugarra said.

Justine thought they might have caught a break, but after Bugarra showed her the barrel of the gun hidden in his jacket, she reached into Kurt's pocket and came out with her keys. Hitting the lock function to beep it, she found her car and led them toward it.

"Can you drive?" Justine said to Allie in a commanding tone that implied an order, not a question. Several scenarios had already played out in Justine's mind. She had caught both Bugarra and Allie off guard. Allie answered yes enthusiastically. Justine couldn't blame her; the ink was still wet on the sixteen-year-old's license.

Bugarra directed Allie to the driver's seat after she helped Justine load Kurt into the backseat. Bugarra was in the front, sitting sideways. There was nothing Justine could do unless Allie read her mind, and as careful as the new driver was behind the wheel, Justine doubted that was going to happen. Without revealing his destination, Bugarra began giving Allie directions.

They turned left onto Atlantic, and when the signs for the airport appeared, he asked her to turn in. Justine couldn't figure out where they could possibly be flying to, until he had Allie pull into the FBO lot and Justine saw the seaplanes.

It had all started at Fort Jefferson, and she supposed that was where it would end. The problem was Kurt, but heading to the fort had its benefits that Bugarra might have overlooked. If she could attract the attention of the park service personnel there, surely they would take care of one of their own.

Justine and Allie helped Kurt up the narrow steel stairs to the plane and got him settled in a seat. A few minutes later, the pilot, a different man than had flown them down a few days ago, stepped aboard and closed the door. Justine had hoped it would be Gary, who knew them from the earlier flight. He would have figured out what was going on and helped them. The new pilot acted familiar around Bugarra—not a good sign. Justine resigned herself to waiting until they reached the fort before taking any action.

It had been a different set of circumstances, almost a mini-vacation, when she had taken the trip before, and she remembered staring out at the water below. There was nothing to be gained by forcing the plane down, if she could have even attempted that. She squeezed Kurt's hand. He responded in kind, allowing her the freedom to close her eyes. Since there was nothing she could do for the next forty-five minutes, she knew whatever rest she could get would benefit her later.

She jostled awake when the plane banked on its approach. Leaning across the aisle, she checked Kurt, who appeared to be okay. Her stomach bounced into her throat when the plane began descending, and when she looked out the window, she saw the last of the sunlight illuminating the whitecaps beneath them. The landing had been scary on relatively flat seas earlier, and now she gripped the armrests as the pilot eased the plane on top of the first wave.

The pontoons hit the water hard, and the plane skidded across the crest of a wave and into a trough. She thought they were going to flip when one pontoon lifted, but the tapered edges of the pontoon gained some traction and settled back in. She looked over at Kurt, who was wincing in pain as the boat slammed into each wave. Finally, the plane slowed, and she breathed out and sucked in the stale cabin air. She was already nauseated, and the short taxi to the beach proved to be harder than the actual landing. She greedily gulped the fresh air when the plane finally came to a stop and the pilot opened the door.

There was no time to recover, as Bugarra again showed the pistol hidden under his light jacket and motioned with his head for them to exit the plane. With an arm around Kurt, Justine helped him out the door, making sure that he had solid footing on the pontoon before she guided him to the beach. Allie came to help after deplaning, and the trio stood staring at the door, wondering what Bugarra was going to do.

He exited the plane and had them walk ahead of him into the fort, where he turned into the director's office. Justine had been banking on the park service seeing Kurt's injury and protecting him, but as they entered the office behind Bugarra, she observed the familiar way the two men greeted each other. The director barely looked at Kurt as he led them to an interior office. Once inside, her nausea returned after just one breath of the stale, clammy air.

The feeling only got worse when he shut the door and threw the bolt.

THIRTY-SIX

Mac sat back and started reading again.

We sailed through the night, finding ourselves off the western tip of Cuba as the sun rose. There had been no rest for me or the crew, as it took all hands to keep the ship running at her best speed. Daylight showed Lafitte's two ships still behind us. We hadn't lost them, but neither had we given up ground. The wind had been in our favor to this point, but there were some high clouds that told me it was going to change. As soon as it did, the schooners in pursuit would have an advantage. Something would have to happen before that. Mason and I plotted our position and course on the chart, both agreeing that the Tortugas was still our best chance to lose Lafitte's men.

Mason had shown me a fuzzy area of the map. He said there was a narrow channel running through, and thought that if we could maintain our advantage and reach it before the wind changed, there would be a good chance at least one of Lafitte's ships would run aground there.

Rhames was with us now, and I asked if there was anything at all we could use for a weapon aboard. He replied that a keg of nails, the diving bell, and the chain rode for the anchor were the only things that were even steel.

An idea came to me that with the chain, it might be possible to rig a boom across the channel. Then we wouldn't have to worry about the pursuing ships finding the channel and not running aground. Our problem was time. With Lafitte's ships less than a mile back, we would only have about a quarter of an hour to rig it, not enough time to fix both ends. After much discussion, we came up with a plan to use the ship as one end of the boom and use the diving bell filled with gold as the other. Shayla and the men had been distressed about my decision to drop the gold we had just recovered back into the sea, but my logic prevailed. After jettisoning our ballast earlier, we needed the weight of the gold to hold the bell in place and knew if the boom failed, we could retrieve it later, as long as it was dropped on some kind of landmark.

Finally, it was agreed. With Mason at the helm, Rhames and I took every able body to run out the chain and free it from the anchor. Laid out on the deck, it spanned two lengths of the ship. The bell was loaded and wrapped in a cargo net. With the ship listing to starboard due to its weight, I had no doubt it would serve its purpose. I only hoped we would be able to recover it as I'd promised. Rhames rigged a block and tackle from a stout spar off the main mast to lower it, and we went back to the chart table.

Mason estimated that we had an hour before we reached what he called the tongue, a feature that, although it wasn't present on the chart, he swore he knew. We dropped sail in order to lure Lafitte's ships closer and made the final preparations.

I watched Lafitte's ships close on our position from high in the rigging, which also gave me a good view of the ocean floor. Mason had said we would be running in between three and four fathoms, and the coral tongue rising ten feet from the bottom was *easily visible. I wanted to see it for myself, so we would be able to return and recover the bell and our treasure.*

Climbing back to the deck, I checked the block and tackle we had rigged to hoist the bell. I studied the chain, trying to antici-pate its route, and saw nothing on deck it could snag on. The list to port became even more noticeable when the men hoisted the bell and swung it over the side. We were ready.

I moved to the forepeak for a better view of the bottom and looked into the clear water. The man working the lead beside me had advised that we were in five fathoms, and the bottom showed the dark blotches I knew to be coral. Ahead was a white patch, and I called back to the crew to be ready. The coral seemed to narrow as we approached the deeper sand, and just before the bow was over the white bottom, I called for the bell to be dropped.

Rhames reached out and cut the rope with his knife, and the bell hit the water with a huge splash. It disappeared below the surface, and I watched the chain follow. I could see the trail leading back to the tongue-shaped section of coral. If we survived this, I was sure I could find it.

Mason steered off to port, and when the chain was played out, we ground to a halt with the bell acting as an anchor. The old ship creaked with the strain of the weight of the bell and chain pulling against the forward pressure of the sails, but I could see the chain taut in the water. Dropping some sail earlier had worked, and the two ships were closing.

Even though they were less than a quarter mile away, it seemed like an eternity. Rhames was correct, surmising that they wouldn't try and sink us with the treasure aboard, and no cannon fired on us, but I could see on deck the flurry of activity that indi-cated they were preparing to board us. The ship groaned again as Mason made a final adjustment to the boom, and I wondered if it would hold up to the collision that was only seconds away.

With a crash, the lead ship tore into the chain, dragging our ship stern first toward it. Rhames was ready and slammed a hammer into the pin holding the chain to the capstan, and our ship bounced back, almost reacting too much to the swing in momentum. Once we righted, I could see the first ship was done. The captain of the second ship steered hard to starboard to avoid colliding with the first, and a minute later I heard the sound of wood being torn apart. He was hard aground on the coral just outside the channel.

A cheer went up from our crew as we sailed away from the doomed ships and set course for Greater Inagua.

With Van Doren's description of the location, Mac opened up the chartplotter and studied the approach from Cuba. He saw it instantly. A reef running in the center of a narrow channel leading out of the Bird Key Anchorage.

There was no mistaking its shape as a tongue.

THIRTY-SEVEN

Mac had finally discovered what he thought was the location of Van Doren's cache. Of course, the fort had not been here back then, but the other islands would have looked the same. Whether he was right or not, he needed Trufante and Ned. Doing anything on the water was harder at night, and if it weren't for Kurt and his family, Mac would have checked it out himself during daylight. The light was fading quickly, and due to the urgency of the situation, Mac was willing to forego the difficulties and dive it tonight. If he was correct about the location, it might be possible to recover it as well, and for that, he needed help.

Bugarra wouldn't expect a night dive. Mac was sure the kidnapper was getting updates from Farnsworth, who would have told him that Mac had abandoned his crew and run. Mac could only hope Trufante, Pamela, and Ned didn't share that opinion and were waiting for him. Sitting behind Loggerhead Key, Mac had an advantage. He put away the journal after placing a waypoint on the location he had found from Van Doren's description, and as the sun started to set, he pulled the anchor and started to motor to the northeast.

His course led him away from the fort, as there was no such thing as a direct route here. Almost three miles of shoal-ridden water separated Loggerhead Key from Fort Jefferson. It would take more than twice that many miles to reach the northern channel without grounding. His choice to anchor on the backside of Loggerhead Key kept him out of the line of sight, but with shallow water extending almost a mile past the beach, it made it even longer to reach the fort.

He studied the water as he passed over the coral patches beneath him. Even in the dimming light, the reefs lying twenty feet below were visible, with some of the coral heads coming to within a few feet of the surface. It was nerve-racking enough transiting these waters with a depth finder and chartplotter to aid him; he could only imagine how Van Doren felt having only his eyes and some lead weights to guide the old wooden ship.

The water turned a dark blue, and Mac glanced down at the chartplotter, which confirmed he was in the southwest channel leading to Fort Jefferson. He had chosen this approach not only because it was closer, but because it was less visible from the fort.

Coming around the back side of the fort, he was soon able to see the steel pilings, all that remained of the old structure. Knowing it previously had been used as a deepwater dock, he'd planned to tie up to the closest piling and swim ashore to find Trufante. Mac didn't know where the Cajun would be, but that didn't bother him—Trufante was rarely invisible, and Mac hoped his crew would be watching for him.

Mac coasted to a stop, looking over his shoulder to make sure this was the best position. He tossed a loop over the piling and tied off the line. After checking the drift, he was able to drop a small anchor off the stern to both stop the swing caused by the tide and to allow him an easy jump to shore. This portion of the pier was just offshore of a small rectangle-shaped island created from the construction spoils. He dropped over the side and waded toward shore.

Water sloshed out of his boat shoes, but they saved his feet from the sharp coral. Climbing onto the island, he stayed low and worked his way through the labyrinth of both old and new construction materials. Several boat trailers were parked close to a small beach that led to the fort, and he briefly wondered what they were doing out here seventy miles from the closest road. Figuring the boat trailers had been brought across on the ferry, he let it go and used them to his advantage as he approached the old fort's crumbling brick walls. Crossing the small spit of land that connected the spoil island to Garden Key, where the fort sat, was the only approach where he wouldn't have to swim the moat. He had noticed how clear it was the other day, but now it was dark, and a moat was a moat. Too easy to imagine sharks cruising the perimeter of the fort with their cold, hungry eyes on him.

Looking for an access point to the fort, he couldn't help but notice how badly the saltwater environment had treated the old brick structure. The walls were in a state of major disrepair, and with a contractor's eye, he saw why. The large openings used to shoot the cannon had been originally designed with huge steel shutters. The steel supports, embedded several feet into each side of each opening, had rusted, and expanded over the years, causing the surrounding brickwork to fail. The mortar mixture used had long ago deteriorated, leaving some bricks loose enough to remove by hand. Mac used this to his advantage as he started to scale the fort walls.

After an easy climb to the first embrasure, he peered over the edge before crawling in. From here, he could see the dim outline of the hundreds of arches forming what were now open corridors, but once had held wooden doors, creating cells for the prisoners. The fort was dark, and he was able to move about easily without any fear of being seen. Reaching the interior section, he looked out on the parade ground. The pathways were illuminated with security lights, but he noticed many routes through the large, grassy area were dark. Most of the lights shone from the living quarters. Only one room in the fort itself had a light, and that appeared to be the office.

Standing there, he wondered where Trufante, Ned, and Pamela were. Ned was a problem. The old man, in his day, had been a strong worker and diver. Mac remembered many salvage jobs where, even in his sixties, Ned had pulled his weight. Now, probably close to eighty, he might not be up to what lay ahead of them. Even escaping the fort might be too much for him; what came after that would be even more taxing.

Looking out over the fort, Mac saw few signs of life, and his gaze drifted upward. The decorative beacon from the old lighthouse and the security lights couldn't begin to compete with the most magnificent skies he had ever witnessed. The Milky Way was so well defined that he could imagine himself inside it, like a starry snow globe. He'd seen many memorable skies at sea. Once you were out of sight of land, without the lights from shore to interfere, the stars reached all the way to the horizon. Here the heavens were even more brilliant.

A disembodied voice came to him as he watched, and at first Mac thought it floated from the sky. But then he heard a woman speak, and he recognized the voice as Pamela's. He followed it, and listened as she explained the constellations to Trufante. Staying to the seaward side of the corridors, Mac was able to remain in the shadows until he was close enough to see the outline of the two figures sitting side by side in one of the embrasures.

"Tru," Mac whispered as he got closer.

"Mac Travis," Pamela said. "I knew you would come."

He walked up to them, and when he could see out the opening, he stopped. The view from the interior of the fort was nothing compared to what lay before him.

"We seen you come up on the pile there," Trufante said. "Figured you'd find us before long."

With one problem solved, Mac stood behind them and told them what he had figured out from Van Doren's journals. "I want to dive it tonight and, if I'm right, salvage what we can."

Trufante rose and nodded. He extended a hand down for Pamela. She took it, and the three of them stood together.

"What about old man?" Trufante asked.

"This is going to be too much for him. I'd like to have his brain along, but his body won't hold up."

"He'd tell you different," Trufante said. "Old man's come in handy more than once."

Mac imagined how he would want to be treated, facing possibly his last adventure. He knew Trufante was right. Assuming Ned was in the living quarters, Mac decided that Pamela should fetch him. There was too much of a risk if Mac went, and Trufante looked suspicious just sitting on a barstool. Pamela hopefully could find Ned and bring him out. Mac explained what he wanted and told her where to meet them, then watched as she disappeared down the circular staircase and, a minute later, crossed the parade grounds. He waited until he saw her emerge with Ned, and then nodded to Trufante.

Staying to the shadows, they reached the meeting point a few minutes ahead of Ned and Pamela. When the pair arrived, Mac guided them back the way he had entered. They reached the embrasure, and he stayed behind to help Ned while Trufante and Pamela descended the decaying structure like cats. Ned went next, with a little help, then Mac dropped beside him.

Climbing down the walls turned out to be more difficult than the ascent, even without having to help Ned, who spat back every piece of advice Mac gave. Ned was unable to see the footholds, and kicked bricks loose as he scrambled down. Most fell into the water, splashing quietly before disappearing. A few fell onto the stacks of old debris with loud thunks that were definitely not natural sea sounds. With each fallen brick, they had to stop and listen. After they realized how unstable the structure was, they moved more carefully and reached the beach and waded to the trawler.

Mac pulled the anchor while Trufante went forward to retrieve the line around the piling. After stowing the anchor, Mac started the engines and idled forward so the lanky Cajun could retrieve the line. Once clear, Mac headed back toward Loggerhead Key.

BUGARRA WASN'T HAPPY. It was pretty apparent by now that, though the park ranger was not in good shape, he wasn't going to die or lose his leg. He and the two women were secure in the office, and Bugarra had Farnsworth's support. What Bugarra didn't know was where Travis was, and that troubled him.

Thinking the best way to find him would be through his mate or the old man, Bugarra had kept his eye on both since arriving. Ned had spent most of the day in the fort's archives and was now in his room. Trufante had spent most of the day in his room and was now sitting up in the old fort with his woman.

Bugarra could just make out their silhouettes in a moonlit embrasure, when suddenly a third figure approached them. After a few seconds, they all disappeared.

Bugarra sprinted across the parade grounds. Looking around, he saw a two people walking toward the opening, but neither looked like Travis or his mate. Of them, there was no sign. Bugarra approached the dark opening for the old circular stairs and started to climb to the second level, where he had seen them before. The sound of his footfalls hitting the worn concrete echoed off the brick walls, but he didn't care. If they weren't inside the fort, he knew where they were.

Exiting the stairwell, he ran to the first embrasure. He stopped short when he heard what sounded like a brick crashing below, and looked out over the old south pier. He could see Travis's boat tied up to one of the pilings and four figures making their way across the spit of sand connecting the fort to the pier. He had seen enough, and ran back down the stairs.

Farnsworth had been paid well, and the hostages would probably be safe if he left them here. He and Bugarra had created an incident report that would provide a coverup of their fake confinement. But Bugarra didn't care much about their safety. He had taken them for leverage, and without them along, he knew he would lose his advantage over Travis.

Entering the office, he slid the bolt back on the inner door and saw the trio sitting against the far wall.

"Get up. We have to go."

"We can't move him. Look at his leg." The woman removed the towel covering the wound, revealing a dark purple mess. "It's infected. If he doesn't get help, he could lose it."

The younger one, the ranger's daughter, looked at Bugarra defiantly.

"You—there's a wheelchair outside in the corridor," Bugarra said, pointing at the teenager.

She looked at the older woman, who nodded her assent, then left the room.

"Where are we going?" the woman asked.

"Your friend Travis is up to something," Bugarra said. Right after the words were out of his mouth, he saw a slight smile ghost across her face. Travis was their ray of hope, and Bugarra now knew he had their cooperation.

The girl arrived a minute later pushing a rubber-tired wheelchair. She and the woman loaded the ranger into the seat and strapped him in. Bugarra had originally been worried about getting the ranger to the boat, but the chair had been customized for the fort's beach. The seat was a sling that looked like it came off a beach chair, and there were no armrests, but the large grey rubber wheels could handle any terrain between here and the boat.

As they exited through the sally port and started toward the dock, he heard the engine of Travis's boat fire up. Just as they reached the dock and loaded the ranger aboard the boat, Bugarra saw the outline of the trawler cross the horizon. Instead of heading for the channel that led to Key West, Travis turned in the opposite direction and started toward Loggerhead Key. For the first time in days, Bugarra felt he was getting closer to whatever was Gross's secret.

THIRTY-EIGHT

WITH EVERYONE ABOARD, MAC STARTED THE ENGINE while Trufante released the line attached to the pile. Staying to the channel, but running dark, Mac retraced his route around the backside of the fort. The white masthead lights of a few sailboats that had chosen to weather the storm in the harbor were visible, but no running lights could be seen on the water.

The fort was mostly a blocky shadow, backlit by the security lights and the decorative lighthouse. Behind them Mac could see the light on Loggerhead Key flashing every twenty seconds. Otherwise, there was nothing except the dark expanse of the sea, and the overhead curtain of starlight. Moving past the backside of the fort, Mac stared at the screens in front of him. Though there were several markers ahead, spotting them on the moonless night without a searchlight would be almost impossible. He had to rely on Trufante's eagle eyesight to spot them. Trusting the chart on the right-hand screen, Mac set the zoom to a hundred feet and steered by the instrument.

The left-hand screen showed the bottom as they passed over it. The channel was fairly deep, almost twenty feet, and he didn't have to worry too much until they reached the Bird Key

Harbor, where they would be forced to run cross-country. Trufante called out the markers as they passed them, confirming what Mac saw on his display. When they reached the last one, the breadcrumbs from the track on his screen ended, and they were on their own.

Mac thought again of Van Doren making this same approach in an old wooden ship with only one or two men forward, dropping lead lines. The trawler could reverse if they got into trouble, but there was no way to stop a ship from Van Doren's time. In the proper conditions backing the sails was possible, but it would only delay the inevitable, not stop it. Mac gained a new appreciation for the men who sailed these waters before electronics.

After passing Garden Key and the fort, Mac saw the open expanse of Bird Key Harbor in front of them. He had to be careful here, as the chartplotter showed the deep water ended in an abrupt shallow bank. In daylight he might be able to discern it from the water color, but in the dark it would be impossible. The journal had described exactly this, and he watched the chartplotter for his turn. Van Doren, along with his navigator Mason, had extensive knowledge of the area, and had found the perfect escape route, a deepwater channel that narrowed to less than a hundred feet. His plan to create a boom and lure Lafitte's pursuing ships into it was brilliant.

"Can you see anything in the water?" Mac called to Trufante.

"Darker than a mullet's belly."

"Stay up there and keep an eye out."

Mac had been so focused on the chartplotter that he hadn't noticed Ned come up next to him.

"Seen some lights moving on the other side of the fort," Ned said.

Mac turned back, but saw nothing. He didn't doubt Ned,

but whatever he had seen had either gone the other way or was behind one of the keys. "Keep an eye out, and tell Pamela, too."

"I don't need any damned help," Ned said, and returned to the stern.

Mac was worried the lights Ned had spotted were from a park service boat, but there was nothing he could do. He was already running dark and had turned the electronics to night mode, so only a small glow emanated from the screens. Looking ahead, he saw nothing but stars, so brilliant that it was hard to turn away, but they shed little light on the water.

The channel was only a hundred feet wide, just over two boat lengths, and without daylight to show the reefs bordering it, he had to rely on his electronics. Switching the left-hand display to the side-scan sonar, he zoomed out until he could see both sides of the channel. A dark path was displayed down the middle of the screen before opening up to a sideways shot of the water below the boat. Mac waited for the turn he knew was coming.

Correcting course as the display changed, he followed the channel as it snaked first to the right and then the left before turning once again. He was close now, and there was no need for the chartplotter. Changing that display to the depth-finder mode, he circled the area, looking for the coral tongue that Van Doren described as the resting place of the diving bell filled with gold. It had occurred to him that the crafty captain might have returned and recovered his riches, but Gross seemed sure that it was still here. Mac looked forward to ending this escapade and reading the rest of the journal.

His focus moved back to the depth-finder. the display jumped, showing a sudden spike, about ten feet high and twenty feet wide—exactly as Van Doren had described it. Mac smiled, knowing they were close, and as he circled the area several times, a picture of the bottom formed in his head.

It took several passes before he was satisfied and called for Trufante to drop the anchor. The rattling of the chain startled Mac. The purring of the diesel was merely background noise, and though sound traveled at night, with the boat running at an idle, it was hard to hear from a distance. The noise the rode made as it passed over the roller could be heard for miles. Ned's eyes caught Mac's as he looked back, and Mac knew the old man felt it too.

"Keep a good watch now," he said, as he dropped the boat into reverse and goosed the throttle to set the anchor.

"Pamela, can you climb up on the wheelhouse and keep watch?" Mac asked. "Tru, let's get geared up. Ned, make sure we're ready up here." He cut the engine, and the dark night settled around them. In the sudden silence, every small noise made him jump. Once they were ready, he and Trufante walked through the transom door and, standing on the dive platform, put their fins on.

"Might want this." Ned handed Mac the spear gun. "This is just the kind of place the big bulls like to hunt at night."

"If I'm takin' it, put the power head on," Mac said.

Ned went back to the cabin and called back, "Only see two rounds."

"All I need is one."

Ned came back with the loaded power head and handed it to Mac. He took a giant stride entry into the water. Not wanting their dive lights to be seen from the surface, Mac fumbled, trying to flip the switch with his gloved hand. He finally turned it on and scanned the water below him. After clearing his ears, he shot a small amount of air into his buoyancy compensator and floated toward the bottom. Trufante was right behind him, and they met at the anchor.

Mac signaled that they should circle the area. They set off, with Trufante just behind and to the right. The sea life was distracting, and his finger itched over the trigger of the spear gun, but he knew he had no time to hunt. At night, the lobsters came out of their holes to feed, and were scattered across the sandy bottom. Predator fish were out as well, and Mac knew he could have gotten his limit of bugs and grouper within minutes. But Ned had been right and one thing, and Mac released the safety when he saw a dark shadow ahead.

Maliciously lingering on the edge of their visibility, it was definitely a big bull shark. Mac silently thanked Ned for making him bring the spear gun, and, releasing the safety, took cover behind a coral head. Trufante was behind him. A second later, the shadow slid by.

Mac looked over at Trufante, who had seen it as well. The shape moved away, but Mac knew it wouldn't go far. He held up two fingers to his eyes, signaling for Trufante to watch for it. Mac's breathing was generally second nature underwater, but with the big predator nearby, he noticed he was gulping air, and tried to relax. Just as he had his breathing under control, Trufante tapped Mac on the shoulder and pointed to the head of the shark coming toward them. It knew they were there, and was either checking them out or coming in for the kill. Knowing sharks had poor eyesight and hunted by smell, Mac readied the spear gun, assuming the worst. Suddenly, just twenty feet away, the shark accelerated. Mac flinched. The big bull was within range now, and he had to make a decision. At five feet away, he squeezed the trigger.

The shark's head muffled the explosion as the twelve-gauge shotgun shell dispersed in its brain, but its muscles continued to propel it forward until suddenly, less than two feet away from them, it dropped to the bottom. Mac slowly swam toward it and released the shaft from the carcass. Sliding it back into the gun, he added air to his BC and floated above it. He checked his air gauge. The incident had caused them to lose precious bottom time, and he knew his air consumption was high. He had jammed the tanks with 3400 PSI to start, and now, with only 1500 PSI left, he slowed his breathing and continued the search. It was hard to look away, but Mac turned his attention to the bottom, looking for any kind of straight line, indicating something man-made.

Mac had dived enough old wrecks to know that anything left would be covered with coral, making it harder to discern its true origin. The night dive, which he expected to be a hindrance, turned out to be a help, as he was able to narrow his focus on the path of his dive light as it swept the bottom in a methodical search pattern. In a groove now, both men worked an area ten feet apart, their lights crossing on the edges of their respective search areas.

They crossed the tongue and came back several times. Mac, looking at his watch, saw that they had been down for thirty minutes. Checking his air, he tapped the brass clip attached his BC against his tank. Trufante turned to him, and Mac signaled with one finger across his forearm that he had a thousand PSI remaining. Trufante checked his gauge and signaled that he had eight hundred left. Mac was never one for dive computers, having long ago memorized the dive tables. He knew they would run out of air and would have to surface before there was any danger of decompression problems.

He was becoming discouraged after crossing the tongue for the third time. Another ten minutes had passed, and he figured Trufante was below five hundred PSI now, their predetermined limit to find the boat and end the dive. He decided on one more pass toward the tip of the tongue that would lead them in the direction of the boat. They had crossed this area once from the opposite direction, but everything had started to look the same a long time ago.

As Mac looked down to where the coral dropped to the flat

sand, a thought came to him. Van Doren would have needed a feature distinguishable from the surface to mark the treasure. He wouldn't have had the resources to search the bottom, as Mac and Trufante were doing. The tip of the coral tongue would be a logical place to drop it.

With a renewed sense of purpose, Mac released air from his BC and descended to the sand. They had been searching the bottom from above, which was the most efficient method of scanning a large area, but now that he suspected where the cache might be, he wanted a look from the ocean floor.

Slowly, hugging the bottom, he moved along the sand, shining his light against the coral. As he crossed the tip of the structure, his excitement started to wane, and he was about to signal Trufante to surface when something caught Mac's eye. At first he thought it was a fish swimming across the light, but when he moved the light back, the reflection was still there.

Mac could feel his heart beating in his ears as he approached the object and, trying not to get his hopes up, fanned the sand away. A small piece of metal emerged, and he fanned harder, exposing more of it. Trufante must have seen the silt, and swam next to him. Together they worked to uncover the object, but with little air remaining, Mac soon realized they would need more firepower than their hands. He gave the thumbs-up signal to Trufante, who nodded back, and both men shot air into their BCs and started to ascend.

"I can tell from the look on your face that you found something," Ned said as he took Mac's fins.

"Bronze," Mac replied. "Looks big—like a bell."

"Really?" Pamela jumped down from her spot above the wheelhouse.

"Gonna need the firehose and some fresh tanks," Mac said, as he pulled himself onto the dive platform, handed Ned the spear gun, and slid out of his BC.

"Y'all are going to need at least an hour before you go back down there. The closest decompression chamber is in Key Largo," Ned said. He looked at the spear gun. "Guess that came in handy after all."

"Big goddamned bull. And I mean big," Trufante said.

"Clock's ticking, then. Let's get everything ready," Mac said. "Might want to reload the power head."

"That'll be the last round," Ned said. "Checked the shotgun, too."

BUGARRA SPUN the wheel to port and headed out the south channel. The park service boat was equipped with a spotlight set in a cradle on the dash, and, steering with one hand, he used the light to guide the boat through the markers. When he reached the last one, he turned to the south and set course for Loggerhead Key, the direction Travis had taken.

He soon realized that he was heading the wrong way. There were no navigation lights or moving shadows that would indicate a boat, only the light from the tower on the key several miles ahead and the fort behind him. Travis was probably running dark, and without the moon, although the night was black, the outline of his boat would still be visible.

Scanning the water, Bugarra thought he saw a trail of bioluminescence off to the east, like the disturbance a propeller makes as it cuts through the water. Turning the wheel, he set a course toward deep water and wide of the mark. There was no reason to run up on Travis. As long as Bugarra had him in his sights, he would let Travis do the heavy lifting and find the treasure.

He sensed movement behind him and looked back to see Justine staring at the same phosphorescent wake. That only confirmed his suspicion, but instead of pushing down on the throttles of the twin-engine boat, he backed off and studied the chartplotter. This area was known for its shoals and coral heads lurking just below the surface. The soft-sided boat drew little water, but one brush against the coral would likely puncture it.

After choosing a fairly straight and wide section of deep water that would use Garden Key and the fort to screen his approach, he started toward where he thought he had seen the boat. Passing the fort and keeping a small island to port, he saw the flash of two lights. They weren't navigation lights, and he puzzled for a second, realizing they were dive lights. He grinned, knowing he was getting closer.

THIRTY-NINE

Mac checked the tanks stowed behind the starboard bench. Six was his usual, and he saw that he had four filled plus the two empties from their dive. There was a compressor aboard, but it was loud and would probably be heard at the fort. During the day, the racket might warrant a visit from a ranger, but that kind of noise at night would surely attract attention, which was the last thing he wanted.

"We've got air for two more dives. I'd like to get another one in now and uncover enough of what we found to figure out how to recover it, then get some rest and dive at dawn." Exploring at night was one thing, but from Van Doren's description, they needed a block and tackle to lift the gold-laden bell over the side. Recovering it at night would be very risky.

"Makes sense," Ned said. "I'd like to have a look before you destroy anything."

Mac couldn't say no. Ned had proven himself capable and actually would be better able to appraise their find. "When was the last time you dove?"

"It's like riding a bike. You worry about you; I'll take care of me."

Mac shrugged and went to the cabin to get a bottle of water. Now that he wasn't diving until morning, Trufante already had a beer in his hand. "I'm going to need you to keep an eye above and below," Mac said.

"You sure Old Man is up to this?"

"We'll see," Mac said, taking the bottle of water back to the cockpit and checking his gear. Trufante followed him onto the deck.

"Think we should get right above it and use the pressure washer," Mac said.

"It'll silt the water up good. Likely bring more sharks; they get all excited. Not much for current, probably still blood in the water from the one you shot."

Having heard enough of Trufante's doom and gloom. Mac ignored him and went to the helm. Not that he was going to ignore the threat, but they had no options—he needed to do another dive tonight. "Where'd we come up?" he asked Ned.

"'Bout a hundred feet ahead."

Mac had dropped the anchor directly over the tongue, but now they needed the stern of the boat there to feed the hose over. "Tru, get the anchor—we're going to have to reset."

Mac waited for Trufante to climb onto the foredeck and release the safety. He called out to stay clear and started the windlass. Line came in as the boat was pulled forward. When they were directly above the anchor, Mac dropped a weighted buoy over the side to mark the position and retrieved the rest of the rode. With the anchor secure, he idled forward about a hundred and fifty feet before dropping it. Easing the engine into reverse, he set the hook and let the line pay out until the buoy was only a foot from the stern. "Clip it off. We're good."

"Might ought to drop a stern anchor so she doesn't swing when the tide shifts," Ned said.

Mac grudgingly admitted Ned was right, and reprimanded

himself for not thinking of it. To retrieve the diving bell, he would need to be on top of his game.

Between resetting the anchor and preparing the pressure washer and gear, the hour had almost expired. Mac and Ned geared up again and, a few minutes later, dropped into the water. They were directly above the bell and, without having to waste any time or air in locating it, went right to work.

Ned stopped Mac several times as he used the pressure washer to clear the sand away from the bell. The wait for the silt to settle seemed like hours, but Mac knew he was right. The bell had rested here for almost two hundred years, bronze was made of copper and tin, and, from what he'd seen so far, there was no indication of the shape it was in. He couldn't assume that it was still intact. Going too fast in this type of operation could easily destroy what they were after.

Mac took over the pressure washer. He could only work for a minute or so at a time before the visibility was reduced to less than a foot. Then they had to wait. Each time the water cleared, Ned inspected the newly uncovered section and nodded. By the time the needles of their air gauges were into the red, Mac had half the bell uncovered. Before they ascended, he motioned for Ned to stand back, and blasted a hole underneath it.

Again they had to wait for the silt to settle, but when it did, Mac pressed his body against the sand and shined the light in the hole. The dull glint of gold flashed back.

"We've got it," Mac said, after climbing back aboard. "First light'll be at six. We'll be in the water shortly after."

Mac knew he wouldn't be able to sleep, and settled into the captain's chair while the others went below to get some shuteye. He would have liked to finish reading the journal, but the risk of using a light overpowered his desire to find out what happened to Van Doren and why he hadn't come back for the bell.

Instead, Mac scanned the horizon for any activity. The

radar would be useful as well, but again, not worth the risk. It was already close to two a.m., and he slouched in the chair, getting as comfortable as possible for the next few hours.

BUGARRA SAT off the end of Long Key, using the binoculars he had found in the console of the park service boat to scan the waters. He had seen Travis head in this direction, but this was the last spit of land he could use as cover for a hundred miles. The newly risen moon was hovering just above the horizon, and its light outlined anything solid above the water. Bugarra focused on the area where he had seen the dive lights earlier. Slowly moving the binoculars back and forth, he finally settled on a dark spot that looked like the outline of Travis's trawler.

The boat was unlit, so he examined the water below it, hoping to catch a glimpse of the dive lights, but none appeared. Bugarra knew the limits of night diving and assumed Mac was waiting for first light before proceeding. If there was cell service, Bugarra would have called Travis, but without it, and after seeing the other boats anchored in the harbor, he was reluctant to air his dirty laundry over the public airwaves.

"Get comfortable. We're going to have to wait for morning." He had thought about going back to the fort and decided against it. There had to be a limit to how much Farnsworth would allow, and with the amount Bugarra had paid, he imagined he was close to that limit. Better to stay out and wait.

He was tired and the thought of grabbing a few hours of sleep was appealing. But looking back at the hostages, he caught Justine's eye and saw her determined look. If it weren't for her husband's wound, she probably would have taken the girl and swum for the point of the key just off their bow. Wanting to remove the temptation, Bugarra pushed the throttles forward and idled toward deeper water. When the depth finder indicated fifty feet, he left the helm and dropped the anchor. Long Key was only a shadow now, and with the temptation to try an escape removed, he brought the binoculars back to his head and watched the trawler.

MAC WOKE his crew an hour before dawn. He was anxious to get started, and there was at least an hour's work before they were ready to dive. Instead of the thin hose for the pressure washer, he broke out a hundred-foot length of firehose, which he attached to the saltwater wash-down. It wouldn't have the pressure of the smaller hose, but the volume should clear the bell quickly. With only two tanks of air remaining, he had to be efficient.

Dropping the end of the hose in the water, he saw the first sign of light on the horizon. Trufante and Pamela were rummaging through the galley, pulling out whatever food they could find, and he decided, along with a mug of the coffee that was brewing, eating was a good idea. The only thing on the menu was peanut butter and jelly, and he waited while Pamela made sandwiches. They ate in silence, waiting for enough light to dive.

"I'm going down myself," Mac said. "Tru, you work the pump. I'm hoping I can get it clear on one tank and use the other to get it ready to lift." He went back to the cockpit, where he laid out and checked his gear. When everything was ready, he started the engine and turned on the pump. It was louder than he liked, and he hoped it sounded like a boat running. There wasn't much boat traffic here even during busy times, but it was traveled, and he hoped the engine wouldn't attract any attention during daylight hours.

When the sun finally broke the horizon, he geared up and walked through the transom door to the swim platform. Between being anchored directly above the bell and having to manipulate the heavy firehose, he had decided on adding weight and using booties only. Checking the gauges, he inhaled through the regulator to check it and was about to enter the water when Ned handed him the spear gun.

"You know all that silt is going to attract something," Ned said. "Better to be ready."

Mac took the spear gun, not really thinking he would need it, and, with one hand on his mask and regulator, stepped off the platform and into the water. It was much easier, even with the low light, to find the bell, and without fins, he was quickly standing next to it with the firehose in hand.

They had decided on a two-minute lag time, and, checking his watch, Mac waited for Trufante to start the pump. As the time ticked down, he braced himself for the blast of water and soon felt the pipe stiffen as it filled. Even underwater, it was heavy, and the water jetting from the nozzle started moving material away from the bell. The current was even weaker this morning than last night, leaving the sand and silt suspended in place. Finally, he caught a glimpse of the chain and started following it across the channel. He knew from the journal that it was attached to the bell, and they had decided to use the chain and the winch aboard the trawler to retrieve the treasure.

Still strung across the open channel, the chain was buried deep under the sand. Mac was slowly uncovering it, but he was almost out of air. Turning the nozzle off, he looked around to get his bearings. He was tired and numb from the vibration of the hose, and as he shook out his extremities before ascending, he thought he heard the sound of a motor, but his hearing had been impacted from the sound of the jetting water. He looked around for the source of the noise.

Without the current running, the typically gin-clear water for which the Tortugas were famous was silted up from the fire-hose, and Mac struggled to see the surface. He dropped the hose, inflated his BC, and with the speargun in hand, started floating toward the surface. At ten feet, he could see the trawler and what looked like the shape of another boat next to it. He shot another blast of air into his BC, floated to within five feet of the surface, and saw the flat bottom and inflated pontoons of the park service RHIB boat.

Dropping back to ten feet, he moved to the anchor line to hold himself in position while he tried to figure out what was happening above. There appeared to be no scenario where this was a routine visit. It had to be either Bugarra himself or his puppet, Farnsworth. The question was, what to do while Mac still had the advantage of being invisible? They certainly knew he was diving, but with the silted-up water, they had no idea where he was. Even if they could track his bubbles, they wouldn't be able to tell what he was doing.

He needed a distraction to get aboard the trawler, and with the spear gun in his hand, he had the means to make one. A shot into the one of the pontoons wouldn't sink the Park Service boat, but would cripple it. He ascended to directly underneath the hard bottom of the RHIB boat. Without fins, it was hard to maneuver, and he released the air from his BC before finally dropping his weights. Swimming to within a few feet of the pontoon closest to the trawler, he drew a breath and felt a restriction. There was no need to check his gauges—he was out of air. He was so close, and pulled hard on the regulator, getting one more breath before dropping his tank and BC. With only the air in his lungs, he aimed the shaft at the pontoon, released the safety, and fired.

A blast of air shot back at him as the power head exploded, and he quickly swam toward the portside of the trawler and surfaced. There were voices, and tearing off his gloves, he put his fingers in his mouth and risked a low whistle. If Ned or Trufante heard it, they would know it was a signal. Treading water, Mac waited until he saw a shadow fall over the water. Ned sat on the gunwale with his back to the water, but had heard him.

"I'm going to cut the anchor line," Mac said. "As soon as you feel the boat drift, fire up the engine and get out of here."

"He's got a gun on Kurt and them, and took our shotgun," Ned whispered over the side.

"The plan stays the same."

Using the hull of the trawler for cover, Mac swam to the anchor line and sliced it with his knife. He kicked up, and when his head broke the surface, he screamed to Trufante to start the engines. There was a long pause, and Mac yelled again, but it was drowned out by the engine starting. Wrapping the anchor line around his arms, he held on as the boat started to move.

After a hundred or so feet, the water cleared, and he could see the edges of the channel on either side as he clutched the line. Soon the boat slowed, and he heard the click of the transmission as it dropped to neutral. Kicking hard, he released the line and swam to the dive platform, where he dragged himself aboard. The boat started moving again the moment Ned called out that Mac was aboard, and he climbed through the transom door.

It took a minute to acclimate himself, but when Mac looked back, he saw the soft-sided boat was just behind them, and Bugarra was looking right at him, pistol extended.

FORTY

MAC LOOKED OVER AT KURT, JUSTINE, AND ALLIE HUDDLED in the back of the park service boat and wondered what he could do. After using the spear gun's last round to shoot out the pontoon, they were now out of ammunition.

Mac saw the muscles in Bugarra's arm tense, and dropped to the deck as two shots went over his head. The two boats were close enough that he heard the click of the empty chamber when Bugarra tried to fire again. Unless he had a spare magazine, the odds had evened.

"He's out," Kurt called from the other boat.

Trufante was at the wheel, and Mac crawled to the base of the captain's chair, where he rose, counting on the protection of the wheelhouse if Kurt was wrong and Bugarra shot again. He was certainly acting like he was out of ammo. The park service boat pulled ahead of them and Bugarra looked back. Mac saw the fire in his eyes, but there was no weapon in his hand. Bugarra turned back to the wheel and set a course that, it appeared, was going to take him back to the channel. Mac took the wheel from Trufante and followed.

A feeling of helplessness overcame him. With one of the

pontoons deflated, he was able to keep pace with the normally faster boat, and he racked his brain for any idea of how to stop Bugarra before he reached the park boundary. Mac could already see the light bars on the T-tops of two park service boats coming toward them. He had to stop Bugarra now and get out of the park waters before the boats reached them.

Fishermen have a built-in radar, and Mac's kicked in. His gaze shifted to the diving birds ahead, and he saw the small silver reflections of the baitfish as they broke the surface, trying to evade a predator beneath them. The school was large enough that one throw of his cast net could fill the bait well.

Mac turned back to Bugarra's boat, but an idea struck him. He called Trufante back to the helm and asked him to maintain the distance between the boats, then told him his plan. The Cajun smiled. The Cadillac grin on his face gave Mac at least some confidence that it would work. Sliding across the deck, he pulled a bucket from underneath the starboard-side bench and carried it forward. He and Trufante exchanged a quick glance before Mac climbed onto the wheelhouse roof. The footing was awkward, and he slid onto his belly, grabbing the antenna mounts to hold him in place as the *Ghost Runner* crashed through the waves in pursuit of the crippled boat.

Bugarra continued on his course, but the damaged pontoon only allowed him to run at about ten knots before the pressure of the water dragged the deflated rubber under the surface and flooded the boat. The self-bailing rigid deck allowed the water to drain and Bugarra proceeded to move forward, knowing, as Mac did, that the damage had been done and it was not likely to get worse. Mac thought about his options. There was nowhere for Bugarra to run except toward the oncoming boats and the fort.

Wedged between the radar dome and the stubby GPS antenna, Mac worked his way to his knees. He brought the bucket between his legs and pulled the line out. Normally he would slide the loop around his wrist, but for what he had in mind next, he would be pulled off the boat if it were attached. Banging on the roof, he got Trufante's attention, and after he felt the Cajun return the signal, he waited as the boats converged.

Several times, as Trufante crossed the crest of the waves, Mac was almost thrown from the roof. Unable to call out directions with the blade of his dive knife in his mouth, he held on and silently rehearsed what he would need to do as the *Ghost Runner* pulled alongside the park service boat. Bugarra was looking over, and Mac stayed low, hoping the angle of the higher boat would block Bugarra's view.

The park service boat swerved as if to change course to avoid the trawler, but with the blown pontoon, it had lost not only speed, but maneuverability. Without having to worry about being shot at, Mac showed himself. He glanced at the three figures huddled by the transom. Kurt was pale and possibly unconscious. Justine had a defiant look on her face. Mac mimicked the motion of throwing a net, and she gave a nod.

The boats were less than ten feet apart now, and Mac rose to his feet, hooking his ankles onto the electronics and hoping that Trufante wouldn't do anything that would knock him off. He reached into the bucket, knowing he only had one chance, then looked up and saw the park service boat was in range.

Looping the nylon line in one-foot circles in his left hand, he grabbed the monofilament brail lines and horn of the cast net. There was no time to check if it was tangled, but both he and Trufante were meticulous with their equipment. Losing a school of baitfish due to a tangled net often ruined an entire day's fishing. With the line and horn in his left hand, he started pulling the mesh net from the bucket until he held two-thirds in his hand. After dropping the weights until they just hit the deck, he took a section of the lead line in his mouth and started tossing the net over his right shoulder. When he felt he had half the net, he dropped his right hand and, with two fingers, took hold of the lead line near his waist. Opening his hand, he grabbed the rest of the split net and brought both hands together by his face. The actions were automatic and took only a few seconds. Before Bugarra could figure out what was intended, Mac turned to the left, drew a deep breath, and recoiled.

He spun to the right, letting the line drop from his mouth at the same time as he released his left hand. After waiting a long second, he snapped his right wrist and let the net fly. It was a perfect pancake, but, used to having the line tied to his left hand, he thought it would fall short. Instead, unhindered, it flew toward the park service boat and dropped over the console, entrapping Bugarra in the fine mesh.

Bugarra held the wheel in one hand as he tried to escape the net, but his actions only entangled him further. Mac watched him for just a second. Before Bugarra could steer the crippled boat clear of trawler, Mac crouched down and launched himself at the park service boat.

His knee slammed into the console and it took Mac a second to gain his feet. Ignoring the pain, he looked up and saw Bugarra was still struggling. Mac hobbled to Justine, grabbed the knife from his mouth, and cut through her bonds. He handed her the knife to release Allie and Kurt, then went to the helm. Bugarra turned as if to fight, but his movements were severely limited by the net. Mac reached for one of Bugarra's hands and twisted it behind his back.

Mac looked back to see if Justine had freed Kurt and Allie. "I need you to take the wheel," Mac called to her.

She cut the last restraint and came toward him. He pushed Bugarra's arm higher and walked him away from the helm, but with the net still draped over him, the quarter-inch mesh snagged on the console.

"Cut it loose. I've got him," Mac told her.

Justine slid the sharp knife through the mesh like it was butter. Releasing the tension allowed Bugarra a little movement, which he immediately used to try to free himself from Mac's grasp. Pulling up harder on the arm, Mac stopped him.

"Is there anything in the console that we can restrain him with?" Mac asked Justine.

With one hand on the wheel, she opened the small compartment and riffled through it, coming out with two flex cuffs. Mac took them from her with his free hand. Placing them in his teeth, he wrenched up hard enough on Bugarra's arm to bring the big man onto his tiptoes and used the knife to cut Bugarra's other hand free. He tried to fight back, knowing once the ties were around his wrists, it was over. Unlike the hardware-store-variety cable ties, which were easy to escape from, the law enforcement versions were bombproof. Still restricted by the net, Mac was able to grab Bugarra's other hand. Needing his own hand free, he dropped the knife, pulled a tie from his mouth, and cinched Bugarra's wrists together.

Somehow, during the struggle, Bugarra had freed one of his legs from the net and, using Mac's grip on his arm to lever himself, executed a sweep kick. Both men were flung to the deck, and as they fell, the net snagged on the leaning post. Their combined weight tore it almost in half, and, Bugarra was freed from it.

Mac had the advantage of using his hands, but Bugarra fought like a bull without his. Using his body weight to his advantage, he was able to slam Mac against the console. Mac's knee, which had taken the brunt of the impact when he landed on the boat, crumpled. Bugarra approached, and Mac saw his leg swing forward. He tried to avoid the blow, but the injury to his knee slowed him, and he tried to roll against the soft gunwale to avoid the side kick. He was too slow, and the kick landed just below the hurt knee, causing him to howl in pain.

Bugarra backed off and went for the knife on the deck, rolling onto his back in an attempt to grab it. Mac struggled forward, trying to ignore the pain, knowing that in seconds Bugarra would not only be free, but have control of the knife, too. Bugarra's attention was focused on Mac, and just as he was about to grab the blade, Kurt slid toward him on his belly. Still lying on the deck, he grabbed one of Bugarra's feet. With a twist of his body, he howled in pain, but still threw Bugarra to the deck. Mac slammed his foot down on Bugarra's hand, and the knife dropped from his grasp.

Bugarra screamed and tried to roll away, but Kurt was not done. Now on his knees, he rained down blows on the rogue treasure hunter, exacting revenge for what he had done to his family. Mac finally made it to his feet and reached out to grab Kurt's shoulder. At first, Kurt pushed Mac away, but, realizing who it was, he relaxed. Mac reached beneath Justine, grabbed a handful of the flex cuffs from the console, and went to Bugarra, who lay in a fetal position, trying to protect himself. Mac added another restraint to his hands and secured his ankles. Once Bugarra was secure, Mac leaned against the gunwale and tried to catch his breath.

"Where are we going?" Justine asked. "The park service boats are closing in on us."

Using the wheel, Mac hauled himself upright. He looked over and saw the boats were only a mile away. Time to ditch the crippled boat and run. After signaling to Trufante that they were okay, he instructed Justine to steer a collision course with the trawler, and within a minute, the two boats came alongside each other.

Justine was still behind the wheel, and Mac ordered them to

abandon ship. Justine and Allie easily made it aboard the *Ghost Runner*, but it took Trufante and Pamela to haul Kurt from the lower boat to the trawler. Mac, careful of his knee, climbed aboard and yelled for Trufante to head toward open water. It would be close, but Mac thought they had a chance.

The tachometer was in the red for longer than Mac wanted, and he could almost feel the fuel tanks emptying as they fed the struggling engine. He'd never had the engine over twenty-one-hundred RPMs, and they were close now. "A little more," he told Trufante, and looked back. They were running thirty-five knots, close to the maximum speed of the park service boats. Slowly, the red line on the chartplotter approached. Finally, they crossed it.

When they were a good mile past the line, he relaxed and turned back to Allie.

"How's your dad?"

"I'm good," Kurt responded.

"We're out of the park, but need to decide what to do about him." All eyes moved to Bugarra, who was still curled up in a fetal position by the starboard gunwale. They all knew that taking him back to the park was not an option and no one knew what awaited them in Key West.

"I've got an idea." Using the gunwales for support, Kurt hauled himself to his feet. Trufante dropped the RPMs and slowed just enough to allow Kurt to make his way to the helm. "I've got a buddy with ICE. I don't know what they did during the hurricane, but if he's around, he'll help out."

"This isn't ICE's jurisdiction," Mac said. Over the years, he'd had several dealings with the different alphabet agencies.

Kurt thought for a second. "As a special agent for the National Park Service, it's within my authority to pursue suspects that have committed crimes inside the park's boundaries, wherever that may lead me. Don't ask me how I know that, but it works."

"That'll play," Mac said. "Stealing a park service boat should get the ball rolling."

Kurt picked up the VHF and called out on channel sixteen. A moment later, a scratchy response could be heard. The ICE interceptor was just offshore of Key West and would rendezvous with them off the Marquesas. Mac relieved Trufante of the helm, leaned forward, and entered the position the ICE captain had indicated into the GPS. The fort soon dropped below the horizon and Kurt moved next to Mac, grasping the back of the chair for support.

"Thanks, Mac," he said.

"Hopefully, he's going away for a long time." Mac glanced back at Bugarra, who lay motionless on the deck. He pushed the throttle just enough so that every wave they hit jostled Bugarra.

"What about the treasure?" Kurt asked.

"Found a lot of it in my day and never helped me any. It's in the park. I'll leave that to you."

Mac wasn't done, though. There was still Henriques treasure lying somewhere. But he would need to read the rest of Van Doren's journal to find out if he had escaped with it.

EPILOGUE

Sitting up in the hospital bed in Fishermen's Hospital in Marathon, Kurt checked his email. Two days had passed since they had left Fort Jefferson, his wound was starting to look better. Surgery to remove the bullet embedded in his leg had been a success, and he had started to wean himself from the painkillers. Slowly the government was coming back to life, but Justine, along with the rest of the crime lab, was still deemed nonessential, and she had stayed by his side. Allie had returned to her mother's this morning after a tearful goodbye.

Justine wondered how this adventure would affect Allie. She was strong, but still only sixteen. It was bound to leave some scars. Time would heal, and Justine would do whatever she could to help. Their bond had grown stronger after being held together. She squeezed Kurt's hand, thinking about how much she loved him, and his daughter, as she watched the steady drip of antibiotics from the IV flow into his arm. A shadow appeared by the door, passed by, and returned.

"Hey," Mac said, standing in the doorway.

"Come on in," Justine said. Mac had seemed standoffish to

her when she first met him, but she was starting to understand him, and a deep respect had grown between them.

"Only have a few minutes. Mel's flight lands in an hour."

"Have you seen your place yet?" Kurt asked.

They turned to the TV, which had been showing nonstop coverage of the devastation the storm had brought to the Middle Keys, expecting Wood's island to be the next location shown.

"That's something I have to do with Mel. I've been staying on the boat, behind the Rusty Anchor. We'll go out in the morning and have a look," Mac said.

Kurt turned to Justine. "Johnny Wells came by when you took Allie back to her mom's. Bugarra's going to be charged by the feds for kidnapping. They'll broker the lesser charges, but that ought to finish him off. I heard the IRS is camped out at his office as well. Add in a dose of tax evasion, and we won't be seeing him again."

"That was a good call to have him taken into custody," Justine said.

"It was unintentional," Kurt said. "I didn't want to deal with Farnsworth."

"What's going to happen to him?" Mac asked.

Before answering, Kurt looked down at his laptop, knowing his status as a park service employee would dictate the answer. After several minutes, his emails began to load. He started to skim through all one hundred of them..

"I guess the storm doesn't stop the world," Justine said with a smile, looking over his shoulder.

Towards the bottom, Kurt found what he was looking for. Martinez had granted his leave. "We're good. When I get back to work, I'll deal with Farnsworth."

"I bet he turns state's evidence and walks away," Mac said.

"I've got some ideas," Kurt said. "You sure you don't want to make a dive on the bell before I report it?"

"Damned sure. It'll be good for you, and if it'll help you deal with that prick, have at it," Mac said.

"Tru and Pamela came by earlier," Justine said.

Mac hadn't seen the couple since dropping them off at the marina in Key West with instructions to bring the *Reef Runner* back to Marathon.

"They said Pamela was going to move back up."

"That's good news," Mac said. "Listen, I gotta go. Y'all take care."

He started to walk away, but Justine grabbed him at the door and gave him a big hug. "You're not just walking out like that."

Mac smiled and nodded to Kurt. "Take care of this one, and bring your daughter down some time."

After Mac left, Justine sat on the bed next to Kurt and took his hand. "He's right about that treasure not helping anyone."

Kurt nodded, his eyes slowly closing. Justine stayed there holding his hand as he drifted off to sleep.

"YOU READY?" Mac asked Mel. They were sitting in the cockpit of the *Ghost Runner*, finishing their coffee. Marathon was a mess, but most of the power had been restored, allowing them a comfortable, air-conditioned night aboard. But they both knew it was time.

"Yeah. I'm pretty much resigned to the fact that it's gone," she said.

"If it is, we'll build it back. Done it before; we'll do it again."

"Spoken like a true Conch," Mel said. "Let's go have a look."

Mac went to the wheelhouse and fired up the engine while Mel cast off the lines. Debris cluttered the canal, and Mac turned over the wheel to Mel while he went forward with the gaff to clear a path. When they reached the end of the canal, he came back to the wheel, and they both looked back at Rusty's. "He's finally got that view he wanted," Mac said. The normally lush vegetation was bare, and they could see the back deck of the bar clearly.

"And Rufus's shack survived," Mel said.

Mac turned back to the water ahead. It was an unusual shade of brown from erosion and already-decaying vegetation. He steered to deeper water and past Sister Creek. Boot Key was barren, and through the bare branches, he could see the normally hidden harbor. They both stared ahead, knowing that they would soon find out their future. They passed under the Seven Mile Bridge—the strong currents running between the Atlantic and Gulf of Mexico had cleared the spans—and Mac pushed down on the throttle. He was tired of waiting and ready to get to work.

The small keys all looked the same; many had been essentially leveled by the storm surge. Mac saw ibis and herons standing on the bare branches looking for fish. For them, this was just a natural process, and life continued, a little altered, but still the same. That was how Mac viewed his own life.

Finally, the island came into view. Wood had chosen well, and it was immediately evident that the island, being higher and drier than many of its neighbors, had fared better. From a quarter mile away, they could see the house.

"It's still there," Mel said.

Mac studied it as he closed on the channel, making sure to slow earlier than usual in case the bottom had shifted with the storm, and once he knew the channel was deep enough, he glided up to the pile.

"That old pile's survived many a storm," Mel said. "Kind of reminds me of Dad."

Mac nodded, too nervous to laugh. "Ready?" he asked, after tying off the boat and shutting down the engine.

Mel walked out the transom door and stepped off the dive platform. "You think we can add a dock?"

"Might be about time for that. It'll be a while before the camouflage grows back."

Together they waded to shore and walked through the opening where the gate had been. The pile of traps remained, but was covered with seaweed. They saw the house well before they would have previously, and Mac was surprised how well it had endured. "If the storm surge didn't make it to the floor, we did pretty well." The water tanks were stripped from the roof and the solar array was gone, but the shell of the house was intact.

Climbing the stairs, they could see where the high-water mark had been, one step short of the floor level. It had been a hell of a ride, but they had survived. Standing on the porch, they looked out over the island.

"I'm so happy, Mac. Giving up the treasure was the right thing to do. It's almost like karma."

Mac fingered the folded papers of the journal in his pocket and took her in his arms. "So far, so good," he said. He'd not had time to read the rest of Van Doren's journal, and still wondered if the captain had escaped—and what he had done with Henriques' treasure.

AFTERWORD

Wood's Tempest is the middle part of a story that spans three of my series. They are all independent stories and can be read and enjoyed by themselves.

Mac's involvement starts with Backwater Tide, where Kurt and Justine work to solve Gill Gross's murder. Wood's Tempest starts where Backwater Tide ends.

Shifting Sands is the story of how Nick Van Doren and his crew find the treasure, the chase, and what happens to them afterward.

Things are never easy when you're labeled a pirate in the Caribbean.

Get the story behind Wood's Tempest

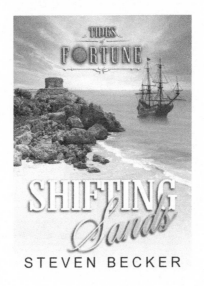

Available on Amazon - http://bit.ly/tofshiftingsands

There is one word that brings out the worst in people: TREASURE.

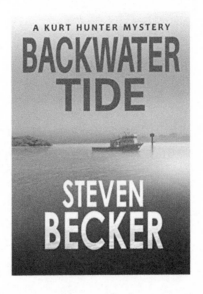

Get it now on Amazon: http://bit.ly/backwatertide

☆☆☆☆☆ ⌄   53 customer reviews

ABOUT THE AUTHOR

Always looking for a new location or adventure to write about, Steven Becker can usually be found on or near the water. He splits his time between Tampa and the Florida Keys - paddling, sailing, diving, fishing or exploring.

Find out more by visiting www.stevenbeckerauthor.com or contact me directly at booksbybecker@gmail.com.

 facebook.com/stevenbecker.books

instagram.com/stevenbeckerauthor

Get my starter library First Bite for Free!
when you sign up for my newsletter

http://eepurl.com/-obDj

First Bite contains the first book in each of Steven Becker's series:

- **Wood's Reef**
- **Pirate**
- **Bonefish Blues**

By joining you will receive one or two emails a month about what I'm doing and special offers.

Your contact information and privacy are important to me. I will not spam or share your email with anyone.

Wood's Reef

"A riveting tale of intrigue and terrorism, Key West characters in their full glory! Fast paced and continually changing direction Mr Becker has me hooked on his skillful and adventurous tales from the Conch Republic!"

Pirate

"A gripping tale of pirate adventure off the coast of 19th Century Florida!"

Bonefish Blues *"I just couldn't put this book down. A great plot filled with action. Steven Becker brings each character to life, allowing the reader to become immersed in the plot."*

Get them now (http://eepurl.com/-obDj)

Also By Steven Becker

Kurt Hunter Mysteries

Backwater Bay

Backwater Channel

Backwater Cove

Backwater Key

Backwater Pass

Mac Travis Adventures

Wood's Relic

Wood's Reef

Wood's Wall

Wood's Wreck

Wood's Harbor

Wood's Reach

Wood's Revenge

Wood's Betrayal

Wood's Tempest

Tides of Fortune

Pirate

The Wreck of the Ten Sail

Haitian Gold

Shifting Sands (January 2019)

Will Service Adventure Thrillers

Bonefish Blues

Tuna Tango

Dorado Duet

Storm Series

Storm Rising

Storm Force